TROJAN

ALSO BY ALAN MCDERMOTT

Tom Gray Novels

Gray Justice

Gray Resurrection

Gray Redemption

Gray Retribution

Gray Vengeance

Gray Salvation

TROJAN

ALAN McDermott

THOMAS & MERCER

Published by Thomas & Mercer, Seattle

www.apub.com

Amazon, the Amazon logo, and Thomas & Mercer are trademarks of Amazon.com, Inc., or its affiliates.

ISBN-13: 9781503942127
ISBN-10: 1503942120

Cover design by © blacksheep-uk.com

Printed in the United States of America

On January 16th 2016, it snowed in Leigh,
Lancashire.
God painted his canvas as only He can, and
He gave us something beautiful.
In return, it was time for Him to take something
beautiful from my life.
I miss you, Mum.

FOREWORD

This is a work of fiction. At the time of writing, it was set twelve months in the future, and so I took certain liberties with elements of the story, such as the refugee reception centre in Lampedusa, Italy. No-one can accurately predict how the migrant crisis will develop over the coming year, nor how countries will adapt to deal with it. The current facilities might change dramatically over the coming months, as might the way the registration process is handled. The rest of the story should be seen to take place in a sort of 'parallel universe' version of the UK. I had no idea what changes there might be to government personnel, or what real-life events might take place during the book's timeline.

I call it a migrant 'crisis' because, while the vast majority are genuine refugees fleeing war zones, there are a few who are heading to Europe for other reasons. Some of them are economic migrants, while the attacks in Paris in November 2015 show that a few have come simply to wage war.

There are those who will read this story and come to the conclusion that I must have something against Muslims, but that couldn't be further from the truth. I dine with my Muslim friends, and I only chose to write about this topic because it is one of those 'could happen' situations that can make fiction feel compelling and relevant.

CHAPTER 1

Monday, 3 July 2017

A lone cloud in the azure sky provided escort to the motorcade thundering along the desert road, its white tendrils seeming to point the way. An opportunistic vulture took to the sky as the trucks rumbled past, abandoning the remains of the lizard it had found minutes earlier.

The lead vehicle was a ten-year-old Nissan Titan with pockmarked paintwork. Behind it, another four trucks fought their way through the cloud of dust thrown up by rubber churning the desert floor.

In the front passenger seat of the middle truck, Abu Hussain stared at the mountains that rose away to his left, then checked his handheld GPS and saw that they were less than a kilometre from their target, a small village in eastern Syria that was home to no more than a dozen families. Intelligence suggested the inhabitants were Shia Muslims, which didn't sit well with the leaders of Saif al-Islam.

The group's name in Arabic translated to *Sword of Islam* – also the name given to the late Colonel Muammar Gaddafi's son. Like the Gaddafis, the men in the trucks were Sunnis, and their task for the day was to convert the villagers, one way or another. Those who chose the

Sunni way would be press-ganged into service, while a more permanent fate awaited those who resisted.

Hussain knew that the 'intelligence' was probably founded on nothing more than rumours, as was usually the case, but he didn't care. He had a job to do, plain and simple, and the fact that it meant taking lives was irrelevant. Scores had already died by his hand, and he felt neither thrill nor remorse when dispatching someone with his sword or rifle.

That those he 'converted' were sent to other parts of the country wasn't his concern. It would have been nice to have them fill the gaps in his own thinning ranks, caused by the recent allied strikes against the unit, but he was merely a foot soldier. He left the bigger picture to those who knew best.

The thought made him glance up at the sky, but he saw no grey jets preparing to unleash their deadly payloads.

Hussain radioed ahead and told the lead car to enter the hamlet and sweep right, with the second to take a position to the left. His own vehicle drove into the centre of what turned out to be a few single-storey, mud-covered dwellings haphazardly staggered around a well. Goats wandered between the buildings and a pair of young children argued over a wooden doll as Hussain climbed out of his vehicle.

'Bring me the elder,' Hussain called out as the other three occupants of his truck decamped.

One of the children pointed towards a house with laundry hanging on a clothes line outside. Hussain's subordinate marched to it, kicked in the door and emerged thirty seconds later, dragging a man in his seventies behind him.

People began to stream out of their houses, drawn by the noise of the arriving vehicles and the shouts of their occupants.

'We are Saif al-Islam,' Hussain bellowed, 'and your village is now part of the glorious caliphate.'

The rest of his men moved from house to house, rousting the villagers. Young women over the age of thirteen were herded off to one side, while men of fighting age were similarly segregated.

Hussain addressed the elder. 'Tell me which *hadith* you people adhere to.'

'We read from the four books,' the old man said defiantly, referring to the narratives purporting to quote the prophet Muhammad. The Shia branch of Islam differed from the Sunni branch, whose collection ran to six tomes.

'That is all about to change,' Hussain told him. 'From this day on, you will all observe the true Quran.'

'This entire valley has been Shia for generations,' the elder told him.

'And I am here to end the blasphemy,' Hussain shot back before turning to address the villagers. 'Who here refuses to denounce their false beliefs?'

He stared at the faces, almost disappointed that no-one stepped forward or raised a hand. It seemed his sword would stay sheathed today.

Until the elder spoke.

'There are no apostates here,' he said. 'We've heard about your rampage through our lands, using your faith as an excuse to rape and murder, but your actions are abhorrent to any true Muslim. We will never bend to your will.'

A humourless smile broke out on Hussain's face. He called two of his men over and gave them instructions, scratching his long, black beard as one readied a digital camera and the other bound the old man's hands behind his back and pushed him to his knees.

Hussain slowly drew his sword from the sheath on his back, the long blade glinting in the sunlight. He took a position to the elder's left, then addressed the villagers once more as he waited for the go-ahead from the cameraman.

'We come to you with a simple choice,' he shouted. 'Those who choose to follow the true Quran will be spared. Those who do not will meet with the same fate as this foolish man.'

The soldier with the camera indicated that he was ready to start filming, and Hussain began a speech he'd prepared for precisely this moment.

He managed two words before a .50-calibre bullet removed the top of his head, and he collapsed like a sack of rocks. A second later, the sound of the round leaving the rifle echoed off the nearby mountains.

～

The moment the sound of the shot reached him, the SAS sergeant issued his order.

'Light 'em up!'

He rose from his position on the roof of the elder's house and picked off two Saif al-Islam soldiers who were staring at their dead leader; his rifle was soon seeking the next target. He found it in the form of a man guarding the young women of the village. Two bullets left his weapon and scored head-shots.

His fellow troopers were also making light work of the opposition. The sniper and his spotter, hidden in the mountains almost a kilometre away, had counted twenty-five enemy soldiers in the trucks. Updates had continued to come in about their locations, and within ten seconds of the leader's takedown, another twenty-two of his men followed him to the grave.

Two remained, however, and had enough wits about them to take cover among the villagers. One rose with his arm tightly wound around a young girl's neck, his pistol jabbed into the side of her head, and he began shouting. The other was cowering among the elderly, raising his head now and again to take a potshot at the men on the roofs.

The sergeant, chosen for the mission because of his fluent Arabic, understood the terrorist's order: drop your weapons or the girl dies. It wasn't an instruction he was about to obey.

'You got the tall one with the girl in your sights?' he asked into the radio.

'Just say the word,' the sniper responded.

'He's all yours,' the sergeant said, never taking his eyes off the target. Within two seconds, half of the terrorist's face disappeared in a crimson cloud, leaving just one X-ray to deal with.

The sergeant knew the sniper couldn't get a bead on the enemy, as a hut lay in his line of fire. It was up to him to end it. Unfortunately, this fighter had learned from his friend's demise and forced three women to stand in front of him, making it impossible to shoot him without striking them first.

The target had his back to a wall. On the roof above him, one of the sergeant's men knelt near the edge.

'Jones, he's right below you,' the NCO said. 'Stand up and move one foot to your right, then get ready to fire.'

'You have nowhere to go,' the sergeant called out. 'Lay down your weapon and put your hands in the air.'

He waited until the terrorist began his response, then whispered into his throat mic: 'Take him.'

Jones leaned over the side of the building, pointed his weapon straight down, and sent three rounds through the target's skull, ending the stand-off.

The sergeant climbed down from his perch and told the sniper to keep an eye out in case any of the enemy had managed to call in reinforcements, then ordered the troops to gather the bodies and photograph them before loading them onto the backs of the trucks. Once the task was complete, he ordered his men to climb into the cabs and went to have a word with the elder.

'We were never here,' he said in Arabic, then pointed to the trucks. 'And neither were they. Hide any bullet holes and throw away our shell casings, just in case they send someone looking for them.'

The old man looked at him, still in shock.

Sergeant Mitchell walked to the lead vehicle and got in the passenger seat, then ordered the driver to take them to the pre-arranged point. The dead would be staged to make it look as if they'd been in the vehicles all along, and an aircraft would be called in to destroy the trucks with air-to-ground missiles. It would look as if the terrorists had fallen to an air strike. Mitchell had originally questioned the order, wondering why they needed to go through the subterfuge when they could simply have the jets take out the convoy en route. The response was that the head shed had a desire to put names to corpses, which was good enough for him.

The ruse meant no-one would know about the SAS patrol operating in the region. The sergeant and his men would simply fade back into the desert and await their next target.

CHAPTER 2

Wednesday, 5 July 2017

Another *boom* echoed across the city as Andrew Harvey steered the car down the ramp to the car park underneath Thames House. After enduring the wettest June on record, London had been blessed with five days of brilliant sunshine, but that had come to an end with the thunderstorm intensifying above the capital.

He parked in his usual spot and checked his appearance in the mirror. His short brown hair could do with a trim, he noticed, but apart from that, he looked okay. His nose was a little bigger than he would have liked, but at least he wasn't developing the jowls that seemed to curse some of his friends who had also reached forty. He put that down to the regular nocturnal workouts his girlfriend put him through.

He looked over at Sarah Thompson and smiled. How he'd ended up with someone so wonderful was beyond him, but he wasn't complaining. A well-toned body was only one of her many attributes, but it was her personality that he missed most whenever they were apart for any length of time. Sarah was whip-smart, and funny as well – especially when she got away from the open office that they shared with half a dozen others.

At least, she had been until the incident a few months earlier.

As time wore on, he was seeing more and more of the old Sarah, but there were still moments when he could see her dwelling on her time in Bessonov's basement . . .

Harvey cast the thoughts aside, fearing that she might read his mind and start recalling those few hours when it had been only her, the Beriya brothers and an assortment of tools.

He smiled at her as they got out of the car. They rode the elevator to their floor, and both swiped their security cards into the slot to give them access to the office. Like most days, they were the first people in.

'Remind me to get salmon on the way home,' Sarah said as she kissed him on the cheek. 'I'll make your favourite tonight.'

'Yum. Any particular reason?'

'I just want you in a good mood tonight,' she said over her shoulder as she sauntered to her desk.

'No need to bribe me,' he laughed. 'You could feed me roadkill garnished with baked beans and I'd still give you all my loving.'

Harvey walked over to his own station and powered up the computer, then went to make them both a coffee while it went through the start-up process. When he returned, he entered his username and password and delivered Sarah her coffee. As he placed it on the desk next to her, he ran his hand through the back of her long, blonde hair and marvelled again at how lucky he was to have her in his life.

They'd been together for over a year and a half, though he'd never have imagined they would become an item after their first meeting. After several fruitless months searching for a fugitive, Sarah had been seconded from MI6 to work as his superior at MI5, and had rubbed

Harvey up the wrong way from the get-go. To make matters worse, Harvey had suspected her of colluding with the man they'd been looking for. As it turned out, both of them had been played.

He seldom thought back to those times, though. When he pictured Sarah Thompson, he always saw the smiling, happy Sarah before him now. The images of her after her encounter with Alexi Bessonov, the Russian gangster who'd had her tortured, remained locked in the deepest recesses of his mind. Her physical scars remained but, thanks to the counselling sessions they'd taken, emotionally she was the same woman he'd fallen in love with nineteen months earlier.

He kissed her on the top of her head and got a smile in return, then walked back to his desk and opened the internal messaging system to see what had been happening in the world while they'd been sleeping.

'There's something here about Hannibal,' he said.

Sarah walked across to look over his shoulder.

Working under the cover name Abdul al-Aziz, Mohammad Abdulrashid was a field operative she had worked with during her time at MI6. Codenamed Hannibal, he'd been undercover in Syria for the last year, and had been instrumental in feeding both Five and Six vital information on activities in the region. Over the last few months, he'd given them the heads-up on a splinter unit he'd infiltrated: SAI or Saif al-Islam.

The message contained details of a recent engagement between SAI and British Special Forces. Appended were the names of twenty-five SAI members who'd been identified by MI6. Next to each was a succinct legend:

Deceased.

'Looks like Hannibal made good again,' Sarah said.

'It's a shame we don't have more like him,' Harvey agreed, and printed out the report so that he could process the names and see if any of them had ties to the UK. A similar mission three weeks earlier had identified two men who had travelled from Manchester to Syria a year earlier, only to die in an apparent air strike.

The buzzer for the door sounded and Veronica Ellis entered the room wearing her trademark pencil skirt, laptop bag over her shoulder. At fifty-four years of age, she carried off the look very well, but underneath the smart appearance she was a double-edged sword. She was polite and affable for the most part, but gave short shrift to those who crossed her.

'Morning,' the Director General said as she headed to her transparent office, known as the glass palace. 'Anything on the wire I should be worried about?'

'Not so far,' Harvey said. 'I'll pop by if anything major comes in.'

Harvey went back to sorting the incoming messages, but couldn't help his thoughts turning to the pleasures – culinary and otherwise – that awaited him at home tonight.

Nabil Karim stood by the window of his apartment and looked out over Aleppo, Syria's largest city. This neighbourhood had survived the recent fighting relatively unscathed, people on the streets below going about their business as if the civil war had never occurred.

But things were far from normal for Karim.

His visitor had arrived minutes earlier with news about Abu Hussain and his men.

'When did this happen?' asked Karim.

'We don't know exactly,' Javad Zarifa said, 'but it appears they were hit before they could complete their mission.'

Karim turned and faced his second-in-command, a small man whose hawk-like countenance and long black beard were in stark contrast to his own blunt and recently shaven face. 'Then it is as we feared.'

'It would appear so,' Zarifa agreed.

Over the last year, Saif al-Islam had lost more than a hundred men to fighting, but the vast majority had been killed in the last few weeks, and it seemed too much of a coincidence that the Western troops, once so inept at finding them, should suddenly be able to intercept his men at every turn.

It was now abundantly clear that Saif al-Islam had a traitor; it had taken the lives of twenty-five good men to confirm it. That aside, finding one man in the three hundred under his command would be no simple task. Time constraints added extra urgency, and Karim was acutely aware of the ticking clock.

The main Islamic group in the region had a rigorous structure, consisting of Caliph Abu Bakr al-Baghdadi and, under him, the religious, advisory, military and security councils. A similar structure existed in each of the provinces, nine in Syria and seven in Iraq, each ruled by the Wali, or provincial governors. Karim had been surprised when ordered to set up Saif al-Islam, but once the purpose of the new unit had been explained, he had taken great pride in the appointment. He'd worked hard during the last twelve months to get things in place, and now it seemed his efforts would be for nothing unless he discovered who was betraying him.

'Bring me a list of our newest recruits as a starting point,' Karim said. 'If we find they are not responsible for this treachery, we can expand the search. In the meantime, I have an idea that should flush out the infidel among us.'

'I took the liberty,' Zarifa said, handing Karim a sheet of paper with twelve names handwritten on it.

Karim nodded. 'I should have expected no less. I also need you to send me a runner. Make sure they have the proper paperwork, and book them a flight to London for this evening.'

He gave Zarifa one final instruction, which was to procure four dozen automobile shock absorbers. 'Get the biggest you can find.'

Zarifa nodded and took his leave.

Karim opened his laptop and typed a query into the search engine. Up came a list of car repair shops in Birmingham, England. He made a note of several small, privately owned companies. He then repeated the search in other major British cities until he had a dozen addresses. That would be enough for the initial stage of his investigation; he hoped it wouldn't have to go beyond that.

If it did, his ultimate mission, the very reason for creating Saif al-Islam, would be in jeopardy, and he was well aware that if the operation failed, his masters would be unforgiving.

CHAPTER 3

Thursday, 6 July 2017

As he entered the workshop, Abdul al-Aziz did his best to hide the shock of seeing Nabil Karim standing next to a man pouring a reddish, viscous liquid into a blue metal tube. Unlike his own, the worker's hands were steady as he added the last drops, and Abdul watched him put the container down and gently wipe the neck of the tube with a rag before inserting a thinner pole inside it and screwing on a stopper. When the man removed the cylinder from the vice, Abdul could see that it was a shock absorber, and he could only imagine that it belonged on a truck, given its size.

Only when the shock absorber lay alongside three others in a wooden crate did Karim look up to acknowledge the new arrival.

'*As salam aleykum*,' Abdul said, doing well to control the pitch of his voice.

'*Wa aleykum as salam*,' Karim replied.

When he'd been told to report to the building to carry out a small task, Abdul hadn't expected the leader of Saif al-Islam to be there, and he couldn't help wondering if this was going to be his last day on the planet. If they'd discovered that he was working for MI6, it certainly would be.

'There is something I'd like you to do for me,' Karim said, as he watched the worker apply a label to the box.

'Of course,' Abdul said.

'I want you to take this package to Port Latakia and give it to a man named Najeeb. He will meet you at the coffee shop on Al Maghreb al Arabi at two this afternoon.'

'It looks . . . delicate.'

'It is fine,' Karim smiled, 'as long as the contents of the tubes do not come in contact with each other.' He banged the red box on its side. 'This is a binary explosive. The two compounds on their own are harmless, but once mixed, they produce an explosive more powerful than C4. Malek was being careful because if even the tiniest drops came into contact with each other, it could destroy this entire building.'

'I shall be extra careful,' Abdul said. 'May I ask what it will be used for?'

'Of course.' Karim smiled. 'I was going to make an announcement in a few days, but as you are to make the delivery, it is best that you know how important it is to us. Do you know why Saif al-Islam was created?'

'No,' Abdul said honestly. He knew the workings of the parent organisation inside out, and when told he was going to be placed into a specialist unit, he'd relished the opportunity. Any specialised information would be of keen interest to his masters back home, but so far he'd gained no new intelligence. The purging of villages had continued, the sacking of Christian enclaves increasing, if anything. He'd started to worry that there was nothing special about the new unit. Until now. At last, it appeared he would have something to pass back to MI6 other than troop movements.

'Creating and expanding the caliphate has always been our priority, and at first we had great successes. However, the West has responded in kind, and it is beginning to take a toll. We have lost over twenty thousand men since our fight began, and we cannot afford to continue taking such losses. That is why we will take the fight to them.'

'But how can we attack their planes? They have air superiority.'

'We can do little about their air strikes,' Karim said, 'but we can punish them for every bomb they drop, every missile they fire. It has taken a year to manufacture enough of this explosive. Now it will be sent to England, where our people have been waiting patiently.'

When Karim didn't elaborate, Abdul knew that he had effectively terminated the conversation.

'I will see that it gets to Najeeb,' he said.

Karim had Malek help him carry the box to his car and told Abdul what Najeeb looked like. With the description memorised, Abdul drove the old Nissan to the M5, the main artery leading to the port. Once on the motorway that would take him west, he drove at just under the speed limit for ten minutes until he was sure no-one was following him.

After all this time, he finally had valuable information to report. Up until now, he'd been forced only to give his bosses scraps, reporting on one in five operations being carried out by SAI. He could have told them about each planned attack, but if every mission were intercepted, SAI would have quickly become suspicious of Karim. As it was, Abdul felt safe, despite the company he kept.

It hadn't always been that way.

Born of Syrian parents, he'd been brought to England at the age of seven when his father had secured a position as a doctor with a hospital in London. The family had lived in a leafy suburb, and Abdul – Mohammad Abdulrashid, as he'd been named then – had been privately educated. His exam results had attracted the attention of the security services, and he'd been the perfect fit for MI6 when the crisis in Syria had kicked off. A kid full of self-confidence, he'd aced the intake process and, when offered the opportunity to return to the land of his birth, he'd jumped at the chance.

Getting into the country hadn't been as easy as he'd anticipated. His handler had insisted first on finding a near lookalike who'd make a likely traveller to the war zone. Despite an extensive UK watch list, it had taken months to find a match. That man had been Abdul al-Aziz, also Syrian and fresh out of university, where he'd hung around with a group of radicals. Six had manipulated al-Aziz into arranging to go back to the land of his fathers, but the young man hadn't even made it to the airport.

What they'd done with him, Mohammad didn't know, nor did he care. He had been busy memorising everything Six had on al-Aziz, from the names of his family members to the man's favourite food.

He vividly remembered that initial journey, from arriving in Turkey to making his way to the Syrian border, where he'd been met by someone called Farooq. It had been a tense time, as his guide had eyed him suspiciously and quizzed him non-stop on the trip to Aleppo. That he hadn't been shot and dumped by the side of the road told him he'd passed the test with flying colours, and he'd been able to relax into his role.

That had been more than twelve months earlier; soon after joining up with the group, he'd been given his first major test.

His first kill.

The unit he'd been assigned to had been engaged in a violent skirmish with Syrian troops. They'd come out of it with a few losses and a couple of prisoners and, as one of the newest members, Abdul had been given the honour of blooding himself.

He'd known it would come at some point. The organisation he'd joined had been created for one reason, and there was no such thing as a non-combatant. It had been something his handler had gone over with him time and again. While still at the theoretical stage, it had been easy to accept. When he'd been presented with a kneeling figure, an actual human being who was someone's son, possibly someone's husband and father, his handler's words suddenly rang hollow.

Abdul had told himself that the man was going to die anyway. If not by his hand, then by someone else's. With no alternative, twenty-two-year-old Abdul had dispatched the Syrian soldier and earned his place within the unit.

It was an incident Abdul had revisited many times, and he'd sworn that the victim's death wouldn't be in vain. It spurred him to be extra vigilant, to cover his every track. So far it had kept him alive, and now it was time to exercise his counter-surveillance skills once more.

Abdul checked his mirror and, with a clear road behind him, he pulled over to the side of the road and climbed out of the car. He walked to the front and popped the hood, and after another glance around to make sure no-one could see him, he felt the underside of the chassis and found the phone that was securely clipped in its hiding place. After unclipping it from the power lead wired to the car's fuse box, he turned it on, then opened the trunk and quickly took photos of the box he'd been entrusted with. He ensured the delivery address was clearly visible, then returned to the front of the car and sent the images to his handler back in the UK, along with a message describing the contents.

A car approached him, and he quickly returned the phone to its hiding place just as the vehicle pulled up next to him.

'What's the problem?' the driver asked.

'Just a loose lead,' Abdul said, slamming the hood closed. 'Time to trade in this pile of junk.'

The other driver waited until Abdul got back in the car and turned over the engine, then waved as he drove off. Abdul made a note of the car and its plate, then gave himself a couple of minutes before pulling back onto the highway. If he saw that same car on his journey, he'd know someone was watching him, but he made it to Latakia without seeing it or any other suspicious vehicles.

At the port, he found the coffee bar and saw the man he was supposed to meet sitting outside, nursing a drink. Abdul approached the large-framed man and introduced himself, and Najeeb got to his feet and climbed into Abdul's car without saying a word.

'Take a left at the end of the street,' Najeeb ordered, and Abdul followed further directions until he found himself outside a small warehouse.

'Open the trunk,' Najeeb said as he got out, and Abdul watched the man lift the box out and carry it towards the building.

Najeeb stopped and snapped a one-word order.

'Go.'

Abdul almost hoped the surly bastard tripped and blew himself to bits, but he knew a better outcome would be for his colleagues back home to intercept the package when it reached British shores.

CHAPTER 4

Sunday, 9 July 2017

Nabil Karim stubbed out his cigarette and blew on his tea before taking
a sip. Opposite him, Javad Zarifa sat patiently, waiting for his commander to continue.

'We will send in fifty men,' Karim said. 'After all this planning, we
cannot afford any mistakes.'

'It won't be easy for so many to approach unnoticed.'

'I appreciate that,' Karim told him. 'Send in a handful to take out
the guards on the gate and the rest can follow once that obstacle is
cleared.'

'As you wish,' Zarifa said, 'though I still think it is overkill. We
know there will be only ten guards on duty when we strike.'

'Indeed, but ten against five will feel confident. When faced with
fifty, panic will set in, and that will be our advantage.'

Zarifa nodded acceptance of Karim's logic, then took a sip of his
own tea. Something appeared to be troubling him; Karim told him to
speak his mind.

'I'm sorry, but I am worried that this is a lot of effort for little reward. I have researched VX nerve agent, and it is easily countered with atropine and pralidoxime. At best we might kill a few who are elderly and infirm, but once the infidels know what they're up against, they will be able to prevent deaths in the numbers we seek.'

'You are correct, my friend. A VX attack against the UK would have limited success, but I have something different in mind.'

Zarifa's eyes narrowed, clearly hurt by not having been told the whole story.

'I'm truly sorry,' Karim said, 'but I had instructions from the military council to share this with no-one, not even my most trusted friend.'

That seemed to appease Zarifa. 'We must all obey our masters,' he agreed. 'When will you be able to share this secret?'

'That's why I asked you to come today,' Karim said. 'I informed the council that, logistics aside, everything else is in place, and once we have the chemical agent we will be ready to proceed. They agreed that I could now involve you in the plans.'

It hadn't been easy keeping Zarifa out of the loop. He was the one person Karim trusted with his life, and their friendship went back twenty years. It had been necessary to tell him about the chemical weapons storage facility outside Homs so that Zarifa could help plan the assault, but he'd been forced to withhold the real target.

'You say you've researched VX nerve agent,' Karim said. 'What do you know about X3?'

'I've never heard of it,' Zarifa told him.

'Not many have. It was developed by the Syrian government four years ago, but few people outside al-Assad's inner circle and the military chiefs know anything about it.'

'What does it do?' Zarifa asked.

Karim spent a few minutes sharing everything he'd been told about the new chemical agent, and he could see the delight on his friend's face.

'Are you sure there's no antidote?' Zarifa asked.

'I'm certain. Once deployed, the casualties will continue to mount and the British will be powerless to help them.'

'Given the method we'll be using to transport it to the UK, we won't have a large quantity to work with. We will have to be selective in finding the right target.'

'Indeed we will,' Karim agreed, 'but the amount we have will be more than enough to get our message across. If the British think our campaign is merely a fight in the desert, they are sadly mistaken.'

Zarifa asked about the time frame.

'We'll wait until we discover who betrayed us. The shipment of shock absorbers will arrive in the UK early on the twenty-first. Once we discover who our mole is, we'll go ahead with the raid.'

'A prudent move,' Zarifa said. 'But what if we don't manage to flush him out this time?'

Karim had already considered the possibility that he might not catch the traitor with his first cast of the net. 'Then we go ahead anyway. I'd prefer it if the X3 remained a secret for as long as possible, but even if the British learn that we have it, they can't stop it from getting into the UK.'

'It is truly an audacious plan.' Zarifa took another drink of his beverage.

'We still have a lot to organise. What are the latest developments?'

'The boat's ready,' Zarifa told him. 'It can easily accommodate fifty people but I've instructed the owner to take half that number. The traffickers get greedy and overload their craft, which is why so many fail to complete the journey alive. We can't afford to let that happen.'

'Have some of our people there when the boat sails. If the captain tries to sneak a few more on board, show him the error of his ways.'

'Certainly,' Zarifa said.

'What about the rest of the journey?' Karim asked.

'Once the women reach Italy they'll be processed at the reception centre. We have someone ready to drive them to the French border. Another truck's been arranged to take them into England. We're just waiting for them to secure the last couple of items. They'll contact us when they have everything they need.'

Karim sat back in his chair and lit another cigarette, blowing a blue–grey cloud towards the ceiling. Just a few weeks to go, and he would cement his place in history. The mass bombings that shook Britain a couple of years earlier should have been a wake-up call, but the country's borders remained porous, leaving it susceptible to further attacks.

He was looking forward to exploiting that weakness to its fullest.

CHAPTER 5

Monday, 10 July 2017

Andrew Harvey opened the maritime website and entered the name of the vessel into the search box. The file next to him had been sent over by MI6 a couple of days earlier, but it had taken the resident technical wizard, Gerald Small, nearly forty-eight hours to get into the Syrian port's computer to see which ship the consignment had been loaded onto.

The screen zoomed in to show an icon with course and speed displayed next to it, and he expanded the view to see the expected arrival date. He jotted down the details, then did some research on the UK recipient.

Half an hour later, Harvey was in a position to update Veronica Ellis on developments.

He walked over to her glass-walled office, and the Director General waved for him to enter. He took a seat opposite her, a sparsely furnished oak desk between them.

'The shipment is due to arrive in ten days,' he said. 'It'll be offloaded in Southampton and collected by an import/export company, which will use a local courier to deliver it to the garage.'

'Let SO15 know,' Ellis said. 'We'll need Bomb Disposal, too.'

'Already notified,' Harvey told her. 'I've also put the Syrian shipping company on the watch list. If anything destined for the UK is sent through them, we'll know about it.'

'Hopefully they won't make another play for a while. I read Hannibal's report, and he said it took them nearly a year to make the binary explosive. I don't know if that includes R-and-D time or was purely manufacturing.'

'I guess we'll know more when the lab's had time to analyse it,' Harvey said. 'Either way, this puts a big dent in their plans.'

Ellis brushed a strand of platinum hair behind her ear. 'What about the final destination – the garage? Any link between the owner and Saif al-Islam?'

'Not yet. I've got Hamad and Sarah looking into everyone who works there, but at first glance they all appear clean. I'd like to set up surveillance to monitor phone and internet use.'

'Put in the request,' Ellis told him, 'and I'll sign it off.'

With the boss updated, Harvey went back to his station.

'Hamad,' he said, looking over his monitor. 'I need you to send me the profiles for the staff at Guler Motors.'

Hamad Farsi sat opposite him, their computer screens separating them. Farsi had been a close friend and colleague for nearly a decade, a likeable and reliable operative who had put his life on the line more than once. He was still recovering from an incident earlier in the year, when a Spetsnaz team working for the Russian mobster Alexi Bessonov had mown him down in their SUV, and the injuries he'd sustained remained evident.

'They'll be with you in a second, though I can't find anything on them,' Farsi said. 'Normally we have a known associate to work with, but these guys look squeaky clean.'

'They're hardly likely to announce their intentions,' Harvey pointed out. 'They've managed to stay under the radar this long, but they always slip up at some point. I've got the go-ahead to tap their phones and internet, but it's going to mean a drive-by using some of Gerald's kit.'

Gerald Small had developed a bit of software that could detect mobile phones within a fifty-yard range and harvest the numbers on them. Going on the presumption that bad guys always use burner mobile phones, it enabled Harvey's people to eavesdrop even on unregistered devices.

'Want me to do it?' Farsi asked.

'Nah, Gerald can handle it. If anyone looks less like a spook, I'd like to meet them.'

Harvey filled out a communications monitoring form using the information Farsi had provided, detailing the information they'd received about the perceived threat. He emailed it to Ellis for her electronic signature, then walked to Small's office, where the lanky technician was busy with a colleague.

'The problem you have there is line of sight, and the brickwork's going to interfere with the signal—'

'Sorry to interrupt,' Harvey said. 'Gerald, I need you to go walkabout.'

Small stood from his desk. 'Sure, no problem.'

Harvey explained the mission.

'That's all, just get their phone numbers?'

'Simple as that. We'll pass them on to GCHQ and wait for the results.'

Small looked disappointed. 'When are you going to let me play real spy?' he asked.

'Sadly, this is what spy shit is all about. Little tasks all adding to the big picture. I've got some data mining that needs to be finished by this evening, if that's more your thing . . .'

'Fine. When do you need the numbers?'

'As soon as,' Harvey said. 'It relates to the shipment you worked on.'

Small picked up a backpack and removed a device the size of two thick slices of bread. He checked the battery level, then replaced it in the bag. 'Who's the target?'

'I'll send the details over to you. It's a garage in Wandsworth.'

Harvey went back to his computer and pinged the details across to Small's terminal, then walked over to Sarah's desk and placed a hand on her shoulder.

'Lunchtime,' he announced.

She looked up and smiled. 'Sure, just give me a second.'

She finished an email and sent it, then picked up her bag and locked arms with Harvey. 'What do you fancy today?'

'I'll let you choose,' he said.

They settled on the little sushi place around the corner and, once seated in a corner booth, Harvey ordered for both of them.

'We've identified the boat carrying the explosives,' he said, after the waitress delivered their mineral waters. 'It'll be here on the twenty-first, which gives us plenty of time to assemble a welcoming party.'

'That's great news, though I'm sure it won't be their last attempt.'

'It might be for the time being. We don't know how long it will take them to get their hands on more explosives, and we've identified one of their routes. I know it isn't quite game over, but we've got their moves covered for the moment.'

'Thanks to Hannibal,' Sarah agreed. 'It's just a shame we can't get more people into their ranks.'

It was indeed. With Hannibal feeding them genuine, reliable information, they were able to stay one step ahead of SAI. Unfortunately, as Sarah had pointed out, Hannibal was one of just a handful of operatives scattered throughout Syria and Iraq. While the intel they sent back about the players in the region was priceless, there was just too little of it.

On top of that, Hannibal's report of SAI bringing the fight to UK soil matched with intel received from one of their other operatives working in Damascus. That report suggested that the major Islamist group operating in Syria had begun sending soldiers into Europe posing as refugees. So far, the Damascus operative said, around a hundred terrorists had made the perilous journey by sea to Greece and Italy. But that was as far as the report went. MI6 had no names or faces to work with, making the task of detecting them almost impossible. Hannibal, thankfully, had fed them the identities of the people he was working with, so if any of them tried to make it into the EU, MI6 had a good chance of stopping them.

'Exactly,' Harvey said. 'Having more people like Hannibal would go some way to help sort the operatives from the migrants.'

'Right,' Sarah said. 'Rather than simply suspecting them all.'

While Harvey held what he considered to be a pragmatic position on the refugee crisis, Sarah had one foot in the 'Let's save them all' camp. He'd found it strange that, given the nature of her job, she failed to see the danger.

'A healthy dose of suspicion is about all we have, lacking better intel from Syria.'

'The PM's policy of only taking in refugees from the camps bordering Syria and Iraq is the sensible way of covering your concerns.'

'In one respect, it does,' Harvey agreed, 'but we can't dismiss the million who made it into Europe last year. That's where the real threat is going to come from.'

Sarah nodded. 'I just feel sorry for the children. It's not much of a start in life when you're forced to risk your life for weeks or months just to find a country willing to offer you a bed and some warm food.'

'I know,' he said. 'And think about the ones who don't make it out at all. And of the dozens of other countries with kids in the same situation. I think it's a crappy time to bring any child into the world.'

Their food arrived, and Sarah fell silent as they ate.

CHAPTER 6

Thursday, 20 July 2017

Andrew Harvey put down the phone and walked round to Farsi's desk.

'They loaded the container onto the truck five minutes ago,' he said. 'It should reach the importer within the hour.'

'Are you sure you don't want to be at the garage when the police pick them up?'

'No need,' Harvey assured him. 'Once they're in custody, I'll go and sit in on the interviews.'

'Okay, but I still think this whole thing has a bad smell about it.'

'I know, but we have little choice.'

After ten days of thorough background checks and sifting through gigabytes of communications data, they hadn't detected much to suggest that any of the staff at Guler Motors Limited were involved in a bombing plot. Apart from one mechanic who attended a mosque that was also frequented by a minor figure on their watch list, the worst transgression they'd uncovered was that the owner was cheating on his wife.

'I still think the idea that they were pressured into accepting the package on someone else's behalf should be revisited,' Farsi said. 'We could sit back and see if anyone we know makes a surprise visit.'

It was a notion the team had batted around a few days earlier, but in the end it had been decided that they would strike the moment the shock absorbers were delivered; they simply couldn't afford to let the consignment sit in the garage for too long. The contents of the shock absorbers could easily be removed and spirited off the premises in any number of ways, and they could hardly arrest everyone who left the building without giving the game away. Ultimately, the mosque attendance coincidence had been enough for Ellis to sign it off.

'We already put that to bed,' Harvey said. 'This way, it's win–win. We prevent the explosives being used on our soil, and possibly expose a cell we never knew about.'

Farsi put his hands up in mock surrender. 'You're the boss,' he said, and rose to walk to the coffee station.

Harvey noticed that his friend's limp was improving. Six months after being hit by the SUV, he was lucky to be alive, never mind walking unaided.

'A tenner says I'm right,' Harvey shouted after him.

'Deal!' Farsi smiled.

Of course, there was always the chance the consignment could be switched or intercepted en route, but Harvey was satisfied that SO15 had that covered.

~

Sergeant Toby Sitwell of the Counter Terrorism Command, also known as SO15, sat in the passenger seat of the unmarked Skoda as it tailed the lorry along the M3 motorway towards Basingstoke. A mile further back, another vehicle carrying four armed team members was ready to move up on his command. Like the driver, Sitwell was wearing plain clothes, but he'd chosen a suit rather than his colleague's denims and casual jacket.

So far, the operation had gone smoothly, but he knew his men would have to remain alert until the package reached its final destination. The next scheduled stop for the truck was the importer's warehouse. MI5 had done background checks on the five personnel known to work there and had found nothing to suggest they were anything but innocent links in the supply chain. Still, Sitwell wasn't about to risk his men's lives by being blasé.

The truck carrying the large blue container signalled its intention to leave the motorway at junction 7, as expected. Sitwell radioed the other car and told them to close the gap.

He found himself one car behind the truck, and though he was now more conspicuous, it didn't really matter too much. The warehouse was less than half a mile away from the motorway, and it would soon be time to make his presence known.

As expected, the truck took a left and then a right into the industrial estate before backing into a loading bay. Sitwell ordered the driver to pull up outside the reception office of Larkin Logistics, and as soon as the car came to a halt he barked, 'Go, go, go!' into his radio and climbed out.

He marched through the office door and flashed his badge at the young female receptionist just as the reserve unit screeched to a stop next to the truck.

'Police,' Sitwell said. 'Where's the manager?'

A man in his thirties emerged from a side office, wearing a yellow shirt and pink tie.

'I'm John Larkin. Can I help you?'

Sitwell held up his badge. 'I've got four armed officers at your loading bay,' he said. 'We need to supervise the unloading of that truck.'

'Could you tell me what this is all about?'

'There's a package on that vehicle that's of interest to us. We just need to ensure it makes the next stage of its journey without interruption.'

'I can assure you, none of the consignments we receive are tampered with in any way.'

'Understood,' Sitwell said, 'but we're not taking our eyes off it. Who's supposed to pick it up?'

'I'd need to know which package and the delivery address,' the manager said as he asked the receptionist to move and sat down at her terminal.

Sitwell gave him the details, and moments later the information appeared on the screen.

'Charlie Fenton, of T & C Couriers. He's due here in about forty minutes.'

'Then I suggest you start unloading. My men will make themselves scarce when he arrives, but if anyone warns him that we're here, there'll be consequences.'

'I hardly think Charlie would be involved in anything,' Larkin said. 'He doesn't even know which parcels he'll be delivering until we receive them and arrange his route.'

'Perhaps not, but I'm not taking any chances. How many deliveries will he be making from this shipment?'

Larkin tapped a few keys and the printer spat out two sheets of paper. 'This is his route. Seventeen stops in all. Your package is number fifteen.'

'Too many,' Sitwell said. 'Has Fenton got a copy of this?'

'Not yet.'

'Good. Scratch the first fourteen items and make ours the first on his round.'

'But our customers are expecting their deliveries today,' Larkin argued. 'We've got a reputation to maintain.'

'Then here's what you do. Have number fifteen ready. As soon as Fenton leaves, call another firm to deliver the rest.'

'That's going to leave me out of pocket. Are you going to pick up the tab?'

Sitwell nodded. 'Sure. Write up an invoice and I'll give it to my superiors.'

With this financial wrinkle ironed out, Larkin led Sitwell through to the warehouse, where unloading was under way. A forklift backed out of the container with a pallet loaded with dried figs, which the driver skilfully stacked in a corner.

'Once the truck's empty,' Sitwell said, 'put number fifteen near the loading bay, then tell everyone to clear out. Send them shopping, or to the pub, I don't care. They can come back when he's gone. I'll be with you all the time, so pretend I'm a potential new customer looking to use your services.'

Within a quarter of an hour, the warehouse staff cleared out and the targeted packages were waiting for the courier to collect them. The second police vehicle had retreated two hundred yards down the road, awaiting Sitwell's instructions. Sitwell's driver joined him and Larkin in the reception area.

'What does Fenton's van look like?' Sitwell asked.

'It's a white Transit,' Larkin told him. 'It's got his logo splashed along the side, so you can't miss it.'

'Okay, then here's the plan. When Fenton gets here, you keep him talking here on reception for at least a minute, then let him go and pick up his packages. Once he's gone, we'll clear out, too. And please don't try calling him later to tell him what's been going on. It'll be easy for us to get all of his phone numbers and see what calls were placed to him. Likewise, if we suddenly get a demand from him for lost wages, we'll know you spoke to him in person and told him why his route is so short today.'

'Well, this isn't going to be fair on him,' Larkin said. 'He's always grumbling how money is so tight these days.'

Sitwell was becoming exasperated. 'Then accidentally pay him what he should get for the original route. I'm covering the other delivery, so no-one's out of pocket.'

Sitwell could see the businessman weighing up the options, trying to select the one which would make him the most money, and he decided Larkin was unlikely to tell Charlie Fenton the real reason for the curtailed route.

He took his driver off to the side. 'Go and get the tracker ready.'

As the man disappeared, Sitwell checked his watch, passing on Larkin's offer of a cup of coffee.

Fenton turned up five minutes early and, while initially chipper, seemed genuinely disappointed with the short list Larkin handed him.

'At least you'll be home in time to watch *EastEnders*,' Larkin pointed out.

Fenton, in his forties and sporting a crew cut, made disparaging noises at the suggestion, but folded the paper and tucked it into his breast pocket. He was heading for the warehouse when Larkin called him back.

'I see Chelsea have put in a bid for Lionel Messi. What do you think their chances are?'

'The way we started last season, we need him,' Fenton said, 'but £120 million is far too much to pay for a twenty-nine-year-old.'

While the men debated the merits of the Argentinian footballer, Sitwell had one eye on the front door. When he saw his driver walk back to the vehicle and climb in behind the wheel, he turned to the manager.

'Mr Larkin, I'm afraid I'll have to be going soon. If you could show me the rest of your layout, it would be appreciated.'

Larkin got the message, and ushered both men into the warehouse. He pointed Fenton in the direction of the three boxes, then started explaining to Sitwell how his company would handle the logistics of getting his Chinese goods from the port to his lock-up garage in London more cheaply than his rivals.

Fenton loaded his packages, waved at Larkin and climbed into his van. Sitwell waited for him to drive away before thanking the manager for his co-operation and jogging to his car.

Inside he saw the screen affixed to the console with their current position marked in green and a red dot moving slowly away from them.

'Don't get too close,' Sitwell said, as the driver reversed out of the parking space and headed towards the exit in pursuit.

An hour and a half later, Charlie Fenton's van pulled up outside Guler Motors. He got out and went round to the back to open up the double doors, then emerged with the wooden box and carried it into the open bay.

Sitwell watched from fifty yards away, preparing to radio his men to move in. From his position he could see Fenton talking with someone, possibly the owner, who looked very confused. Fenton put the box down and offered a shrug, and once his docket was signed, he got back into his van and drove off.

The moment the Transit van disappeared from sight, Sitwell told his driver to floor it and ordered his men into action. By the time he reached the open work bay, the other vehicle was right behind his, disgorging armed police officers who ran into the workshop, barking instructions.

Sitwell ran to where he'd seen the manager carry the box, a small office with dirty glass windows. He barged in, with a gun-toting officer close behind him.

'Armed police. Hands where we can see them!'

The man had been in the process of opening the box with a flathead screwdriver, and he froze with the tool sticking out of the underside of the lid. Slowly, he raised his hands and took a step backwards.

Sitwell ordered him around the desk and forced him up against a wall before searching him. The man found his voice and began protesting, but Sitwell ignored him. After confiscating the man's phone, Sitwell had another officer cuff the suspect and load him into the van, which had arrived seconds after the raid began.

Sitwell called in the bomb-disposal team and left the office while they assessed the package. Three minutes later, they declared it safe to transport, and carried it to their vehicle while Sitwell made a call.

'The suspects are in custody, Mr Harvey, and we have the explosives.'

'Thanks. I'll meet you at the station in thirty minutes.'

From his position next to the window of the café thirty yards away, Ahmed watched the raid unfold. He'd been tasked with keeping an eye on the garage, and in the last four hours he'd been through more coffee than he normally drank in a week.

His order had been simple: keep an eye on the place and report any unusual activity, especially anything involving the police.

Why, he had no idea, but the day's surveillance work had earned him an easy hundred.

Ahmed activated his phone and began filming the scene. After ten minutes, he reckoned he had enough to show the man who'd given him the assignment. With his mission complete, he made a long-awaited trip to the bathroom before heading to the mosque to share his findings and collect his reward.

CHAPTER 7

Thursday, 20 July 2017

Nabil Karim looked at Javad Zarifa with more than a little astonishment.

'Really? Abdul al-Aziz?'

'We got confirmation fifteen minutes ago. There is a video available if you wish to view it.'

'No need,' Karim said. 'It's just that Abdul is the last person I would have suspected.'

'I must admit, I was surprised, too. How would you like to handle this?'

Karim had thought about the punishment for several days, and he shared his idea with Zarifa.

'Also, check to see if we have any video of Abdul in action. It could be useful.'

Zarifa hurried away to carry out his orders, leaving Karim relieved to have found the traitor, but annoyed at having been duped in the first place.

The one redeeming note was that only he, Zarifa and the military council knew what he had planned in the coming weeks. Not even the people carrying out the most hazardous part of the mission knew their roles.

Not yet, at least.

It would soon be time to take control of the chemical-weapons storage facility, and once he had the X3, he would share the details with the five who needed to know. As far as everyone else involved was aware, including those helping to facilitate the travel arrangements, he was simply helping a handful of people to be reunited with their families in the UK. Now that Abdul had been exposed, he was confident that he could keep things that way.

An hour later, he received a call from Zarifa to say that the meeting had been set up, and he walked down two flights of stairs to his SUV. He told his driver, a huge man of few words, to take him to an address on the outskirts of the town, then settled back in his seat and contemplated the pleasure to come.

Abdul al-Aziz pulled up outside the building he'd been told to report to and saw Karim's right-hand man, Javad Zarifa, waiting by the door. Half a dozen vehicles already dotted the area around the two-storey stone building, beyond which lay a vast expanse of desert. Two German shepherds chained to a wall snarled as he approached the door.

He'd never been invited here before. He hoped he'd have something worthwhile to report home afterwards.

After the usual greetings, Zarifa showed Abdul inside, where a dozen others were already gathered. They were lining the walls of the room, and on a long wooden table a video was playing on a laptop.

'Ah, our guest of honour,' Karim said, opening his arms wide and smiling. 'Come, sit. You are just in time.'

Immediately, Abdul sensed something was wrong, but before he could react, two men grabbed his arms and forced him into a chair facing the old Dell laptop. He recognised the person on the screen, a man with an AK-47 standing over a kneeling figure.

It was him.

'I see you recognise yourself,' Karim said. 'This was taken shortly after you joined us, remember? It was your initiation, your way of showing me that you were one of us.'

Abdul nodded, trying to hide the panic invading every sinew of his body. He wanted to convince himself that his worst fear wasn't about to come true, but one glance at Karim told him everything he needed to know. The smile was gone, replaced with a glare that could strip paint from walls.

He remained silent, hoping that by playing dumb he could find a way out of the situation.

'This film has never been released,' Karim said. 'No-one knows that you killed this man. That is all about to change.'

'I don't understand. It was a simple headshot. How will that instil fear in our enemies?'

'It won't,' Karim told him, 'but it should come as a shock to the British public when they discover that the man who pulled the trigger is one of their spies.'

Before Abdul could fashion a response, he was hoisted to his feet and the laptop was moved out of the way. The others in the room crowded in as he was picked up and thrown onto the table, where four men held his legs and two others pinned his shoulders to the wooden surface.

Abdul could see a video camera being set up on a tripod, and he began pleading with his captor.

'Nabil, this is a mistake! Why are you doing this?'

'I suspected there was a traitor among us for some time, and it was simply a case of finding him. That's why I let you and certain others believe you were delivering explosives to England. Only one of those packages was intercepted. Yours.'

'It's not true!' Abdul shouted. 'Maybe the explosive was detected by customs.'

'Unlikely,' Karim said, drawing closer. 'We switched packages before they were shipped out. The consignment that the police picked up contained normal shock absorbers. There was nothing in the box to raise any suspicion at all.'

Abdul realised there was little point in further protestation. It was now just a matter of how Karim chose to deal with him. Any hopes of a swift death with a bullet to the head were quickly dispelled when he heard the roar of a small engine starting up. The men around him started masking their faces, and it was obvious his demise was about to be filmed.

'We are going to send a message to your masters,' Karim said. 'They can send as many spies as they like, but this will be the fate that awaits them.'

Karim stood aside to make way for a soldier wielding a chainsaw.

~

'For the tenth time, I have no idea why it was delivered to me!'

'It had your name on it, Mr Guler,' the police officer said, sounding bored.

Andrew Harvey watched the interview on CCTV, and so far had seen nothing to convince him that the garage owner had anything to do with a bomb plot. The interviewing officer had been all round the houses, trying to trip the suspect up, but the answers always came back the same. Usually the guilty ended tying themselves up in knots as they wove their webs of lies, but this man seemed genuinely surprised that the parcel had been delivered to him.

'I don't even know what was inside,' Guler continued.

'But you were in the process of opening it when we arrived.'

Alan McDermott

'Of course! Someone sends you a parcel, all paid for, what else would you do?'

'You could have reported it to the police.'

'Are you serious?' Guler asked. 'That has to be the most stupid suggestion I've ever heard. What if one of my mechanics orders something that I'm not aware of? Do you expect me to call the bomb squad just in case?'

'This package clearly originated abroad,' the officer continued. 'Doesn't that strike you as strange?'

'Not strange enough to call the police without first checking the contents.'

Harvey's phone rang, and he stepped away from the console to take the call.

'You have to get back to the office,' Farsi said when he hit the 'Connect' button.

'What's up?' Harvey asked, already moving towards the door.

'Bomb Disposal called and told us what was in the shock absorbers. Nothing out of the ordinary. They were the real thing.'

'It can't be. SO15 had the shipment covered from the moment it reached the dock. There wasn't time to switch it.'

'I don't think they did,' Farsi said. 'We got played. A few minutes after BD called, we received a video from Nabil Karim. They killed Hannibal.'

Realisation hit Harvey like a heavyweight boxer.

They'd been set up, and all to expose their man in Karim's ranks. Harvey massaged his temples, knowing that their spy hadn't suffered a swift death. Reluctantly, he asked Farsi what they'd done to him.

'They amputated his arms and legs with a chainsaw, just above the knees and elbows, then dragged him outside and let two German shepherds finish him off.'

Harvey could hear the tension in his friend's voice, angry and bordering on tears.

'They ate him alive, Andrew. That bastard fed him to the fucking dogs!'

Harvey gripped the phone until he nearly cracked it. He could almost hear Hannibal's screams.

'I'll be there in twenty minutes.'

Harvey ended the call and went in search of Sergeant Sitwell. He found him in the canteen.

'Kick Guler loose,' he said. 'It was a trick, and we fell for it. There were never any explosives; they did it to root out our operative.'

'You'd better get word to your man, then. Tell him to get his arse out of there.'

Harvey just nodded and turned on his heels. There was little point in telling Sitwell that his suggestion was already too late. No, it was time to get back to the office to see what they could salvage from this mess.

Half an hour later, he had his team assembled in the conference room. Veronica Ellis sat near the head of the table, next to a teary-eyed Sarah Thompson. Sarah had known Hannibal personally from her time with MI6, and was taking his demise hard. Also present were Hamad Farsi, Eddie Howes, Elaine Solomon and Gareth Bailey.

'Hamad, please tell us what we know so far.'

Farsi tapped a couple of keys on his laptop and an image appeared on the fifty-inch wall-mounted screen. 'This is Mohammad Abdulrashid,' he said for the benefit of those who didn't know the young operative known as Hannibal. He had a thin face and the beginnings of a beard. 'He was deployed in Syria where he went by the name Abdul al-Aziz. He had infiltrated a unit called Saif al-Islam – Sword of Islam – headed by this guy, Nabil Karim.'

Another picture appeared on the screen. This one showed a man in his forties, with a moustache and swept-back hair.

'We recently received news that Karim had killed Mohammad, and they sent video evidence to prove it. I won't be showing that, but they also sent this.'

A video began playing, and it showed Mohammad standing over a kneeling figure with a rifle in his hand. Unlike the others on the screen, Mohammad's face was clearly visible. As he raised his weapon, Farsi paused the footage.

'There's no need to show the rest of it. You can guess what he does next.'

'Why did they send us this?' Howes asked.

'They copied in all of the news channels and told them who pulled the trigger. We can expect the phones to start ringing any second now, but that's the least of our concerns. Mohammad told us early on that SAI was created to strike the UK. More recently, he led us to believe that a shipment of explosives was being sent here, but that turned out to be a ruse. It cost Mohammad his life.'

Harvey stood and began pacing. 'That's what we have so far, but the chain of events suggests that SAI already have people sympathetic to them here, in London. Someone was watching that garage when the police swooped in, and we need to find out who. I want CCTV from the area combed to see if anyone left the scene shortly after the police arrived. I don't care if it's a kid or an old woman, they had to be reporting to someone, and that someone fed the information back to Karim. We need to find them, and fast. Eddie, you check CCTV. Gareth and Elaine, I want you to scour social media and see if anyone uploaded footage of the garage being raided. If you find a video, identify the person who took it. The rest of us are going to go through everyone on our watch list and put tails on anyone with the remotest ties to SAI.'

He walked towards the door, signalling an end to the meeting and, back at his computer, opened the communications-monitoring form template. He had a feeling he was going to be filling them out for the rest of the day and into the night.

CHAPTER 8

Monday, 24 July 2017

At 3 a.m. precisely, Wahid gave the signal for his men to make their move.

The chemical-weapons storage facility, a huge, one-storey building surrounded by a ten-foot wall made of reinforced concrete, was situated near a village on the outskirts of Homs.

Wahid's men had been making their way towards the compound for the last four hours, crawling slowly on their bellies while covered with sand-coloured sheets. He had traced their painstaking progress, moving inches at a time to preserve the advantage of a surprise attack. A Syrian military unit was based less than three miles away, giving them minutes to carry out their mission before reinforcements arrived.

Wahid had been sweeping the walls of the compound for hours with his night-vision glasses, but there were no signs of CCTV cameras and no-one had stuck their heads up.

Still, he wasn't taking any chances.

Seven of his soldiers were now ten feet from the wall, and he watched from six hundred yards away as they prepared rappelling ropes with rubber-coated hooks on the end. The first man swung his towards the top of the wall and Wahid saw it come tumbling back down. The man tried again, and this time the hook caught. Three of his people were already halfway up the wall, and he heard nothing from inside the facility to suggest they'd been compromised.

He watched as the men disappeared over the wall, then ordered his reserve to move up. His own driver was the first to crank his engine and gun the truck towards the gates. In the darkness, Wahid could see flashes of light dancing off the top of the wall.

By the time he reached the gate, it was already open, with two of his men standing guard. The bodies of four Syrian soldiers lay on the ground. Wahid walked over to one of the dead and removed a plastic card from a chain on the corpse's waist, then jogged to the glass double doors and swiped it. A click signified that they had entry, and he stepped aside as his men poured into the building.

Gunfire erupted as Wahid's soldiers pushed forward, then subsided as he entered the building. Three more guards lay dead, leaving another three to contend with. He jogged down the hallway to the junction and looked both ways. The right was clear, and he ordered two men to cover it. To the left, his people were already working to open the door he'd ordered them to look for. He ran to join them just as it burst inwards.

Wahid let the soldiers check the room for guards, then walked inside and looked at the bank of large refrigerated cabinets. Third from the left on the top shelf, he'd been told, and when he looked at the labels, he confirmed that the intelligence his master had paid for was accurate. The cabinet door was locked, so he used the grip of his pistol to shatter the glass and carefully lifted the tray of phials off the shelf. He placed it on a workbench and extracted a leather case from inside his combat jacket.

He'd been instructed to take five phials, no fewer. He stole a look at his watch and saw that it had been two minutes since the first gunshots.

The army would have been alerted by now: he had to get his men out of here.

With the small bag now full of glass tubes, Wahid told his men to follow him, and he ran back out into the night.

'They're coming,' his driver told him as he jumped into the passenger seat of the truck.

Wahid snatched up the NVGs and saw the army convoy in the distance. He stuck his head out of the window and shouted to his lieutenant. 'I must get this safely to Karim. You know what to do.'

Without waiting for a response, Wahid told the driver to floor it, and he left the scene trailing a cloud of dust in his wake.

His men would fight until he was well clear of the area, and many of them would die before sunrise. Whatever he was carrying in his small bag, he hoped it was worth the price they would pay tonight.

CHAPTER 9

Thursday, 27 July 2017

These last few frustrating days weren't showing any signs of improving.

Harvey was trawling through the mountain of communications data that GCHQ had sent over that morning, but none of it mentioned SAI or Nabil Karim. His team had spent hours scouring the CCTV coverage of the garage raid and had seen one person leave a nearby café and take a bus to a mosque. They hadn't been able to identify him, but others associated with the place of worship included Imran al-Hosni, the imam and a person of special interest.

He'd been recorded months earlier at his mosque in Stockwell Green giving a sermon that praised the destruction of the temple at Palmyra in Syria. In his speech, the imam suggested that the brave young men who had travelled abroad to help their Muslim brothers should be seen as heroes, not criminals, for their support of Islam.

As a result, MI5 had placed electronic surveillance on al-Hosni six months ago, but there hadn't been enough evidence to charge him with any offence. The Crown Prosecution Service had listened to the original recording but hadn't deemed it enough to arrest him on a charge of incitement. Since then, al-Hosni had gone quiet, his preaching more mainstream and his meetings with a few members of the mosque infrequent, and although Harvey and his team had expanded their surveillance to incorporate his cohorts, no-one was making any noises to indicate an imminent threat.

Harvey rose from his desk and went over to Ellis's office, knocking before entering.

'I'd like to put some people on Imran al-Hosni,' he told her. 'We're getting nothing from phone or internet chatter, so it would be useful if we could have eyes on him for the next few weeks.'

'I'll see what I can do,' Ellis said, 'but don't get your hopes up. Maynard is still pissed at me, and I'll need him to authorise the overtime.'

John Maynard, the Home Secretary, was becoming the bane of their lives. He'd wanted to see Ellis kicked out of the service for the way she'd handled the Milenko affair at the start of the year, but the PM – with input from Tagrilistan's president – had seen fit to keep her in the role, much to Maynard's chagrin. His promise to make life miserable for Ellis had been no empty threat, and he did everything within the law to make her job as difficult as possible.

'Does he understand the severity of the threat Nabil Karim poses?'

'I'm sure he does,' Ellis said, 'but what better way to get rid of me than to have me screw up on the job? I'm sure that by withholding the resources we need, he's hoping we drop the ball and give him the opportunity to replace me.'

It wasn't just Ellis who suffered from Maynard's petulance. Harvey's own team had been hamstrung by dwindling staff and budget cuts that made a tough job a lot harder. They should have had a new intake of trainees at the start of the year, people who would free up Howes and Solomon to do some fieldwork, but that had been put on the back burner indefinitely.

'I think you should at least try. Let him know that, if there's an SAI cell in the UK, then al-Hosni's the man most likely to be behind it.'

'As I said, I'll do my best.'

Harvey could tell that Veronica Ellis didn't relish another trip into the lion's den.

~

Heat haze made the desert road look like a river as Karim glared into the distance. Night would soon be falling, and he was anxious to see how the latest stage of the mission was progressing.

The doctor's house was in a small town east of Aleppo, and it was dark by the time Karim's driver pulled up at the gates. Two of his men were standing guard, having been sent there the day before, and they recognised him as he approached, swiftly opening the gates to allow him ingress.

Karim walked through the front door, opened by the doctor himself, and the two men exchanged greetings.

'How are the patients doing?'

'Very well. They are all young and fit, so the recuperation period should only be a couple of days.'

'They have a tough journey ahead of them,' Karim said, walking into the living room. 'Will they be able to handle two weeks of travelling?'

'It shouldn't be a concern, as long as they don't lift anything too heavy. I have prepared painkillers and antibiotics, just in case.'

'Very good. I'd like to see them.'

The doctor led Karim down a hallway to a dimly lit room containing five beds. In each lay a woman, at least two of them sleeping. Probably a result of their recent surgery, Karim assumed.

He went to the first bed and stood over the woman. She looked calm despite her recent ordeal, and the empty phial of morphine on the wheeled trolley beside her went some way to explaining why.

'How are you feeling, Ramla?' Karim asked.

The woman offered a weak smile and touched her abdomen. 'It hurts, a little.'

'That is to be expected, but the doctor assures me you should be up and about in a couple of days. Are you ready to make your journey?'

Ramla nodded.

'Good. And are you sure you know what you have to do?'

Ramla went over the role she would play in the coming weeks, and Karim listened intently, ready to pounce if she made an error. He was pleased to discover that she could recite every aspect of the plan, despite having just undergone surgery.

This one wouldn't let him down.

Karim thanked her, then moved on to the next bed, where the occupant was waking from her slumber. He went through the same process with her, and again she knew exactly what was expected of her in the coming weeks.

Forty minutes later, he arrived at the last bed. In it lay the youngest of the women, and the one closest to his heart.

'Malika, are you prepared for what lies ahead?'

'I am,' she replied.

'You know it will mean you can never come back.'

'It is Allah's will.'

She seemed confident, as were the others, and Karim smiled as he stooped and kissed her on the forehead. As with the others, he asked her to go over her role, and she gave a faultless delivery. He interrupted from time to time with questions, but her answers were always the ones he wanted.

Karim took her hand. 'This will be the last time we see each other, but what we do in the coming days and weeks will shape history.'

Malika squeezed his hand and smiled.

'I won't disappoint you.'

CHAPTER 10

Wednesday, 2 August 2017

Nasir Qureshi handed over his Turkish passport and stood with a bored expression as the immigration officer studied the visa.

'How long do you plan to stay?' the official asked.

'Just a few days,' Qureshi told him.

'It's a long way to come for just a few days. What's the purpose of your visit?'

'My cousin is celebrating his twenty-fifth wedding anniversary. I would like to stay longer but I have a business to run back home.'

'How will you be supporting yourself during your stay?'

Qureshi pulled a roll of hundred-dollar bills from his pocket and handed them over. The man counted them and made a note of the amount on his computer, then handed the cash and Qureshi's passport back.

'Enjoy your stay.'

Qureshi picked up his hand luggage and followed the signs for the baggage reclamation area, where he picked up his small suitcase and headed through customs.

The decision to fly on a Turkish passport had been a wise move. Getting a visitor's visa had proven no problem, and he would attract a lot less interest than if he had used his Syrian documents.

Outside the terminal, he took a coach to London Victoria station, where he put his suitcase in a locker. It contained nothing he would need for the next forty-eight hours, by which time he would be on his way back to Aleppo via Turkey.

He took the Tube to Aldgate East, the house he was looking for a twenty-minute walk from the station. As he walked down the street, he looked for signs that he was being watched, but all the vehicles he passed were empty, and there were no suspicious figures lurking in any of the upstairs windows.

Qureshi found number thirty and knocked on the door of the two-storey, terraced house. Curtains in the bay window twitched, and a minute later the door opened a crack, a chain crossing the small gap from which a woman's face studied him.

'I'm looking for Imran al-Hosni,' Qureshi said. 'Please tell him his cousin Habibah gave birth to a baby girl.'

The female face disappeared to pass on the introductory message Qureshi had been given by Nabil Karim. The previous day, he'd spent an hour with the leader, listening to the instructions he would now pass on. He'd been forced to recite them over and over, but his eidetic memory hadn't let him down. He'd been able to repeat word for word the contents of the sheet of paper, which had then been thrown on a fire. When Qureshi closed his eyes, he could see the writing as if he was holding it in his hands.

There were a dozen ways Karim could have passed the message to al-Hosni, but his distrust of phones and email ruled out all forms of electronic communication. Qureshi knew that he was only one of several messengers Karim used, and this was his second visit to England. The first had been three months earlier, when his brief had been to pass on details of where the latest fundraisers should send the money they'd gathered.

The woman returned to the door and removed the chain, then opened it fully and stepped aside so that Qureshi could enter. He walked down a short hallway and into the living room, where a man sat on a sofa.

Imran al-Hosni was in his late forties and had a greying beard that reached down past his chest. The imam's head was covered by a *kufi*, or prayer cap, and the *salwar kameez* consisted of a light grey top over baggy white trousers.

'*As salam aleykum.*'

'*Wa aleykum as salam*,' al-Hosni replied, and motioned for Qureshi to sit.

The woman reappeared with a tray of tea, then left and closed the door behind her.

'What news do you bring from Nabil Karim?'

Qureshi recounted the first part of the message exactly as it had been written, and when he'd finished, he waited for a response.

Al-Hosni removed his glasses and wiped them on his shirt before replacing them on his nose. 'This is going to require a great sacrifice,' he said.

'That is not for me to know,' Qureshi said. 'I have been instructed to take back a simple answer. Will you do this, or not?'

'Of course I will do it!'

Qureshi put up his hands in defence. 'I was told to ask that question. Now that you have accepted, I can give you details of what Nabil expects from you in the coming days.'

It took another fifteen minutes for Qureshi to impart the remainder of the message, and once he was sure al-Hosni understood every aspect, it was his turn to gather information.

'I have been instructed to take certain details back with me. I don't expect you to have them all to hand, so I will meet you again in a few hours. And please, do not use the telephone or internet. You must meet with these people in person.'

He told al-Hosni what information he needed to take back to Syria, and when he was sure his host had committed his instructions to memory, he thanked him for the tea and walked to the door.

'It is better that I do not come back here. Let us meet up again at the mosque on Allen Street in four hours.'

Qureshi walked out into the street with his mission only partly accomplished. Al-Hosni's was only one of the messages he'd been ordered to deliver. He now faced another hour on the London Underground in search of the second man on Karim's list.

~

Dave Lucas let out a yawn and looked over at his colleague, who was engrossed in the game he was playing on his phone.

'You should try this,' Stewart Toner said. 'It helps keep me awake.'

Lucas understood the impulse. The endless hours of watching nothing happen took its toll, no matter how much sleep you had the night before. He often struggled to keep his eyes open during the first couple of hours of a surveillance shift, and today was no different.

'I've got better things to do with my life than crush some stupid candies,' he said, replacing his flavourless gum with a fresh piece. He picked up his book and angled it so that he could read it while keeping an eye on the target on the six-inch monitor. The camera, atop a lamp post forty yards from al-Hosni's house, sent its live feed to their van two streets away.

So far, al-Hosni had had one visitor all morning, and that had been the postman. It had been the same for the past three days, and apart from his twice-daily visits to the local mosque, the man appeared to have no social life whatsoever.

A male figure came into view, and Lucas was immediately alert. He knew just about all of the locals after seeing them time and again, but this was someone new.

'We might have something.'

He used the camera controls to zoom in on the subject, a man in his late twenties who was looking at each house as he strolled down the street towards al-Hosni's place.

'Keep coming,' Lucas muttered to himself, hoping the man would stop at the target house and make the ten-hour shift worthwhile. His wish was granted when the figure entered the unkempt front garden and knocked on the door.

Lucas hit a button to enter a timestamp on the recording, then another that would take a dozen still photos every second. Once the door fully opened and the man stepped inside, Lucas sent the images to Thames House, where an analyst would be given the task of identifying the newcomer.

Half an hour later, the man emerged once more, and Lucas took another set of shots for the team back in the office. After watching the suspect retrace his steps back down the street, he picked up his book and prepared to battle the next round of fatigue.

CHAPTER 11

Friday, 4 August 2017

Malika cuddled the infant as the bus took them south of Al-Hamidiyah along the Syrian coast. She knew the Mediterranean Sea was away to her right, but in the darkness it was hard to spot.

Her companions remained silent, apart from one woman who was comforting her own child. The little boy had recently fed, but was demanding more.

They had only been together for a short time, brought into each other's lives to carry out Nabil Karim's wishes. Ramla, at thirty-five and more than a decade older than the others, had a kind, round face. Khadija was the opposite, her thin face making her look like she was bordering on anorexia. All in all, they were a good bunch, and it was a shame that not all of them would get to live a full life.

Malika adjusted her position to take the weight off her abdomen. As promised, the pain had relented a few days after the surgery, and the painkillers they'd been given seemed to work well, but it was still tender to the touch.

She busied herself by memorising the latest information Karim had given to her prior to departure. The details were handwritten on a sheet of paper, and she read the information over and over until she could recite it without error.

The bus pulled off the road and stopped short of the sandy beach, and the driver got out and opened the sliding door on the side of the bus. A burst of cool air invaded the space, and Malika stuffed the paper into her pocket and pulled her shawl tighter as she climbed down and started walking towards the water. Apart from carrying Jalal, she had a bag containing enough snacks, baby food, formula and water to feed them both on what promised to be a long journey, as well as changes of clothes and a thick, warm blanket.

At the water's edge, she was helped into a small boat, where she waited patiently for the others to join her. Ramla, Inas, Jalila and Khadija each carried their own children, all boys apart from Jalila's. Once they had been seated on the rough wooden planks, the boat was pushed out into the water and a small motor chugged as they headed out into the darkness. Three minutes later, it rendezvoused with a larger vessel that had no running lights.

The pilot called Malika forward and took the boy from her, handing him to the deckhand who was reaching over the side of the fishing boat. She made the short climb up the rope ladder, each step a huge effort that put pressure on the fresh wound just below her navel.

Once aboard, Malika took hold of Jalal and waited for the other four women to join her. The smell of rotting fish seemed to envelop her, reaching into every pore and clawing at the back of her throat. She estimated the boat to be about ten yards long, and there were around twenty others on the deck, huddling close to retain as much warmth as they could. Most were men, but she spotted a handful of women with children clinging to them. She knew that these people would have paid a handsome price for the journey, all desperate to get their families away from a war that had already displaced more than four million.

Once the tender was empty, the pilot tied it off to the stern while the deckhand led them into the bowels of the boat. Below deck, the women were led through a narrow gangway and shown into adjoining cabins. Each contained three bunk beds, and it was clear that they would have to sleep with their children by their sides. The rooms were cramped, and although the fishy smell wasn't so strong here, it remained noticeable.

'Cute boy,' the deckhand said, looking at Jalal. 'How old is he?'

'Eleven months,' Malika said.

Jalal was the youngest of the children making the journey. The others were all able to walk; Ramla's son was almost four.

'Well, I hope he doesn't get seasick. We're expecting some rough weather in the next few hours.'

'How long will it take to get there?' Malika asked.

'This boat will do twenty knots on a good day. We would normally expect to make Lampedusa in just over two days, but it will be closer to three with the storm sitting in our way.'

The young man showed them where they could find the toilet, which he referred to as the 'head', then made his way back upstairs as the huge diesels powered up and pushed the boat away from the coast. The ride was smooth as they headed out into deeper waters, but soon the room began to pitch as the growing waves pummelled the side of the craft.

'I feel ill,' Inas said, and disappeared in the direction of the head. She returned a short while later and collapsed on her bed.

'I don't think I can stand three days of this,' Ramla said.

Malika felt much the same. At least they had a berth to hunker down in, unlike the other passengers, who were forced to sleep on the deck. Once the storm hit, those caught out in the open were in for a miserable ride.

'Try to sleep,' Malika said. 'Hopefully we'll be through the worst of it by the time morning comes.'

She tried to heed her own words, but after a couple of hours, sleep still evaded her. The boat was rolling heavily by this time, and she'd already been sick twice, the last time dry-heaving for close to five minutes. Thankfully, Jalal seemed to enjoy the rocking movement, and had dropped off shortly after the journey began.

The intensity of the storm increased as the night wore on, and a couple of times Malika was almost thrown from her bunk as the ship crested a wave and plunged into a trough. Eventually, fatigue forced her eyes closed, and when she woke she discovered that the storm had passed and the boat was once more on an even keel.

Malika prepared food for herself and a bottle and baby food for Jalal, and after visiting the head to clean up, she ventured upstairs into the pilot house, where she found the captain smoking. Judging by the full ashtray, it wasn't his first of the day, and the smell, combined with the pervasive fish stink, was enough to set her stomach churning once more.

'Morning,' he said. 'Sleep well?'

'Eventually,' Malika said. 'Are we likely to go through that again?'

'No, smooth sailing the rest of the way.'

Malika was grateful to hear it. It was her first time on board a boat, and she wasn't yet enamoured of life on the high seas. She opened the hatch and walked out onto the deck, where she was greeted by blue sky and serene waters. The storm had cleared the air and taken with it much of the noxious odour that emanated from the deck. She soaked in the tranquil setting, and it was almost five minutes before something struck her as strange. She went back inside to ask the captain.

'Where are the others?' she asked.

'Gone,' he said, stubbing out his cigarette. 'I had orders to lose them on the journey.'

'Then why bring them in the first place?'

The captain rubbed his thumb and index finger together. 'To make it worthwhile.'

It at least answered one of the questions about the mission that had been bothering her. She'd been instructed to tell the authorities that their initial destination had been the Greek island of Crete, which was over 350 miles from their kick-off point at the refugee camp in Lebanon. She was to claim that engine trouble had seen them drift for days. At the time, she'd wondered how Karim would prevent the other passengers from contradicting her story, and now she knew.

She couldn't help but feel a little sadness for those who had met a watery end, especially the children, but she had a job to do.

And if she did it properly, many deserving infidels would lose their lives.

~

At just before ten in the evening, the captain knocked on Malika's cabin door and shouted that it was time to go.

She and her companions had suffered two days of boredom as the ship chugged its way across the Mediterranean, venturing on deck now and again when there were no other vessels on radar. It had given Malika more time to commit the latest information to memory, and the paper had been tossed overboard earlier that day. Now, the worst part of the journey was almost over, but they still had to make land. No easy task for five women with no experience on the open seas.

She gathered her meagre possessions and carried Jalal up the stairs and into the cooling darkness. A starry sky and sliver of moon offered scant illumination, but Malika could see lights on the horizon and guessed it was the south-west tip of Lampedusa, an island barely five miles long some 120 miles south of the Italian mainland.

The deckhand climbed down into the smaller boat that was tied up against the hull and motioned for Malika to pass Jalal down to him. She handed the boy over, then climbed down the rope ladder and took him back before settling down on the wooden seat. The other women followed, and the sailor jerked the outboard motor into life.

'Just point it towards the lights and you should reach the shore within thirty minutes. It's a rocky coastline, but the water will be flat by the time you reach it. Use this handle to steer, and twist this grip to go faster. Just remember to reduce speed as you near the rocks, otherwise you'll hit too hard and you could capsize.'

Malika was sitting closest to the engine and took it upon herself to do the steering, and once their host had clambered back up the ladder and untied the ropes, she fed in a little fuel and eased away from the fishing vessel.

Despite the calmer seas, the small boat translated every tiny crest into a judder, and the vibration from the engine brought on a new wave of seasickness that Malika couldn't shake off. Five minutes in, she heaved over the side.

As promised, they reached the shore within half an hour. Malika searched for a landing spot that wouldn't require much climbing, and after ten minutes she saw a break in the rocks where sea met sand. She pointed the bow towards it and grounded the craft on the beach. In the darkness, she had difficulty finding the cut-off switch, so she left the engine running as she and her companions clambered onto the sand.

'Where's the reception centre?' Ramla asked as she handed Jalal back to Malika.

'I think it's at the north end of the island. We should keep walking until we meet someone and ask for directions.'

After three days at sea, it took them a few minutes to get their land legs, each step trying to compensate for imaginary pitching and rolling. It took them just a couple of minutes to find a road that ran parallel to the airport, and after skirting the perimeter they saw a harbour off to their left, with dozens of fishing boats moored up for the night.

They followed the road until they came to residential streets. It was after eleven in the evening and few lights lit the surrounding buildings. The streets themselves were almost deserted, but Malika spotted a couple out for a walk and decided to try to enlist their help. She asked for directions, first in her native tongue, then again in English, but just got shrugged shoulders in reply.

Undeterred, she went in search of others, and heard the sound of voices laughing and speaking Arabic. She hurried around the corner and saw three young men, a strong odour of alcohol emanating from them. One of the men grinned and sauntered over to her, a good-looking young man whom Malika might have found attractive under different circumstances, but today she wanted nothing more than to know where the camp was. Any lascivious thoughts on his part ended when the other four women came into view.

'We're looking for the reception centre,' Malika said.

'It's closed,' the man said, his grin returning. 'But you're welcome to stay with me tonight.'

'Thank you, but my sisters and I really need to get there as soon as possible.'

His advances clearly rejected, he pointed up the road and told her to continue to the main junction, then gave directions from there.

'It's a long journey,' he said. 'Are you sure you won't change your mind?'

Malika shook her head, then started walking. She could hear the other women following her, but didn't want to look back in case it gave her suitor the wrong impression. At the junction, she slowed her pace and stole a backwards glance, relieved to see that the amorous young man had given up the chase.

His warning that the walk would be a long one was correct, though. It took almost three hours to reach their destination, and Malika was dismayed to see at least a hundred tents and other hastily erected shelters outside the wire fence that surrounded the sports hall that had been transformed into a reception centre. The plan called for them to be at the Italian border with France in four days' time, but with this many people to process, they were unlikely to make that deadline.

They approached the tented village, where some people were still awake despite the hour. One man looked up at them, then threw his cigarette away in disgust and mumbled to himself as he retreated into his makeshift shelter. A few feet away, a couple in their forties huddled together under a blanket, a young child asleep on the mother's lap.

'Ignore him,' the woman said. 'He's just angry that you've jumped ahead of him in the queue. I'm Anila.'

Malika gave her a puzzled look. 'I don't understand.'

'They're processing single mothers first,' Anila said. 'He's a single male from Algeria, and has already been here for more than a month. The Italians are prioritising families over individuals.'

That eased Malika's concerns a little. 'How long have you been here?'

'We arrived this morning – yesterday morning, I should say. We hope to make the flight out later today.' Anila explained how things worked on the island. 'Every day, two flights leave for the Italian mainland. They carry five hundred people between them, but twice that number arrive here each day. Orphans are dealt with first, followed by single mothers and then families. It protects the more vulnerable, but it means the camp is filling up with men who are not happy at being kept waiting. There have been many fights since we arrived, and one man was killed earlier this afternoon. This is not a good place to be right now.'

Malika agreed, but the news that she and her fellow travellers were likely to be on their way sooner rather than later was comforting. She thanked the couple and guided the four others towards the main gates, where they found a patch of grass. Malika dug out her blanket and settled down with Jalal for some much-needed sleep.

The hardest part of the journey was now behind them; once they reached the Italian mainland, they would be guided every inch of the way until they reached England. That would give her a few days to prepare herself for the most important part of the mission.

CHAPTER 12

Tuesday, 8 August 2017

Andrew Harvey was finishing an email when the internal messaging system flagged a new message from MI6. It was marked 'urgent', so he stopped what he was doing and clicked on the link. After reading for a couple of minutes, he called Farsi and Sarah to his desk.

'It looks like Nabil Karim has got his hands on some chemical weapons,' Harvey said, moving aside so that they could read the communication.

'What's X3?' Sarah asked.

'Very nasty stuff.'

They turned to see a short man in his fifties with military-cut hair who had just entered the office alongside Veronica Ellis.

'This is Frank Dale from Porton Down,' Ellis said. 'I want you all in the conference room in two minutes.'

Harvey locked his station and grabbed his bottle of water, then walked to the room with his colleagues. Dale was already there, setting up a laptop and pairing it to the fifty-inch monitor on the wall.

Ellis stood at the head of the table. 'As you'll probably know by now, Nabil Karim has managed to get his hands on five phials of something called "X3". Frank is going to explain what that means to us.'

She stood aside, and Dale started his presentation.

'How many of you have seen a film called *The Rock*?'

'Was that the one where American terrorists hold a load of people hostage on Alcatraz?' Harvey asked.

'Correct. They claim to have VX nerve agent and are prepared to fire it at San Francisco. If you remember the opening scene, one of them gets exposed to it and his face begins to peel off. Well, let me tell you, VX doesn't do that. It kills through asphyxiation. X3, on the other hand, does exactly that, only more so. The Syrians developed it a few years ago.'

'Weren't they supposed to have destroyed their chemical weapons stockpiles in 2014?' asked Farsi.

'They were, but only the ones the UN inspectors knew about. The facility that was hit last week didn't have the security you would associate with a weapons-storage site, presumably to keep it off the radar. The US satellites would have flagged it up as suspicious if it had been crawling with soldiers, but al-Assad's decision to keep it low-key looks to have backfired. The identity of the person who reported it to the West is unknown, and al-Assad officially denies any knowledge, obviously, but through backchannels we've confirmed the quantity taken and the chemical make-up.'

'So what exactly is X3?' Sarah wanted to know.

'It combines VX with mustard nitrogen,' Dale said. 'It causes almost instantaneous blistering of the skin and attacks the respiratory system. The usual antidotes that combat VX, atropine and pralidoxime, are not effective against this new agent as it not only causes damage to the skin, but also once it penetrates and reaches the blood vessels, it destroys them. Death occurs within an hour through internal bleeding. It is viscous, like motor oil, and can be delivered as an aerosol.

The amount stolen, if dispersed in the air, would kill anyone within a two-mile range.'

'If atropine doesn't work, what does?' Ellis asked.

'Nothing,' Dale said. 'If this stuff gets loose, be somewhere else.'

For Harvey, it was the ultimate nightmare scenario. Nabil Karim had signalled his intention to bring the fight to British soil, and if his weapon of choice were X3, the outcome would be devastating. If released near a football stadium or a major music festival, the number of dead could reach 100,000.

What was of a greater concern was that they no longer had Hannibal to feed back details of how Karim planned to use the agent. It could already be in the country, or on its way.

'Is there any way to detect it?' he asked Dale. 'Does it show up on airport scanners or would sniffer dogs be able to spot a person carrying it?'

'It was stored in glass phials, so metal detectors wouldn't be any good. And it's odourless, so there would be nothing for the dogs to pick up on.'

'Why store something so deadly in little glass tubes?' Sarah asked. 'That's just inviting trouble.'

'I'd normally agree, but we've been told they are made of toughened safety glass. You could drop a hammer on one and it wouldn't even scratch the surface.'

'You've mentioned aerosol dispersal,' Harvey said. 'Are there any other ways it could be deployed?'

'Other agents have been used in warheads, but X3 was designed specifically to be an airborne threat. An explosion would send people scurrying away from the area anyway. In aerosol form, it could be released and no-one would know until it was too late.'

Dale fielded questions for another five minutes, after which he handed out photographs of phials similar to those that had been stolen. He also gave them his contact details at the government's military science park.

The team headed back to their desks while Ellis showed Dale out of the building. In a couple of minutes, she came to Harvey's station.

'I need you to consider every possible way of getting X3 into the country,' she said. 'In order to stop Karim, we have to think like him.'

'I'm already making a list, though I have a feeling it'll mean stepping up security at every major port. Do you think Maynard will sign off on that?'

'The PM wants to see us both later this afternoon. When he understands the seriousness of the situation, he'll order Maynard to toe the line.'

As Ellis retreated to her office, Harvey finished his list and sent it to the team so that they could pick up their assigned duties. He then sent Sarah an internal message asking her to draw up a list of possible targets, starting with anything involving the PM, then the armed forces and, finally, upcoming public events likely to attract large crowds.

The task facing them was colossal, but the penalty for failure didn't bear thinking about.

CHAPTER 13

Tuesday, 8 August 2017

Malika woke with a start as feet trampled past her head. She sat up and saw that a huge crowd had already gathered at the gates of the reception centre, and she checked her watch to see that it was just approaching six in the morning. The first rays of the sun were just breaching the horizon, the chill of the night already dissipating.

'Wake up,' she said, tapping Ramla on the arm. 'We have to get in the queue.'

In truth, there wasn't so much a queue as a throng, with the stronger ones starting to push their way to the front.

Malika stood and got her first real look at the camp. There were scores of shelters, some free-standing tents, others cobbled together from whatever the locals had provided. The ground was littered with empty bottles and food wrappers, as well as discarded clothes and soiled nappies. It was truly a desperate place, more like the aftermath of a tornado than the gates to sanctuary.

Malika gathered her things and picked up Jalal, then joined the ever-growing crowd. She asked a woman what time the gates opened and was told that she faced a three-hour wait. With time on her hands, she fed the child before snacking on the last of the dried fruit from her bag. She had some money and could have ventured to the local shops, but figured they could do without for a couple of hours. Best to keep her place in the line than have to rejoin at the back.

The sun was doing its best to melt the ground she stood on, and it was a relief to see uniformed figures approaching the fence from the inside of the compound. The last of her water had run out an hour earlier, and Jalal was making his own thirst known.

At ten o'clock, a minibus arrived and volunteers began handing out bottles of tepid water. Malika gladly accepted a couple and let Jalal have his fill, all the time looking at the reception building. The crowd was trickling through the gates, all women and children, and she heard shouts as three Eritrean males demanded to be let in. It soon turned into a crush as more and more men had the same idea and pushed forward, urging the officials to take their details and send them on their way to the airport.

With the increase in tension, it was inevitable that violence would follow. A group of Eritreans, unhappy that Syrians seemed to be getting preferential treatment, began scuffling with a bunch of males from Homs. Within seconds, objects were flying through the air as both sides used anything they could get their hands on as missiles.

The battle intensified as more men joined in, and it raged for ten minutes before the police arrived in sufficient numbers to restore peace. It was another hour before the combatants were dispersed, allowing the gates to be opened once more.

Malika and her four friends gained access at two in the afternoon, and she was shown to a room where a woman sat behind a desk piled high with paperwork. The small space was at least air-conditioned, a blessing after hours spent standing under the summer sun. She took a seat opposite the curly-haired woman and handed over her passport.

The clerk flipped the document open and entered the details onto a laptop.

'You're from Syria. Why didn't you travel to Greece? Why come hundreds of miles when Rhodes is half the distance?'

'That was our original destination, but the boat we were on suffered engine trouble during the first night at sea. We drifted for days, and when we finally saw land, they put us in smaller boats and told us to make our own way here. It was only when we landed that we discovered where we were.'

The clerk entered this information, then asked why Malika was fleeing Syria.

'I am a Shia Muslim. Last month, a group of men went from house to house looking for anyone who wasn't Sunni. I was in the backyard when they turned up, washing my son. I heard them shouting at my husband and father, and then the shooting started. I took Jalal and hid, but then the whole house shook with an explosion. I ran back inside and saw that the roof had collapsed. I didn't know if it was a bomb from the sky or a hand grenade, but the roof timbers had fallen in and one of them trapped my father. He was still alive, but my husband was already dead. I tried to lift a burning beam off my father, but it was too heavy and I burned the skin on both hands.'

She held them up for the woman to see. The palms and fingers showed the classic signs of third-degree burns, the skin taut and pink, like epidermal lava that had cooled in random, jagged patterns.

The clerk showed no emotion as she added this detail to Malika's record.

'We'll still have to fingerprint you,' she said. 'We'll be taking a DNA sample, too.'

'I wasn't able to move the beam,' Malika continued. 'I had to watch my father die. After that, I went to stay with neighbours who let me stay in a hidden cellar. They were Sunni, but not like the men who killed my family. They kept me safe for a few weeks and helped me with my injuries, but I knew I couldn't stay with them forever. They retrieved what they could from my house and sold everything to raise enough money for my journey here.'

'And where do you plan to live?'

'I would like to go to France,' Malika said. 'My friends told me that there is a Syrian community on the outskirts of Paris. My son and I will be safe there.'

The clerk asked for Jalal's details, which she typed into the computer.

'There wasn't time to get him a passport,' Malika explained.

More questions came Malika's way: how many people were aboard the boat when it set sail? How many survived the journey? Where did they set off from? Who was the captain? How much did she pay to the people smugglers?

Malika gave the prepared answers to each question, and once the paperwork was complete, the clerk printed out two copies and asked Malika to sign both, then stamped one and stapled another document to the front of it. She then swabbed the inside of Malika's mouth before doing her best to extract prints from Malika's disfigured fingers.

'Go out of the door and turn right. At the end of the hallway, you'll see a set of double doors. In there you can get something to eat and they'll call you when the bus is ready to take you to the airport.'

Malika thanked her for her kindness and followed the directions she'd been given, ending up in a vast room. Tables lined three walls, where more volunteers were handing out food parcels and offering tea and coffee. There was also a station where hot food was being served, and Malika got a packed lunch for later and two bowls of vegetable soup. She went in search of somewhere to eat it and found that Inas had beaten her through processing. She sat down and began feeding Jalal.

'They seemed to believe my story,' Inas whispered. 'Did you have any problems?'

Malika shook her head. 'The real test will be when we get to England.'

Ramla soon joined them, and within half an hour, the quintet was reunited. They chatted in low voices until a man with a clipboard appeared in the doorway and began calling out names. They dutifully lined up when requested, and once the man had exhausted his list, he led them outside, where five buses were waiting. Twenty minutes later, they arrived at the airport.

The sun was kissing the horizon by the time the plane left the runway, and Malika finally felt that she could relax. This was the only time-sensitive part of the journey, and it now seemed that they would reach the mainland with two days to spare.

Malika sat outside the café with Ramla, both nursing tea. The other three members of the party had gone to buy provisions, and they were due to meet their escort within the hour.

After landing at Lamezia Terme International Airport, they'd been given temporary accommodation and food, and the next day they'd been driven almost the entire length of the country by the Italian authorities. Their destination had been Ventimiglia, a small place that was one train stop from France. The 760-mile journey had taken more than twelve hours, and Malika felt grateful for the money Karim had given them. After the confines of the bus, she'd been able to afford a room in a small hotel for the night, where she had showered for the first time in a week and changed into fresh clothing. They'd spent the intervening hours talking in the local parks until the time had come to meet up at the rendezvous point.

The others had finished their shopping and were sipping their drinks when a VW camper van pulled up outside the café. The driver, a balding man in his forties, got out and walked over to them.

'Malika?'

Malika stood and nodded, and the others followed as she climbed into the back of the van.

'How long will we be on the road?' she asked as the man took his seat behind the wheel.

'Five hours to reach the border, then another five to Lyon. The truck will meet you there.'

Malika settled into her seat and watched the countryside roll past. They had a couple of toilet stops before they reached the Strada Statale 25 del Moncenisio, the road that took them up into the Alps and across into France. Malika's concern now was that French border officials might try to stop them, in which case they'd be forced to turn around.

The Schengen Agreement between EU member states allowed free movement of people between countries, but that had been strained two years ago when several nations had erected fences along their borders to combat the tens of thousands of refugees pouring into Europe from Africa and the Middle East. Fortunately for Malika, that had been in reaction to the refugees landing in Greece and travelling up through the former Yugoslav states; the French–Italian border remained largely unchanged.

As she saw the tiny sign welcoming them to France, Malika put her hand on her stomach and felt the lump where the surgeon had sliced into her abdomen. The skin itched as it healed, but it was a minor inconvenience. Soon she would be going under the knife again, and her ordeal would be almost over.

CHAPTER 14

Friday, 11 August 2017

A chill greeted Malika as she climbed out of the VW van. Still another four hours until the sun would rise again. She hadn't yet become accustomed to the milder climate.

They had parked behind a lorry in what looked like a disused industrial estate: a row of drab buildings, many adorned with signs alluding to companies long since closed or moved to pastures new. There were no streetlights but, more importantly, no cameras to watch over them.

The women gathered at the back of the lorry, and the driver climbed out of the cab and walked the length of the vehicle. He was a short, elderly man, with pockmarked skin from an acne-ridden youth. At the rear, he opened the doors and climbed inside to switch on an internal light.

'Listen up,' he said. 'In here are five industrial heating units, one for each of you. You have to climb inside, and I'll seal it shut with this.' He pointed to an acetylene torch propped against the wall.

'How will we be able to breathe?' Ramla asked.

The driver went to the first unit and pulled out a cylinder attached to a tube that ended in an oxygen mask. 'There's two in each heater. One for you, and one for your child. They have filters containing a form of soda lime built in, so when we go through the port, they won't detect your CO_2. They'll last for five hours, which is more than enough time. Only use them when I seal you inside, which will be when we're close to Calais.'

'What if our children cry while we're in the port?' Malika asked.

The driver put his hand in his pocket and took out a small bottle of pills. He gave one to each woman. 'These will knock a child out for four hours. Just before I seal you in, give them to your children. You might as well be the first to try things out,' he said to Khadija, and took hold of her child while she climbed aboard the truck.

He guided her to a heater at the back, which stood five feet tall and was long and wide enough for a couple of people to lie down in side by side.

'The rest of you, gather round.'

He handed Khadija's child back to her and demonstrated the breathing apparatus, showing them all how to get the oxygen flowing and how to turn it off again. He had Khadija try it, and when she showed that she could handle the simple task, he told her to get into her unit and put the end piece back in place.

One by one, the women showed that they could operate the oxygen tank, and the driver told them to make themselves comfortable.

'It'll be nearly seven hours before we stop again, so if you need to go to the toilet, do it now.'

Two of them disappeared behind a wall and returned a few minutes later, climbing into the back of the truck and settling down for the long drive north.

The trip was conducted mostly in silence, with most of them grabbing a little sleep. Night had given way to a bright morning by the time the doors were opened once more.

Their driver jumped up into the back and took a strip of different tablets from his pocket. 'These are for you. Travel sickness pills. Take them now.'

Malika took a strip of four pills and popped one in her mouth, then handed the others out.

'Who hasn't got one?'

Khadija Tawfeek put her hand up and the driver took another pill from his pocket and gave it to her, along with a bottle of water to chase it down.

'If you look inside, you'll see that there are slats at the bottom of the side panel. They're covered with Perspex to stop any smells leaking out, but it will enable you to see when the light is turned on. If it comes on, it means the truck is being inspected by the port authorities, so it's important to be completely silent.'

He told them to get into their units, then began sealing them in. It took an hour before the last one was ready, and the driver went back to the first and brushed grey paint over the fresh welds to make it look like they'd been applied in the factory.

Happy with his handiwork, he turned off the light and locked the outer doors securely with massive chains and a tamper-free tag, then got behind the wheel and set off for the port and the ferry that would take them across the English Channel and on to a secluded place just north of Canterbury.

The driver was keenly aware that getting across the border, despite the measures he'd taken, was by no means guaranteed. It was still an easy task compared to what he would face on the other side of the Channel.

CHAPTER 15

Friday, 11 August 2017

Veronica Ellis stood and adjusted her pencil skirt, then strolled to the glass wall to look out on the main office. She caught her reflection and saw that the recent strain had taken its toll. The lines around her eyes seemed more pronounced these days, and her platinum blonde hair looked dull and lifeless. Whether it was the stress of the job or just the natural passage of time, she felt a lot older than a woman in her mid-fifties.

She saw Andrew Harvey walking over to her, and she opened the door for him.

'We're seeing lots of increased activity,' Harvey said. 'Al-Hosni's up to something.'

'Anything specific?'

'Not yet, but his routine has changed over the last couple of days. In the past week, he barely left his house. Now he's going to the mosque four times a day and staying for half an hour after prayers end. Three people on our watch list have suddenly started worshipping at the same mosque, always when al-Hosni's presiding. This all started after he got a visit from a guy called Qureshi. We matched his photo with airport CCTV, but we just heard back from the Turkish National Intelligence Organisation. They've got no record of him.'

'Then who is he?'

'We don't know,' Harvey admitted. 'The passport was a fake, and clearly a very good one, too. Good enough to fool their own border security. They doubt Qureshi is even a Turkish national, which makes me think he hopped across the border from Syria. The fact that he came all this way just to talk to al-Hosni suggests something big is on the horizon. He could be the main man or just another link in the chain.'

'How many people do we have watching him at the moment?'

'Just two on the day shift and one at night,' Harvey said. 'Given the recent activity, we could do with a few more. We'll also need resources on the people he's been meeting with.'

'That may be wishful thinking,' Ellis said. Her meeting with Maynard and the Prime Minister a few days earlier could have gone a lot better. While the PM had recognised the seriousness of the situation, he had only issued instructions for additional funds to be released as and when it became critical to the investigation, and he'd left the Home Secretary to make those calls. She'd had to fight simply to get authorisation for the three men currently monitoring al-Hosni's activities; even with the recent change in the imam's habits, Ellis knew she would have a tough time selling further expenditure to the Home Secretary.

'If we can get an idea of what he's up to, I might be able to put a few more feet on the ground, but as things stand, I don't have enough to approach Maynard. The funds are available, but he has final say on their allocation.'

'It strikes me as too much of a coincidence that al-Hosni starts making contact with people suspected of being members of banned organisations, and at the same time the X3 is still unaccounted for.'

'That had crossed my mind, too. Do we have any informants that could shed some light on what al-Hosni's up to?'

'I'll put the word out,' Harvey said, 'but usually they come to us. If they haven't heard anything yet, chances are they never will.'

If al-Hosni were planning to take delivery of the chemical agent, he obviously wouldn't discuss it in public. He also hadn't mentioned anything about it in his phone conversations, and the traffic they'd intercepted from his broadband provider had amounted to nothing more than benign chatter.

'Okay,' she said, 'give me a breakdown of how many you need and get them to work right away. I'll put in a retrospective request to Maynard once we have something to report.'

'Are you sure you want to do it this way? He's not going to be happy.'

'He can have kittens for all I care,' Ellis said. 'Just make sure you get me something to justify the overtime.'

Harvey left her office and returned to his own desk, while Ellis considered ways to squeeze some more money out of the Home Secretary.

~

Malika was approaching full-blown panic.

She'd been in the cramped container for more than six hours and the stifling heat and stink of her own sweat – not to mention the contents of Jalal's nappy – had created a creeping sense of claustrophobia. She'd never feared enclosed spaces, but the pitch-black interior of the heating unit had her pulse racing now.

She told herself to be grateful for the cool oxygen from the tank – that the ordeal was almost over. She'd sensed the transition from land to sea and back again, but the ride had been stop–start since then. The truck would move a few yards, then the air brakes would hiss and the engine would idle for a few minutes. She assumed they were still in the port at Dover, the last barrier before entering England proper. Once on the open road, she would be able to relax a little, but for now she fought off another bout of fear, this time the thought of being discovered. To be caught at this point would mean an abrupt end to the mission, and failure would not only affect her, but also those back in Syria who had spent so long planning it.

Malika cuddled the child closer. Jalal was sleeping soundly, the pill working as expected. She couldn't see him in the darkness, but she gently stroked his brow as she wondered what would happen to him in the months and years to come. The British were no fools, and eventually her part in this would come to light, at which point she would lose Jalal forever.

Karim had explained that this would happen, but he'd assured her that the boy would be taken care of. The British, for their many faults, took the welfare of children seriously. Jalal would be put into the care system, and Karim had promised to ensure a good Muslim family would adopt him as their own. Malika hoped they would be a professional couple. Doctors or lawyers. People who could give him a decent upbringing.

But that was beyond her control. All she could do was make the most of the short time they had left together.

She started to sing Jalal a song, but her throat froze as the truck's engine shut down. *Was she about to be discovered?* Her fears intensified as the interior light came on. She could see down the small slats in the side of the unit, and a pair of black boots walked past. Voices echoed around the compartment, and Malika held her breath and prayed that the inspection would be brief. The units were far enough apart for the customs officers to clearly see that no-one was hiding among them, and after a minute she saw the light go out and heard the doors slam shut once more.

It was only when the engine started and the vehicle lurched forward that she let out the breath she felt she'd been holding for a lifetime.

Malika held her son tightly. For a while, it seemed that only she and Jalal existed, but she soon sensed the truck slowing, and after a couple of turns it stopped and the engine shut down. When the doors opened again, she heard the driver's voice.

'We're here. Sit back while I release you.'

Malika pushed herself to the back of the cramped compartment and heard the sound of a power tool roaring into life. Her container juddered as the driver went to work on it and, within a couple of minutes, he pulled the end panel aside and beckoned for her to get out. She did so gingerly and stretched her legs as she stood by the open doors, gulping in fresh air.

The driver was already working on the next unit. When he opened it, Inas blinked as the sunlight invaded her little space. Jalila was next to be freed, followed by Ramla.

When the last unit opened, Malika recognised the smell immediately. She'd been around death enough to know the sulphurous odour of blood and evacuated bowels.

'This one didn't make it,' the driver said, reaching inside to take the little boy who was sleeping on his mother's still body. 'Looks like she haemorrhaged.'

Malika took the child and handed him to Ramla.

'Poor Khadija. What will happen to her?'

'I'll deal with it,' the driver said, climbing down and helping the women off the truck.

They'd parked up in a wooded area, and Malika saw a minibus parked close by. The truck driver told them to get aboard their new ride.

Once seated, Malika turned to the others. 'The hardest part is over,' she said. 'Khadija will be sorely missed, but Allah has different plans for all of us. We are now approaching the end of our journey, but we are not finished yet. Do you all know what is expected of you from this point on?'

The three women assured her that they were aware of their remaining duties, and Malika smiled as she looked down at Jalal. It would indeed soon be over, but she had one major task to complete.

~

The truck driver watched the other vehicle drive away and pulled on a pair of gloves to prepare for the clean-up job. He climbed back into the truck and heaved the woman's body to the open doors, then jumped down and gently eased the corpse over the edge. It was too heavy to lift, so he dragged her over to some nearby undergrowth and prepared a shallow grave. He pushed the body into it, then covered it with soil and foliage.

It wasn't the neatest grave, but that wasn't his concern. Distancing himself from the scene was all he had in mind. He used a tree branch to obfuscate his footprints and hide the blood trail, then cleaned out the heating unit and truck bed with water. His final task was to re-seal the heating units. It was unlikely that he'd be checked on the crossing back to France, but the extra effort gave him peace of mind.

He finished up and locked the back doors, then drove twenty miles to the motorway services, where he spent a couple of hours enjoying a meal and some much-needed coffee. After making a quick phone call, he set off once more. It would be another half a day before he was back home in Lyon, but first he had to ditch the fake plates and restore the truck's original livery. Not an easy task, but the payment for his participation more than made up for it.

~

Malika rubbed her abdomen; the wound was beginning to itch again. There was little she could do about it, though, as the discomfort was inside, which made it even more annoying.

The minibus had already reached the suburbs of London, and as she stared out the window, she saw nothing but shops on either side. A few houses appeared, before giving way to more businesses hawking a plethora of goods and services. Traffic was heavy as the sun retreated for the day, thousands of commuters heading home to enjoy the weekend.

The bus driver turned down a side street and took another left, stopping at the back of a parade of shops. He got out, opened the door for the women and told them to head through a gate that led to a small walled garden. The rear door to the building was already open and a man with silver hair beckoned them inside.

Malika went first and found herself in a tiny kitchen. Beyond that lay a deserted reception area adorned with banners proclaiming it to be one of London's premier cosmetic surgeries. Pictures of women with pert breasts looked down their perfect noses at her, and she fleetingly wondered what it would be like to live in a society where looks were worshipped more than deities.

Their host appeared and showed them up the stairs to the operating theatre. It was a small room, but clean, and smelled of antiseptic.

'Is there anyone else here, Doctor . . . ?' Ramla asked.

'No,' the man said. 'Just me. And names are not important.'

'Who will look after the children while we recover from the surgery?'

'I won't be using a general anaesthetic, just a local to numb the area. It will be a very small incision, and you'll be able to leave shortly afterwards. Who's going first?'

'I will,' Malika said, handing Jalal to Inas.

The doctor ordered the others to leave the room, then instructed Malika to get undressed and lie on the bed. She winced as he pressed down on her abdomen none too gently until he located the phial, then marked the spot and prepared the local anaesthetic. He scrubbed the area with antiseptic and emptied the syringe into her flesh, then opened a sterile pack containing a scalpel and forceps.

He waited a couple of minutes for the drug to kick in, then began making the incision. Malika felt only a slight pinch and some tugging as his forceps retrieved the glass phial. He put it in a kidney dish and began the process of closing up the wound. Five minutes later, he helped Malika to her feet and walked her through to a recovery room, where four beds had been prepared.

'Take two of these every four hours if the pain gets too intense,' the doctor said, handing her a bottle of tramadol as she lay down. 'It'll hurt for a couple of days, so don't do anything strenuous.'

Malika asked Ramla to pass Jalal to her, and she cuddled him as Inas took her turn under the knife. Soon, all four women were resting following their surgery, and the doctor came in to check up on them.

'You can stay for another two hours, then you'll have to go,' he told Malika as he checked her dressing. 'The minibus will be back to pick you up at ten this evening.'

He pulled the side of the bed up so that she could sleep without fear of Jalal slipping onto the floor. Malika closed her eyes and tried not to think of what was to come in the next few days.

~

Dr Kamal Bousaid powered up the mobile phone he'd been given and looked up the only number in the contacts list. The call connected immediately.

'Everything went as planned. I have your goods and you can collect them after eleven.'

'I'll be there,' the voice said, and the line went dead in his hands.

That was exactly how Bousaid felt inside. Dead. In his thirty years in practice, he'd been asked to perform a variety of bizarre procedures, but he'd never been called upon to do anything like this.

It wasn't as if he'd had a choice. The £15,000 in cash he'd be paid for less than two hours' work wasn't a factor; it was the threat to his family that had convinced him to take the job and keep his mouth shut afterwards.

Bousaid rinsed the phials and placed them in a metal container that he'd already padded with cotton wool. He had no idea what they contained, but assumed it wouldn't be used for a noble cause. He'd been warned not to open them, and that was good enough for him.

The next couple of hours seemed to last forever, but eventually the minibus reappeared at the rear of the surgery. He woke the women and sent them on their way. One of the things that had concerned him was that they would be able to identify him and implicate him in the plot, and as he watched them leave, he did not feel comforted by the assurances he'd been given.

The women are mules, nothing more. They will be back in Syria before the weekend is over.

That still left the minibus driver and the man who had first contacted him, both of whom could identify him as being complicit. Anxiety gnawed at the doctor as he waited for the man to arrive and take delivery.

Perhaps it was time to retire. He had enough in the bank to start again in a non-extradition country, and he could instruct his solicitor to sell the house and business in his absence. That would give him and his wife more than enough to live off in whichever country they chose to settle.

He was still considering this option when a knock came at the back door. Bousaid picked up the metal container and went downstairs to answer it. When he opened the door, he saw the same man that had forced him into performing the illicit surgery.

'This is what you asked for,' Bousaid said.

The man accepted the small box and verified the contents before slipping it into his coat.

'Let's go inside so I can pay you.'

'There's no need,' Bousaid assured him. 'I trust you. We can handle this.'

'I insist.'

Reluctantly, Bousaid turned, leading the man into the reception area. He hadn't taken more than a few steps when a hand clamped over his mouth and he felt the tip of a knife against the base of his skull.

Before he could fight back, the blade had sliced through his spinal column.

Kamal Bousaid was dead before his body hit the ground.

The anaesthetic was beginning to wear off as Malika and the three others sat outside a room in the mosque in Woolwich. She popped a couple of the pills the doctor had given her, then slouched in the chair to make herself as comfortable as possible.

They'd been dropped off ten minutes earlier and, after introducing themselves and explaining their situation, had been given seats and asked to wait.

'I really need to sleep,' Ramla said.

'Me, too,' Malika said. It had been a long journey. Having reached her destination, she wanted nothing more than some decent food and a comfortable bed.

The door opened and the imam appeared.

'I have found accommodation for all of you,' he said. 'They are local families who will put you up for a few days, and they will help you with your asylum claim. Wait here, and they will come and pick you up within the hour.'

He disappeared inside the room once more, and Malika stared at the opposite wall. There was nothing left to say to each other; soon they would split up, unlikely to see each other ever again.

Midnight came, and Malika was the last one to be picked up. The others had already been collected and taken to their new homes, and the man that entered the mosque and called her name seemed nice enough. She followed him outside and into a car, and half an hour later she was being escorted into a grand-looking house, complete with its own drive.

The woman of the house greeted her and showed her into the dining room, where food awaited. Jalal was taken care of while Malika ate, and she spent the next couple of hours telling her cover story about why she'd left Syria. It turned out the couple had emigrated from Homs fifteen years earlier, and they felt devastated by what had become of their homeland.

When Malika began yawning, they escorted her upstairs and into a room that used to belong to their daughter, now away at college. Malika put Jalal to bed, then took a shower before climbing under the duvet.

She was asleep within minutes.

CHAPTER 16

Sunday, 13 August 2017

When Andrew Harvey returned from the shops, Sarah was already at work in the kitchen, preparing for that evening's get-together. Hamad Farsi was coming round, along with two of Sarah's friends and Harvey's squash partner.

He loved being in her company, and most nights were spent cuddled up on the sofa, watching television or chatting about nothing in particular. For Harvey, she was the perfect companion; not only beautiful, but also witty and sharp as a tack. His previous relationships had all been short, fuelled initially by mutual lust, but the fires had soon faded. His erratic work pattern was partly to blame, but in truth he hadn't had that much in common with the other women. Sarah had become more of a soulmate than a lover, and the hours they spent alone were the happiest of his life. Because she liked the company of others, too, they held dinner parties a couple of times a month. This time it was Sarah's turn to cook.

'You're gonna have to pull something special out of the bag if you're going to top my seafood dish,' he said. His meal a fortnight earlier had consisted of lobster, langoustine and scallop pasta with a fish stock and white wine sauce, undoubtedly the best dish he'd created in their ongoing competition to crown the best chef in the house.

'No problem. I'm doing lamb three ways.'

'Sounds like you're serious this time,' Harvey said. 'How are you going to cook it?'

'Herb-crusted lamb cutlets, ballotine of lamb stuffed with chestnuts and mushrooms and pan-fried lamb sweetbreads.'

'Someone's in a competitive mood,' he said, kissing her on the neck and running his hands over her hips.

'If you're trying to sabotage me, it's not going to work. Now go and wash those mushrooms.'

Harvey peeled himself off her and took the shitake over to the sink, but before he could get his hands wet, his phone rang.

'Harvey.'

'I need you both in the office,' Ellis said without preamble. 'The X3 made it over here.'

'We're on our way.'

He relayed the message to Sarah, who put the lamb back in the fridge and threw on her jacket.

'Did she say if they found it all?'

'No, just that it's here. I guess we'll find out when we get there.'

Fifty minutes later, they swiped their way into the office. It was the busiest Harvey had seen it on a weekend, with almost every desk occupied. He hung his jacket on a hook as Ellis approached.

'We found a phial of X3,' she said.

'Where?'

'Near Canterbury. Some kids riding dirt bikes yesterday came across a woman's body in a shallow grave. She'd been there a couple of days.'

'Origin?' Sarah asked.

'Middle East.'

'And she had the X3 on her?'

'Actually, it was *in* her,' Ellis said. 'An autopsy was performed this morning and it was discovered inside her abdomen. Naturally, the pathologist was concerned and called it in. We had Dale check it out and he confirmed the contents.'

'Who's the woman?' Sarah asked.

'We're working on that. Fingerprints don't show up on our databases, so we're expanding the search.'

'Canterbury's just north of Dover,' Harvey pointed out. 'Sounds like she crossed the Channel.'

'Hamad's checking that out,' Ellis said. 'If she's an illegal, she must have made her way through Europe, which means landing in Greece or Italy.'

'I'll go and see how he's getting on,' Harvey said, and walked over to Farsi's station.

'I'm guessing dinner's cancelled,' Farsi said as he typed another search command into a database.

'If we get out of here before midnight, I might be able to rustle up some beans on toast.'

'I think I'll pass.'

'So what do we know about this woman?' Harvey asked.

'No name yet, but we know she's mid-twenties. The pathologist said the scar on her abdomen was at least two weeks old, so the X3 must have been implanted shortly after it was stolen.'

'Give her a couple of days to recover, and she would have had nearly a fortnight to get from Syria to here. Easily done, especially if she had help along the way.'

'Well, we've ruled out air travel as her method of entry. No matches through airport facial-recognition systems, and the smaller airports have reported no-one matching her description.'

Harvey felt vindicated for requesting extra security at the regional airstrips. If he hadn't done so, their search would have to be expanded even further, wasting valuable time. With flights into the country ruled out, there was only one realistic way she could have reached England.

'Are customs still checking every lorry that crosses the Channel?'

Farsi nodded. 'Anything that arrives by ferry or through the tunnel.'

'Well, she got through somehow. I'll ask Ellis to get in touch with the border agency and have them step up the searches.'

Harvey went round to his own desk and powered up his computer.

They had one of the phials, which was a start, but there were four others out there somewhere. What he really needed to do was determine if the rest of the X3 was already here, or still on its way.

The best place to start would be the port of Dover. Someone obviously helped the woman across the border: corpses didn't bury themselves.

He signed in on his workstation and searched for the number of trucks that had passed through the port in the last three days. To his dismay, the total came to more than 15,000 with half of those inbound. According to the graph on the screen, the number was usually higher, but the recently implemented security protocols had created a backlog that the ferry companies were struggling to clear. It was still going to be a tough ask to identify one lorry from the 7,500 that had arrived, and he couldn't discount the possibility that the woman had come in by car or bus with fake papers. Qureshi had managed to get his hands on a false ID, so why not the woman?

What he really needed to do was positively identify the woman and retrace her steps, but the boring stuff couldn't be discarded.

It could, however, be delegated.

He brought up a map that showed the location where the body had been discovered, then overlaid it with the national traffic camera network. There was one camera that would catch vehicles travelling north to the burial site, but the next one was over two miles away, and between them were two turn-offs that weren't covered by CCTV. It was going to take a lot of effort to find and eliminate every vehicle, but he had the perfect man for the job.

Gareth Bailey had been with the team less than eight months, and in that time he hadn't fulfilled the potential Harvey had seen in his training scores. His work had started off at a good standard, but recently he could have applied himself better. His reports had become sloppy, as if the initial buzz of the new job had worn off. Harvey had tried his best to give him tasks that would stretch him in an effort to recapture the excitement, but those were few and far between.

This one wasn't going to set him on fire, either.

He called Bailey over to his desk to break the bad news.

'I need you to check CCTV of all lorries that took the A2 past the point where the woman was found.'

'Can do,' Bailey said. 'How many are we talking about?'

'Hundreds, possibly thousands, but the cameras are too far apart to make it easy for us. Once a truck goes past the point we're concerned with, it could take one of two turn-offs that aren't covered. What I need you to do is, first, collate all licence plates that passed this camera on Thursday and Friday, then go to the next camera and see which ones didn't make it there within an acceptable time frame. It should take them two minutes, so anything that takes half an hour or more is of interest to us.'

'That could take days,' Bailey said, his demeanour exactly what Harvey had expected.

'In that case, you better get started.'

Bailey returned to his desk and Sarah sidled up to Harvey with two cups of coffee.

'Aren't you going to say I told you so?'

Harvey blew on his drink and took a sip. 'This is one of the times I would have been happy to be wrong.'

Their disagreement over the immigration issue had come to the fore in recent days, with Harvey adamant that the other European countries weren't doing enough to distinguish true refugees from economic migrants and terrorists. That someone had managed to get all the way across Europe and into Britain proved his point, though he could perhaps excuse the other nations for focusing on males as potential threats. He himself would not have pegged a female as a target, which was obviously why she'd been chosen to transport the toxin.

'I've got her!'

Harvey almost spilled his drink when Farsi shouted in triumph.

'Who is she?'

'Khadija Tawfeek. At least, that's the name she gave when she registered in Lampedusa. Her passport and fingerprint details were on the Italian SIF system.'

The *Sistema Informativo Frontiere*, or SIF, was the database used to collate information on visitors from Africa, Asia and the Middle East, but had been pressed into service to handle the huge numbers of refugees that had flooded the country.

Harvey walked round to Farsi's desk and digested the information on the monitor.

'I'm betting she didn't come alone,' he said. 'Can you click on the name of the boat and see who else arrived on it?'

'No, this is just a screenshot the Italians sent us. I'll send a request to the AISI, though.'

'Do it, and print out a copy of that. I'll go and update the boss.'

As he waited for the printer to spew forth the information, Harvey hoped his counterparts in the *Agenzia Informazioni e Sicurezza Interna* worked equally unsociable hours.

Armed with the printout, he walked into Ellis's office without knocking.

'We have a name,' he said when she looked up from her computer.

'Real or alias?'

'We don't know yet, but given that Qureshi had an authentic-looking forged passport, I'd say it was bogus. I'll see if MI6's people in Syria can make some discreet enquiries.'

Going straight to Syria's General Security Directorate would be counterproductive. They would most certainly want to know why MI5 were interested in one of their citizens, and if the name turned out to be real, the woman's family would almost certainly be taken in for interrogation as al-Assad sought to find the people who had stolen his secret weapon. If Tawfeek were merely a hapless mule, it would put her entire family at risk for nothing.

'Hamad is working on who she arrived in Italy with. Chances are, the other four phials travelled with her.'

Ellis read the printout. 'I agree. It says here she had a young son when she turned up in Italy. That means someone is looking after the boy.'

'And if they all travelled together, then the rest of the X3 is already here.'

~

It was five hours before the AISI got back to Farsi with the details of Khadija Tawfeek's companions on the boat, but after extensive enquiries, they had no new leads.

None of the women had been seen since being dropped off in Ventimiglia. Harvey had instructed the team to contact all of their informants, asking them to report on any new women within the Arab community, but so far they'd drawn a blank.

The only certainty was that they would have to have the X3 removed from their bodies at some point, and it would most likely be sooner rather than later. Whether it was done by a skilled surgeon, or simply hacked out of their lifeless bodies, was another matter entirely. He'd informed all police forces and hospitals to report any bodies matching the women's descriptions as soon as they were discovered, but he was really pinning his hopes on finding them alive. If the women were dead, the trail would disappear. The only real chance of finding the X3 was to bring them in for questioning.

Bailey had made little progress identifying the vehicle that they were suspected of arriving in. More than a thousand potential trucks filled his spreadsheet, and Harvey had taken three other team members off their assigned duties to help, but it was a time-consuming task, and every passing minute meant more time for the X3 to be weaponised.

Harvey checked up on Sarah, who looked as tired as he felt. She'd spent most of the day sifting through the electronic data gathered by GCHQ on their prime suspect, Imran al-Hosni.

'There's been nothing,' she told him, 'and that's really worrying.'

'What do you mean?'

'When I say nothing, I mean no phone calls, emails, Skype, anything. It's as if he's abandoned all forms of communication apart from face-to-face meetings.'

'That *is* worrying,' Harvey agreed. 'What about his known associates?'

'Same story. Everyone's gone offline.'

'Then what about human intel? Have our operatives reported anything?'

'Lots of meetings have been taking place, but always at short notice, and we haven't been able to listen in.'

It certainly sounded to Harvey as if al-Hosni were up to something, but they didn't have anywhere near enough to bring him in.

While his actions were highly suspicious, making no phones calls was hardly a criminal offence, and neither was abstaining from surfing the internet.

Harvey jumped when Ellis put her hand on his shoulder.

'Go and get some sleep, both of you.'

Harvey checked his watch and saw that it was almost one in the morning.

'I mean it. They're unlikely to get up to anything at this hour, and the night shift can alert us if they do.'

Harvey agreed. You couldn't overestimate the value of a rested mind. After a while, facts and figures start to blur, and the decision-making process suffers.

'Okay, we'll be back in at nine.'

He shut down his terminal and put on his jacket. Sarah wasn't far behind him.

'I hate leaving when I'm in the middle of something,' she said as a yawn escaped.

'It'll still be here tomorrow, but Veronica's right. We need some sleep.'

They rode the elevator to the underground car park and Harvey took the wheel.

'I'm worried that we won't find it in time,' Sarah said as he pulled out onto a near-empty street.

'We have to.'

The thought of an X3 attack in London was enough to banish any thoughts of sleep. The death toll would be staggering, and any blame would fall on MI5 for failing to prevent it. That's how things worked, and Harvey knew it. John Maynard would use the opportunity to unseat Ellis, and he couldn't let that happen.

Ellis might look like she would be more at home leading a Fortune 500 company, but her heart was with the service, and her loyalty to her staff was legendary. True, she could be blunt at times, but there was nothing she wouldn't do to protect her people from any flak.

As section lead, Harvey knew his own job would be far from secure, as well.

He tried to put such thoughts aside. People always slipped up, be they street muggers or criminal masterminds, and al-Hosni's time would come. When it did, he would be there to pounce.

'We have to,' he repeated, 'and we will.'

CHAPTER 17

Monday, 14 August 2017

Within minutes of arriving back in the office, it seemed as though he'd never left. The only difference was that he felt more alert, and Ellis didn't seem to mind that he'd skipped his morning shave.

Gareth Bailey and his three helpers had already eliminated half of the trucks that had been near the woman's grave, but it would be another twenty-four hours before that task would be completed. There'd been a flurry of excitement when one truck had taken more than an hour to drive the three miles between cameras, but it turned out to be a false alarm. The driver had reported an overheating engine, and the breakdown service had confirmed his story, as well as placing him a mile away from where the body had been found.

Harvey was about to give Ellis her hourly update when Elaine Solomon called his name.

'Andrew, we've got a hit!'

Gerald Small, the resident technical wizard, had set up repeating SQL query statements that constantly polled myriad governmental databases, and it appeared they'd come up trumps.

'Who do we have?' Harvey asked her.

'Ramla al-Hassad and her son and daughter. She registered an asylum claim a few minutes ago.'

It was the break they'd been looking for.

'Send a team to her address and pass along the photos we got from the Italians,' he told her. 'Once we pick her up, we'll get her to tell us where the others are.'

'Will do. Hang on . . . we've got another. Malika Ali and her son.'

'In that case, cancel the first order. Get on to Lunar House and tell them to hold the women until I arrive. Get them to conduct a fake interview, anything, but they're not to leave.'

'Understood,' Solomon said, picking up her phone.

'And give them the names of the other two. Chances are they'll be turning up today, too.'

Sarah was already at the exit by the time Harvey had updated Ellis.

'I called the Met,' she said. 'They're sending a couple of vans and an armed unit will be standing by, just in case.'

'Better let Social Services know, too. Someone will have to look after their kids while we question them.'

Sarah made the call on her mobile while Harvey took the wheel and merged into morning traffic. What should have been a fifty-minute drive turned into an hour and a half as roadworks hampered their progress, but on the upside, Solomon had called to say all four women were now at the asylum registration centre in Croydon.

Harvey found a space in the car park at Lunar House and saw that both police vans and a couple of squad cars were already waiting outside. After introducing Sarah and himself, he asked four officers to accompany him. Inside, he went to the reception desk and asked for the person Solomon had spoken to earlier.

'Mr Shaw is expecting you,' he was told. 'Down the corridor, turn right at the end, third door on the left.'

Harvey found the room and was greeted by a tall man with a military bearing.

'Where are they?' Harvey asked.

Shaw led them to the stairs and up to the first floor. 'One in each of the first four rooms,' Shaw said, and Harvey knocked on door number one and entered, with Sarah in close attendance.

A Home Office official was sitting across a table from a young woman who wore a *hijab*, and Harvey's first thought was that she was stunningly beautiful, with dazzling eyes and perfect skin. On her knee was a young child, fidgeting and clearly bored.

Harvey picked up the piece of paper the official had been writing on. 'Malika Ali?'

'Yes.'

'Do you speak English?'

'She's very proficient,' the interviewer said.

'In that case, I'll have to ask you to leave.'

The man closed the door on his way out, and Harvey stood behind the empty chair.

'My name is Andrew, and this is Sarah. We work for the British security services. Do you know why we are here?'

Malika shook her head.

'I think you do,' Harvey said. 'I'm going to leave the room for a moment, and I'd like you to show Sarah your stomach.'

Harvey saw Malika's eyes dart to the side and knew he had the right woman.

'Alternatively, you can save yourself the embarrassment and admit that you had something concealed inside you when you entered the country.'

Malika remained silent, her eyes on the desk in front of her.

'Suit yourself.'

Harvey nodded to Sarah, then walked out of the room and closed the door behind him. The four police officers, two of them female, were awaiting his instructions.

'We're going to be taking them to Thames House rather than the station,' he told them. 'We'll complete the handover paperwork when we get there.'

The door opened and Sarah joined them in the hallway.

'She refuses to show me.'

Harvey sighed. 'Then we'll have to do it the hard way.' He turned to the officers. 'Be careful. She recently had surgery, and she has a young child with her.'

He let them in and watched from the doorway as one female officer took the boy from Malika and another read her her rights.

The prisoner said nothing. Instead, she looked at the child with longing, a tear forming in the corner of her eye. Harvey saw the motherly instinct kick in, and filed it away for later use.

They took Malika down to the van in handcuffs, and the little one was placed in a child seat in the back of a police car. Once both were strapped in, they went back upstairs to repeat the process with the other three women.

Half an hour later, the vans and cars were full, and Harvey led the convoy back to Thames House. Sarah called ahead and asked that the interrogation suite be readied for their arrival and the holding cells stocked with everything the women would need for what promised to be a long stay.

CHAPTER 18

Monday, 14 August 2017

'What have you got out of them so far?' Ellis asked when Harvey reported to her office.

'Nothing yet. Clearly, they were instructed to stay quiet. It could be that they're just mules and someone's holding their families back in Syria to make sure they deliver the goods, or they could be doing this for idealistic reasons.'

'Either way, we need them to talk.'

'The obvious approach would be to use the kids as leverage. How do you feel about that?'

'Uncomfortable,' Ellis said. 'But if we have to hurt their feelings in order to save thousands of lives, it has to be done.'

'I'll get on it. Sarah is downstairs with them now. I'll fill her in on our approach.'

Harvey rode down to the sub-basement, where one of two armed officers seconded to them from SO15 was guarding the door. Harvey showed the man his ID and was given permission to swipe his way inside.

He entered the newly built corridor, where two more armed officers were stationed. There were five doors set into the left-hand wall and another on the right. Harvey took the one on the right and entered a room with a large one-way mirror that gave him a good view of the interrogation chamber. Inside he saw Sarah sitting across a metal table from one of the prisoners, whom he recognised as Malika.

Elaine Solomon and Gerald Small sat at a desk, watching the two women. Small was monitoring a screen that showed telemetry from the sensors placed on Malika's head and chest, as well as the probe on her right index finger.

'Has she said anything?' Harvey asked.

'Not a word,' Solomon told him.

Over the speaker, Harvey heard Sarah asking another question, but Malika simply stared blankly ahead. They were getting nowhere fast, and an urgent change of tack was needed.

He swiped his way into the interrogation room and stood next to Sarah.

'Malika, you're facing the rest of your life in prison,' he said. 'It's in your best interest to co-operate with us.'

The prisoner remained silent, head bowed.

'If you help us,' Sarah added, 'we can ensure that the courts go easy on you, and you'll be able to see your son again. What's his name? Jalal?'

Malika looked up. 'Where is he?'

'With Social Services. They're taking good care of him, but that won't last forever. If you don't help us, he'll be put up for adoption with a new identity and you'll never see him again. I can't guarantee that the couple who take him in will be Muslim, or even man and woman.'

'You can't do that!'

'Oh, but I can, and I will,' Harvey assured her. 'By the time's he's two, he'll be eating pork and learning about Jesus from both of his fathers.'

'Only you can prevent that,' Sarah said, playing the good cop. 'You need to talk to us.'

Tears were rolling down Malika's cheeks, and Sarah handed her a tissue.

'I'll give you five minutes to think about it,' Harvey told her. 'Then the offer is off the table.'

He motioned for Sarah to follow him, and they left Malika alone to ponder the threat.

'If she doesn't go for it, take her back to her cell and bring one of the others in,' Harvey said when they were out of earshot. 'One of them has to care enough about their child to talk.'

After the allotted time had passed, Harvey went back into the room.

'Well? Have you made your decision?'

Malika maintained her silence, and Harvey sighed as he called for a guard to escort her back to her cell. While he waited for the next suspect, he flipped through the women's records, which he'd had sent to his phone.

He saw that, according to the information gathered in Lampedusa, Malika had no living family. That meant it was unlikely she had been coerced into bringing the X3 into the country. Of course, her story could have been a complete fabrication, but he wouldn't be able to ascertain that until she broke her silence.

The door buzzed and the guard ushered the next prisoner through the door. Harvey recognised her as Inas Abdullah, and while she was being connected to the polygraph, he read through her file. Like Malika, Inas was in her mid-twenties. Her story was also comparable in that her family had supposedly died in recent fighting, leaving only her and her son. As with Malika, since she supposedly had no remaining family, it would have been difficult to force her to transport the nerve agent. And the similarities didn't end there: Inas also claimed to be a Shia Muslim, which didn't add up. Why would a Shiite, of her own volition, help an organisation that was entirely Sunni, a sect that had vowed to eradicate her branch of Islam?

Harvey asked Sarah to start the interview while he went into the other chamber and made a phone call.

'Hamad, you're a Muslim, right?'

'Last time I looked.'

'Which branch?'

'Shia, boss. Why?'

'Do you use a different Quran from the Sunnis?' Harvey asked.

'No, it's the same book. It's the *hadith* that are different. They were written generations after the prophet Muhammad died, and they contain many elements of traditional Islam that aren't mentioned in the Quran, such as stoning adulterers.'

'How well do you know your *hadith*, and are they very different from the Sunni version?'

'To answer both questions, a lot.' Farsi said. 'Is this going somewhere?'

'These female prisoners all claim to be Shia, but I'm not convinced. Could you pop down and see how well they know your *hadith*?'

'No problem. Be there in a couple of minutes.'

While Harvey waited, he watched Sarah try to get Inas to open up. The questions were simple and non-incriminating, but apart from confirming her name, Inas answered every question with a stern 'No comment'.

When Farsi arrived, Harvey swiped the lock and asked Sarah to leave so that their colleague could take over.

'This softly-softly approach isn't going to work,' Sarah said once the door closed.

'That's my feeling, too, but we have to try. I'll give Hamad a couple of minutes, and if she won't talk, we'll go back in and make the same offer we gave to Malika.'

They watched and listened as Farsi did his best to get something – anything – from Inas, but after a few minutes of questioning her on the religious tomes it was clear the woman wasn't going to answer him. Harvey swiped the door open and beckoned his colleague to leave before closing it again.

'We're wasting time,' Harvey said. 'Hamad, go and see how we're getting on with the families they were staying with. We'll have to backtrack and find out who helped them into the country.'

Teams had been sent to the addresses the women had given on their asylum applications forms, and Harvey expected them to have something to report by now.

Farsi left, and Harvey and Sarah went into the interrogation room to perform their good cop/bad cop routine. Unlike Malika, Inas showed no emotion when they threatened to take her son away forever. There wasn't even the slightest flicker when it was suggested he'd be brought up worshipping another deity, and Harvey quickly realised they were wasting their time.

He swiped his way back into the control room and asked Small how her polygraph readings looked.

'Total apathy,' the technician replied. 'Malika's were all over the place, but this one doesn't seem to give a damn about her kid.'

Harvey opened the door to the hallway and asked the guard to swap Inas for the next prisoner. He had a feeling that the remaining two interviews would go much the same way, and that wasn't going to benefit either party. If he couldn't get anything out of the women, then Home Secretary Maynard would take the matter out of MI5's hands, and the prisoners would face a lot more than empty threats.

Harvey ended his call and placed another one to the team that had been sent to the mosque in Woolwich. The families that the prisoners had been staying with all told the same story: the imam had called, asking them to put the women up for a few days. They'd never seen them before and had no idea how they'd managed to reach England beyond what the young mothers had told them. Harvey had people following up on those stories, but he didn't expect they'd turn up any solid details to confirm or deny the women's stories.

His call connected, and the operative recounted his conversation with the imam.

'He got a phone call a few minutes before the women turned up at the mosque, asking him to find accommodation for them. He doesn't know who called, but he gave me the number from his call log.'

Harvey entered the digits into his computer and the result wasn't a total surprise.

'It's an unregistered mobile,' he said. 'Looks like another dead end. Give me the time of the call, though. GCHQ might have a recording that we can use for voice comparison.'

Harvey fired off an urgent request to the Government Communications Headquarters, then went to update Ellis on the lack of progress. He was about to knock on her door when his mobile phone rang.

'Andrew, one of the prisoners wants to talk to you,' Elaine Solomon said.

'Which one?' he asked, already heading towards the exit.

'Malika Ali.'

'I'm on my way. Have her taken to the interrogation room.'

By the time he arrived downstairs, Malika was already sitting at the metal table, a guard affixing sensors to her body.

'Did she say what she wants?' Harvey asked Solomon.

'Nope, just that she needed to speak to you.'

Harvey waited until the woman was wired up and Small confirmed that everything was working before he swiped his card to gain access to the chamber.

'You wanted to see me,' he said as he took a seat opposite Malika.

'I want my son.'

'I'm sure you do, but you won't see him until you've answered all of my questions truthfully.'

'No, I want my son now. If you bring him here and let him stay with me, I will tell you whatever you want to know.'

'It's not that easy,' Harvey told her. 'First, you answer a few questions, and if I think you're being honest, I'll pass your request on to my superiors.'

Malika continued as if he hadn't interrupted her. 'I also want him to stay with me while I'm in prison.'

'No can do. That's only allowed until they're eighteen months old.'

'Then he stays with me for six months, but I get to choose who looks after him for the remainder of my sentence. I also want a new identity, and one for Jalal, too. When I'm released, I want our asylum requests to be granted.'

Her requests sounded reasonable, but Harvey didn't want to seem too keen to agree to her demands, otherwise she might decide to demand further concessions in exchange for her co-operation.

'I understand,' he said without committing. 'Let's start with an easy question. Is Malika Ali your real name?'

'It is.'

'And who asked you to bring the phial to England?'

'His name is Nabil Karim,' Malika said. 'My husband is a member of his group, Saif al-Islam.'

'Who were you supposed to deliver the phial to?'

'Bring me my son and I will answer the rest of your questions.'

'First, you tell me who you were supposed to deliver it to.'

'Not until I am holding Jalal in my arms.'

Harvey could see the determination in her eyes, and decided not to push it. The sooner she had her son, the less time she had to change her mind.

'Okay, I'll make arrangements now. He'll be here within the hour.'

'And he stays here with me?'

'Yes, I'll have a cot brought in, plus anything you need to make him comfortable.'

Harvey left her alone and called Ellis to inform her of the latest development.

'Do you think she can be trusted?' the Director General asked.

'It's a small concession, if you ask me. She knows about SAI and fingered Nabil Karim. I think we should give her whatever she asks for.'

'Okay, I'll have Sarah make the calls.'

Harvey hung up and asked Gerald Small what the polygraph told them about her responses so far.

'Hard to tell. Next time you speak to her, mix in some control questions about her age, her height, things that she can't lie about.'

'Will do,' Harvey said. 'You guys might as well get some lunch. It's going to be a long day.'

~

'So who were you supposed to deliver the phial to?'

Malika looked up at Harvey, then back down to Jalal, who was feeding from a bottle.

'I wasn't given that information,' she said. 'We were all told that once we arrived in England we would have it removed. Then we'd be housed until we were well enough to return to Syria.'

Harvey could understand her response, even though it wasn't the one he wanted to hear. If she were merely a mule, it made sense that she wouldn't know the bigger picture.

'Tell me why you agreed to have a phial implanted in your stomach and bring it here.'

'As I said, my husband is a member of Saif al-Islam. When Nabil Karim asked for volunteers – mothers only – he put my name forward.'

'Why just mothers?'

'I assume it was because we would be the most likely to be offered asylum and given quicker passage through Europe. We saw many young men who had been on Lampedusa for months.'

'What is your husband's name?'

'Yousef Ali.'

Harvey knew Sarah would be passing that information upstairs to see if it tallied with any of the names Hannibal had fed them before his grisly death.

'Do you love your husband?' he asked.

'It is my duty. When I was chosen to be his bride, I had no choice but to agree. I have seen what happened to those who refused such an offer.'

Harvey had seen them, too. The sanitised images shown on the news channels were little compared to the real atrocities being carried out.

'So it was an arranged marriage.'

'I think "forced" is more appropriate,' Malika told him. 'There is no place for Jalal amid all the conflict back home. I saw it as an opportunity to be rid of the fighting forever. That is why I claimed asylum when I arrived here. There is nothing for us in Syria.'

'What made you change your mind? You said you were only supposed to be here until you were well enough to return home.'

'I discussed it with the other women on the journey over here, and we all agreed to stay. Not all Muslims believe in killing innocents in the name of Allah, and we want our children to grow up learning the true messages of the Quran.'

'What arrangements were in place to get you home? Were you supposed to meet up somewhere?'

'We were only told that someone would come to us once transportation was in place. I have no idea how they planned to get us home.'

Jalal had finished his bottle and Malika gently rubbed his back as she held him close.

'Who removed the implant, and when?'

'It was done on Friday,' Malika said. 'The doctor didn't mention his name.'

'Where was it done?'

'A place in London where people go to get new noses.' Her expression turned to disgust. 'And fake breasts.'

'A plastic surgeon? What was the name of the place?'

'I didn't see it. We were taken in through the back and came out the same way. I only know it was that kind of place because of the posters on the walls.'

'Think hard,' Harvey urged her. 'They usually have the company name on the adverts.'

'They were not the kind of photographs I wanted to study too closely.'

Harvey thought that was understandable, but finding the man who carried out the surgery could be vital.

'If I showed you photos of the front and rear of every plastic surgery boutique in London, do you think you would recognise it?'

Malika assured him that she would, and Harvey looked over at the one-way mirror. 'Someone arrange that as soon as possible.'

While his colleagues got to work on that task, Harvey turned his attention back to Malika.

'I'd like to know if any of the information you gave in Lampedusa is true. You've already admitted that your husband is in Saif al-Islam, so the part about him being killed is obviously a lie.'

'It was mostly a fabrication,' Malika admitted. 'A story created to help me get here. This is the only part that is true.' She held up her hands, palms facing Harvey. 'I was at home with my father when a rocket hit the house. He was trapped underneath a burning beam, and when I tried to lift it off, my hands were badly burnt. The only lie was that it happened over a year ago, not last month.'

'The scars look fresh,' Harvey said.

'I know. To make my story more believable, Karim put a pot on a fire for an hour and made me pick it up.'

'Why? He could have just altered your cover story to include the truth, that it happened a long time ago.'

'I suggested that,' Malika told him, 'but Karim insisted. He said he had his reasons, and I was in no position to argue.'

Harvey wondered what kind of monsters would do such a thing, especially to a woman, but to people like Nabil Karim, lives meant little. He certainly wouldn't have lost any sleep over the pain he'd inflicted on Malika.

'I need you to tell me everything, from the moment Karim approached you to the time we picked you up at Lunar House.'

'I'd like a drink before we start,' Malika said.

'Sure. Tea, coffee or water?'

'I've always wanted to try Coca-Cola. It wasn't deemed acceptable during my childhood.'

Harvey signalled for someone to fulfil her request, and while they waited for the beverage to arrive, he asked her to begin her story.

'The first I heard about it was when Yousef told me about Karim's request. We were at home and he brought the subject up during dinner. At first he made it sound as if I was just going to be doing some travelling, and I was happy to help him, but it was only when I was taken to see Karim that I discovered what he really had in mind.'

'Was that the first time you'd met him?'

'Yes.'

'Where did the meeting take place?' Harvey asked. 'Was it at his home?'

'No, some kind of warehouse. He was there with several others, but he took me into a room to explain what he wanted me to do.'

'What was your first reaction when he asked you to have something implanted in your stomach?'

'Please,' Malika said. 'It is better if I explain everything that happened, and then you can ask questions.'

It wasn't the way Harvey wanted to handle the interview. His plan was to keep probing, often rephrasing the same question in the hope of tripping her up, then flitting back and forth, testing earlier statements to see if her story changed. As it was, he had to balance his own wishes with the need to keep her talking.

'I'm sorry. Please continue.'

'Karim took me to a separate room so that we were alone. He impressed on me the importance of the mission, and let me know in no uncertain terms what would happen if I refused. By agreeing to meet him, I had already given my implicit consent.'

Harvey was struck by her excellent grasp of the English language. She was clearly well educated, which only added to her mystery.

'And so he told you that you had to undergo surgery as part of the deal?'

'Not at that point,' Malika said. 'He did tell me that parts of the journey would be hazardous, but that he would provide as much assistance as he could. It was only a few days before we travelled that the five of us were told the full story.'

Sarah buzzed the door open and walked in with a glass of water for Harvey and a plastic cup filled to the brim for Malika. The Syrian woman looked at the contents, and then placed the cup on the table.

'Can I please have an unopened can and a fresh cup?'

'Why?' Sarah asked. 'What's wrong with that?'

'I would just like to be sure that you haven't added anything to it.'

'We have no reason to do that,' Harvey said. 'You're helping us.'

'All the same, I would prefer an unopened one.'

Sarah seemed put out, but Harvey nodded that she should comply with Malika's request.

'I'll get you a can,' said Sarah. 'But first, you tell me why you were reluctant to talk to us earlier. You say you don't love your husband and you have nothing to go back for, so what was stopping you?'

Malika looked down at her hands, while Harvey kicked himself for not asking such an obvious question.

'I did it for Inas,' Malika said. 'She has two sisters, both in their teens. Karim told her that if we were caught we must say nothing, otherwise the girls would be punished for our disobedience.'

'But you're talking now. Why the sudden change of heart?'

'Because I have never met those girls, and if it is a choice between my son and two strangers, I would choose Jalal every time.'

Sarah's face said she wasn't convinced by the explanation, but she turned on her heels and disappeared through the door. She returned two minutes later with a fresh cup and a can of Coke. After putting them on the table, she motioned for Harvey to follow her into the other room.

'I don't buy it. She's holding something back.'

'I agree,' Harvey said, 'but if we push her too hard, she might clam up. I'll keep her talking and you make notes if you think something sounds a bit off. We can go over those points with her later.'

'Okay, but I think she's just telling you what you want to hear so that she can keep her son.'

'We'll know soon enough,' Harvey said, and let himself back into the chamber. Malika had opened the drink and was sipping directly from the can.

'One thing strikes me as odd,' Harvey said as he took his seat across from her. 'Why would Inas agree to stay here and claim asylum if it would put her sisters in danger?'

'We spoke about this at length, and she finally agreed to claim asylum and then tell her sisters to find somewhere safe to stay until she could have them brought over here. We had no idea you would find us.'

Nor did we, Harvey thought. If they hadn't tripped over the body of Khadija Tawfeek, the women would still be free and they would have had no inkling that the X3 had made it to England. The first they would have known about it was when the casualties started overwhelming the emergency services. It pained him to think it, but he was glad that Khadija had lost her life.

'Okay, go back to your meeting with Karim. What did he tell you about the item you would be transporting?'

'He simply stressed the importance of making sure it was delivered safely. I asked him what it was but he just said it was safe. I think that wasn't the case for Khadija.'

'She wasn't killed by that,' Harvey said. 'The phial was intact when we found it. Did Karim say anything else? Did he mention any names?'

'No, just that everything was arranged to make our journey as comfortable as possible. He also said . . . Wait, there was something. Before we went in the room, one of his men gave Karim a phone and said someone needed to speak to him. He said a name . . . What was it . . . ?'

Harvey wanted to scream at her to spit it out, but he knew that adding pressure wouldn't help her memory.

'I'm sorry,' Malika eventually said, shaking her head and yawning. 'I just can't remember.'

Harvey wanted to slam his fist on the desk; instead, he stood and walked to the door. 'I think that's enough for today. I want you to try and remember the name you heard. If it comes to you during the night, let the guard know. If it doesn't, I'll see you first thing in the morning.'

In the outer chamber, he ran a hand over the two days' worth of stubble that had covered his chin. The night shift had already relieved Solomon and Small, and the clock on the wall showed it to be almost midnight. Apart from not wanting to wear Malika out, he was ready for a few hours of sleep himself. Ideally, he would have pushed her until she had something they could work on, but they'd been at it for more than nine hours and tired minds weren't the most reliable.

'Do you think she's telling the whole truth now?' Sarah asked.

'Let's see.'

Harvey had asked Small again what the lie detector indicated, but the answer remained inconclusive, despite the control questions he'd slipped in. It could be that she was being truthful, or that she knew how to manipulate the test.

'My brain's too fried to make sense of this,' Harvey said. 'Let's get some sleep and try again in the morning.'

~

Ayad Badawi watched the traffic crawl by as he sat outside the café, sipping an espresso. The clock on a nearby building told him his ride was a few minutes late, but that was to be expected as the offices began closing up for the day.

As the minutes ticked by, he wondered if something had gone wrong. What he'd been asked to do was undoubtedly illegal, and despite the assurances he'd been given, he couldn't help but feel nervous.

His ride turned up ten minutes late, a black cab with an advert for a West End theatre emblazoned on the side. It pulled up outside the café and Badawi climbed in. A man was sitting in the back, and Badawi recognised him as Ghulam, the one who had recruited him for the job.

'Is everything ready?' Ghulam asked as the taxi pulled back into traffic.

'It is. All I need is the agent and I can get to work.'

Ghulam reached into his jacket and produced an inch-thick metal box the size of an A5 sheet of paper. He undid two clasps and showed Badawi the contents.

Badawi removed one of the phials from the padded interior and examined it. The top had a one-inch screw-on cap that prevented him from seeing the neck of the vessel. 'Are you sure there's a rubber diaphragm in place?'

'We haven't checked, but that was the information we were given. If there isn't, will it pose a problem?'

'Yes, it will. I am set up to expect it in a certain condition. If it differs, I will have to come up with a new method of making the transfer.'

'Why not take the top off and see?' Ghulam smirked.

'I think not.' Badawi replaced the phial in the box and secured the clasps before placing it in his leather briefcase. 'It should be ready by midnight. How should I contact you?'

'No need,' Ghulam said. 'I will stay with you until you have completed the task, just in case you have . . . second thoughts.'

Badawi made his displeasure known. He wasn't accustomed to having people doubt his integrity, but Ghulam placed a soothing hand on his arm.

'It was not my decision. I have my orders, as do you. Believe me, I don't like the idea of being in the same room as this stuff, especially once the top comes off.'

'You will be quite safe,' Badawi said, still angry. 'I wouldn't be doing this if I thought there was any personal risk involved.'

'My friend, there are always risks. All we can do is try to mitigate them, and this plan has been well thought out. After the attack, though, the security services will be looking for people with your particular skills. I trust you've made the necessary arrangements?'

'I have,' Badawi said. He'd contacted a cash-for-homes company that would give him a quick sale on his house, albeit at only 70 per cent of market value, and his flight to Turkey was booked and paid for. It was then just a short journey across the border into Syria and then south to Palmyra, where he would stay with his cousin while he arranged a new place of his own.

Leaving England wasn't going to be that much of an upheaval. He'd lived in London for fifteen years, but there was little about it that he liked. The area he lived in was quiet enough, but the centre of the capital was too busy for his taste. He was looking forward to returning to his homeland and spending his remaining years in tranquillity. As things stood, he was unlikely to find peace anywhere in Syria, but after the attack, the Western allies would think twice about bombing his country.

They drove for forty minutes until they arrived at a storage unit built into some railway arches. The two men got out, and Ghulam instructed the driver to be ready to pick him up later in the evening.

Badawi unlocked the door and waited until Ghulam joined him inside before locking it and switching on the lights. Fluorescent tubes hummed into life, revealing the meagre contents of the room. A table occupied the far wall, and on it was a Perspex box, while to the right stood a small, glass-doored refrigerator containing bottles of water.

The men approached the bench and Badawi removed the metal case from his bag and placed it inside the Perspex chamber.

'What's this for?' Ghulam asked, pointing to a metal canister that fed into the side of the box.

'The incinerator,' Badawi told him. 'If I flick this switch, a flame is ignited in that corner. Once I am finished, I will purge the air inside. Petrol vapour will be sprayed into the tank, and when it hits the flame, any agent that manages to escape will be destroyed.'

Badawi opened the catches on the small box, then placed a rubber-edged lid on the large chamber, ensuring a tight fit before sealing it on all four sides with adjustable grips.

'I'm sorry I can't offer you a seat,' he said, sitting on the only stool in the room. 'I wasn't expecting company.'

Ghulam assured him that it wasn't a problem, and Badawi placed his hands into the large rubber gloves that were fitted into the front of the unit. He took a moment to compose himself, then removed the first of the phials and carefully unscrewed the top. He was pleased to see a four-millimetre rubber stopper jammed into the top, preventing the deadly agent from escaping.

Badawi picked up a small syringe and gently forced the needle through the rubber until the point was visible in the clear liquid, then inverted the phial and slowly withdrew ten millilitres of the X3. He took his time pulling the needle back out, then put the phial down and picked up a stainless-steel canister. It looked like a miniature version of a scuba diver's air tank, but instead of a valve at the top, it had a rubber diaphragm similar to the phial. Badawi inserted the needle into it and pushed down on the plunger until the syringe was empty.

'If you use a bigger needle, we can be out of here by seven,' Ghulam said.

'If I do that, there's a strong possibility that I will displace the rubber rather than penetrate it. If that happens, I will be forced to purge the chamber, and you will lose the agent. Now please stop interrupting and let me get on with it.'

Badawi immediately sensed it wasn't a good idea to vent his frustration at his paymaster, but he'd never been one to suffer fools gladly. He particularly hated to be second-guessed by those who knew nothing about his chosen profession.

'I'm sorry,' he said as he picked up the phial for the second pass, 'I get cranky when I'm nervous.'

'Don't be,' Ghulam told him. 'I shouldn't be questioning your expertise. Please, continue.'

The words sounded hollow, and Badawi knew he was in for a stressful few hours.

CHAPTER 19

Tuesday, 15 August 2017

Harvey stifled a yawn as he swiped his way into the outer chamber at eight o'clock. The previous night had brought little sleep, and what he had managed had been filled with dreams of melting faces and a mountain of dead bodies. He envied Sarah for looking her usual stunning self; in an effort to compete, he'd finally taken a razor to his face.

Malika was already sitting in her usual position, wired up and ready to go. Her son Jalal was playing in a portable crib that Malika had requested, along with toys to keep him occupied.

'She's really making herself at home,' Sarah said disapprovingly.

'I'm happy to make concessions, as long as she gives us what we want. The first sign she's playing us, the kid will be removed.'

'Are you sure it has nothing to do with her looks?'

Harvey's forehead furrowed as he looked at his girlfriend. 'Are you serious? We're trying to foil a major attack and you're jealous of our prisoner?'

'I've seen you in there. You can't keep your eyes off her.'

'It's called maintaining eye contact,' Harvey said, lowering his voice. 'I'm trying to win her confidence.'

Sarah crossed her arms tightly across her chest. 'Huh. I guess that's one way of describing it.'

Harvey was stunned. He'd never seen this side of Sarah, and she wasn't displaying a particularly endearing quality. They'd been in the company of many pretty women during their time together, but this was the first time she'd reacted in such a way. Had he missed something to bring on such behaviour? It wasn't her birthday, and their anniversary was months away, so it couldn't be that. She'd been quiet at home that morning, but he'd put it down to the short sleep and huge workload. Whatever it was, he needed to nip it in the bud before she drove herself crazy with unnecessary worry. She was the only woman he wanted, and he certainly wasn't going to swap her for a suspected terrorist.

'You could lead the interview today,' he offered.

'And let you ogle her through the window? No, thanks.'

This seemed one of those arguments he was never destined to win.

'Look, whatever has got into you, it'll have to wait. We've got work to do.'

Harvey swiped his way into the second room and took his seat across from Malika. After announcing the time and date, he skipped any pleasantries and asked her if she could remember the name that Karim had used during the meeting.

'No. I thought about it all night but it wouldn't come to me.'

It wasn't the best start to the day, but Harvey knew there was more that she had to offer – it was simply a case of pressing the right buttons.

'What can you tell me about the people who helped you to get here? Do you have names for them?'

Malika shook her head. 'They rarely spoke to us. They would just confirm who we were then drive us to the next handover.'

'Then what about descriptions? Was there anything distinctive about them? Extremely tall or short? Strange tattoos, anything like that?'

She thought about it for a moment, giving Harvey time to wonder once more what the hell had got into Sarah. He glanced over to the mirror and could feel her eyes burning into him. He didn't believe he'd been flirting with Malika. He'd been civil, and that was about the limit to the warmth he'd shown the young woman. He couldn't understand why Sarah would take that the wrong way.

'The truck driver in France was missing the top of his ear,' Malika said, bringing him out of his ruminations.

Harvey assumed Sarah would be working that lead up straight away, despite her sudden hostility towards him.

'What else?' he asked.

'That's all. The rest were just . . . normal.'

'Tell me about the truck. The colour, the size, everything.'

'It was very long, and blue, I think. I don't remember the name on the side.'

'There seem to be lots of little details that you can't remember,' Harvey said.

'I didn't know I was going to be quizzed about every aspect of my journey, otherwise I would have been more attentive. As it was, I had more pressing matters to occupy me.'

Harvey let it slide and pressed for more information about the journey in the truck.

'We were picked up somewhere in France by a truck driver. We sat in the back of the truck until we neared the port, then we stopped and were told to climb inside some kind of metal container, which the driver welded shut. He gave us an oxygen mask and a pill to put the children to sleep, then took us across the sea on a ferry. When we got to England, the driver freed us, and that was when we discovered that Khadija was dead.'

'How did she die?' Harvey asked.

'The driver said she'd haemorrhaged. I wasn't about to go and inspect the body to check his diagnosis.'

That detail would soon be revealed, he knew. A post-mortem was being carried out to determine the cause of death, and it would be more accurate than any guess Malika could offer.

'What did they do with her body?'

'I don't know. A vehicle was waiting for us, some kind of small bus, and we were told to get in. Khadija was still in the truck when we left, and Ramla took care of her son.'

Harvey asked her to recall everything she could about the driver of the minibus. She said he was young, in his mid-twenties, and clean-shaven with short hair brushed backwards. Not a lot to go on, but he'd be showing her some mug shots later, and hopefully she'd pick him out.

'We were taken to the surgical centre,' Malika continued, 'and after the thing was removed from my body I was able to rest for a couple of hours before the bus came back and took us to the mosque. The imam there found us someone to stay with.'

'I want to know everything the driver said to you.'

'Nothing. Get in, get out, that was it. The doctor said even less.'

Jalal started to cry, and Malika asked for a break so that she could feed and change him. The session was barely an hour old and Harvey wanted to press on, but he knew he would get nothing further out of her until the boy had been seen to.

He swiped his way into the other room and saw that Sarah had disappeared.

'She went to check on the truck driver with the missing piece of ear,' Elaine Solomon said. 'I also sent her the description of the minibus and truck drivers. Be sure to get a description of the doctor too.'

'I will. Did Sarah say anything else?'

Harvey was hoping that Sarah had confided in Solomon – that she might have an explanation for his girlfriend's offhand behaviour.

'Nope, just that she'd be back down when she had something.'

Determined to know what had got into Sarah, Harvey headed up to the office to confront her. He found her desk empty, as was Farsi's, but saw her through the glass wall of Ellis's office, sitting opposite the Director General.

Deciding that it wouldn't be a good idea to interrupt their discussion to resolve a domestic matter, Harvey returned to the interrogation suite and saw that Malika was finishing up Jalal's new nappy. He entered the room to the overwhelming smell of baby formula and infant poo and took his customary seat.

His chat with Sarah would have to wait until later, but he had difficulty shaking it from his mind as he returned to the questioning.

Hamad Farsi sat on a park bench as he ate his sandwich while browsing the internet on his phone. The call to meet up had come from Samir, a low-level snitch who had been providing the security services with local information for a few months. At first Farsi had blown him off, telling him he was too busy to meet, but Samir had insisted that he had big news that couldn't wait. He'd refused to divulge it over the phone, so Farsi had been forced to take an al fresco lunch. There was a chance that it could tie in with their surveillance of Imran al-Hosni, though Samir wasn't known to be one of his entourage.

Samir turned up five minutes late and took a seat next to him. The informant was young, barely out of his teens, and his gaunt expression suggested a dependency on recreational chemicals.

'What've you got for me?' Farsi asked.

'Depends. How much did you bring?'

It was always the same with Samir. Now and again, he provided little jewels of information, but most of the time it was mere speculation and third-hand gossip. The only thing Samir had going for him was his addiction, which kept him coming back for more handouts.

'I'll give you fifty if it's anything other than something you found on Facebook.'

'Fifty?' Samir moaned. 'Come on, man, I need at least two hundred.'

'Fifty's all I got. You want it or not?'

Samir made a face like a child confronted with broccoli at lunchtime.

'If it's any good, I'll be back tomorrow with another two, how's that?'

Samir perked up slightly. 'Okay, but if I have to wait, I want five hundred. I'm telling you, it's really big.'

Farsi would have to run that amount past Ellis, and he wasn't convinced that she'd be happy with the payment.

'I can't authorise that much, but you start talking, and if it's anything we already know, I'll stop you and you take the fifty. If it's as big as you say, I'll see what I can do.'

'Oh, it's big, man, but I've got these guys on my ass chasing me for money. I need to square them away, otherwise I can't spend my time helping you out, know what I mean?'

Farsi knew exactly what he meant: he'd borrowed from drug dealers and they were demanding payment. These weren't the kind of people who sent you letters threatening court action, either.

Farsi nodded non-committally. 'Start talking.'

He could almost hear the informant's brain working as he mulled over the options. 'Okay,' he said at last. 'You know Muhammad Khan, from Tower Hamlets?'

'I think I've heard of him,' Farsi said. In fact, Khan, the imam at the local mosque, was near the top of their watch list. Until recently, they'd had a man watching him, but he'd been pulled off that duty once their focus had shifted to Imran al-Hosni.

'Well, he's working on something huge,' Samir said.

'You already said that. I'm paying for details.'

'Yeah, well, I don't have them yet, but I'm working on it.'

Farsi rose to leave. 'You're wasting my time. Crawl back under your rock and don't call me again unless you've got something concrete.'

'This is big!' Samir jumped up and grabbed Farsi's arm. 'Khan's stopped talking to anyone. He's closed himself off from everyone but a few of his closest mates. No-one can get near him anymore. And there's a meeting set up for tomorrow night where he's going to make an announcement.'

It wasn't exactly the same communications blackout al-Hosni was undertaking, but it was enough to suggest that Khan had something planned. Whether or not it warranted resources was for Ellis to decide, but Farsi would need much more to go on than Samir had told him so far.

'I want you to get into that meeting and let me know what he says,' Farsi told him, handing over the fifty pounds.

'Impossible! I'm not that close to him.'

'Find a way,' Farsi said. 'If you get me a recording and it's something we weren't aware of, I might be able to stretch to a thousand. Otherwise our relationship ends here.'

The look on Samir's face said he was hooked. Unfortunately, Farsi didn't trust the snitch as far as he could throw him, and without the stipulation of an audio recording, Samir would likely turn up in a couple of days with a fabricated story to try to collect his bounty. Now that he'd spelt out the mission parameters, he would see whether Samir was up to the task.

'Remember, I need a recording,' he said as he turned on his heels. 'Or the deal's off.'

~

'What's the problem?' Sarah Thompson asked as she entered Ellis's office.

'I was hoping you could tell me. Is there something going on between you and Andrew that I should know about?'

'It's nothing,' Thompson said, and immediately began wondering who had brought it to Ellis's attention. Only Solomon and Small were in the same room, so it must have been one of them. Unless Ellis had been watching the feed from the detention area . . .

'Why don't you take a seat and explain it to me.'

'I'd rather not,' Thompson said. 'It's kind of personal.'

Ellis gestured to the chair anyway. 'We're in the middle of a serious situation right now, and I can't afford to have you two at each other's throats. Tell me this is something you can work out.'

Thompson took a seat, and as she did, the emotion that had been building up all morning finally overwhelmed her. The tears came first, followed by uncontrollable sobbing. She took a tissue from her pocket and blew her nose, doing her best to get herself together, but her body wouldn't listen. For two minutes, she bawled into her tissue before Ellis came round the desk and placed her hands on her shoulders.

'Take the rest of the day off. Go home, catch up on some sleep. We can discuss this tomorrow.'

'I don't want to lose him!'

The words were out of her mouth before Thompson could stop them, and Ellis strode back to her seat.

'What makes you think that's going to happen? From what I've seen, you're the perfect couple.'

Thompson finally managed to stop the tears and she blew her nose once more. 'Because I'm pregnant.'

Ellis sat back in her chair. 'And what did he say when you told him?'

'I haven't. We were chatting last month and he made it clear he didn't want children. If I tell him now, he's sure to leave me.'

Ellis looked confused. 'So why were you accusing him of having a thing for Malika? If you're desperate to keep him, why start a fight over nothing?'

'I don't know!' Thompson said, her voice louder than she'd expected. She took a couple of breaths and tried again. 'I don't know. I've just been feeling . . . strange lately. More emotional. I keep trying to imagine what he'd say, but every time it comes out different. Sometimes I think he'll melt into my arms, others I picture him storming out of the house. I'm just so confused.'

'How many weeks are you?'

'Eight. I took a home test last week but only got confirmation a couple of days ago.'

'You're going to have to tell him eventually,' Ellis said.

'I know, but I'm scared of what he's going to say.'

'Trust me, I've known Andrew longer than you have. He's a good man. I suggest you go and apologise for your earlier outburst and, when you get home, break the news about the baby.'

The advice made good sense, especially coming from someone she respected. Thompson took a couple of minutes to compose herself, then thanked Ellis and headed to the bathroom to fix her make-up.

A quarter of an hour later, she swiped open the door to the interrogation suite and stuck her head inside.

'Andrew, can I have a word?'

She held the door open and let him into the other chamber, then closed it and pushed him up against the wall. Her lips met his in the hottest kiss she could muster, and when they parted, she nuzzled her face into his neck.

'I'm sorry,' she said.

Andrew wrapped his arms around her and kissed her shoulder. 'If that's how you make up, we should fight more often.'

CHAPTER 20

Tuesday, 15 August 2017

Andrew Harvey waited impatiently as Malika flicked through the pile of images on the table. They'd identified more than fifty plastic surgeons operating in the London area, and the prisoner was looking through Street View images taken from the front and rear of each surgery.

Harvey suppressed a yawn and looked at his watch. They'd been at it for more than eight hours, though most of that time had been taken up with numerous breaks to tend to Jalal. In the moments when he'd been able to question Malika, details had been thin on the ground. He'd gone back over earlier questions in an effort to try to trip her up, but her story remained consistent, and he still didn't have anything that could lead to the X3.

'This might be it,' Malika said, bringing Harvey back to life. She studied the photo again, then handed it to him. 'Yes, I'm pretty sure that's the one. I recognise the crescent moon cut into the door.'

Harvey took the photo to the door, and when Sarah opened it, he stepped through.

'I want to take her there to confirm that it's the same place. Can you please arrange for an armed unit to meet us there?'

'Will do,' Sarah said. She turned to make the arrangements but Harvey called her back.

'So what was all that about earlier?'

He'd wanted to ask her about it before, but Sarah hadn't given him a chance before he'd had to go back into the interrogation room. Afterwards, whenever he'd stepped out for a break, Sarah had been upstairs, working on other aspects of the case.

'Let's talk about it tonight, when we get home.'

'You can't tell me now?'

Sarah looked at the others in the room. 'No, later.'

She disappeared, leaving Harvey to wonder once again what the spat had been about. Unfortunately, he knew Sarah well enough to know that he wouldn't be able to prise it out of her until she was ready, so he concentrated on the matter in hand.

He asked Solomon to take care of Jalal while Malika and he were away, and went back into the interrogation room.

'We're going now.'

'Now? What about Jalal?'

'It's after four. We need to get to the surgery before it closes. Jalal will be well looked after. We should only be gone for an hour.'

He escorted Malika to the door, then asked the guard to take her back to her cell to get her coat. They returned just as Sarah appeared in the corridor.

'Scrub that,' she said. Then, to the guard: 'Take Malika back to the interrogation room.'

'What's wrong?' Harvey asked.

Sarah waited until Malika was out of earshot. 'I asked SO15 to meet us there with an armed unit and they wanted to know what interest we had in a murder case.'

'Murder?'

Sarah nodded. 'Apparently the surgeon, Dr Kamal Bousaid, was found dead yesterday morning. The receptionist found him when she opened up. It looks like a professional hit.'

She described Bousaid's death, the single stab wound to the neck that had severed his spinal cord. 'It was meant to look like a robbery, but the way he was killed suggests he was targeted. Given that Malika was there on the day he died, I'd say someone was trying to cover their tracks. My guess is that the killer took the X3.'

'What have the police got so far? Any suspects?'

'Nothing. They checked CCTV covering the front of the building but all they saw was lights going on at around the time Malika said she got there. There's nothing covering the back entrance, and that's how they think the killer arrived and left.'

'Then I'll have a word with her and see if anyone else was there when she had the X3 removed.'

He rejoined Malika and asked who else had been present when she'd undergone surgery.

'No-one, just me and the other three girls, plus the doctor.'

'You didn't see anyone else that night?'

'No.'

It was yet another dead end, and Harvey was becoming increasingly frustrated with the way the case was panning out. Despite having the women in custody, they still had nothing more than two bodies and a tenuous link to Imran al-Hosni. If Malika didn't come up with something soon, they might be forced to pull al-Hosni in for questioning, and no judge in the land would sign an arrest warrant on the basis of best guesses.

The door to the room opened and Hamad Farsi entered and placed a folder in front of Malika.

'These are all the people we could find who have damage to their ear. Hopefully Malika can pick out the truck driver from the photos.'

Malika opened the folder to the first page and studied the photograph for a few seconds, then flipped over to the next mug shot. Harvey watched for signs that she'd recognised someone, but it wasn't until the eighth page that her expression changed. She looked at the photo for at least a minute, then pushed the folder towards Harvey.

'That's him. He's the one that drove us into England.'

'You're sure?' Farsi asked. 'Don't you want to check the others?'

'No, that's definitely him.'

Harvey looked up at Farsi. 'Do we know him?'

'Anjam Shah. He's a truck driver by trade, and frequents the same mosque as al-Hosni.'

'Al-Hosni!' Malika said, startling them both. 'That's the name Karim mentioned when I first met him. Imran al-Hosni!'

It was Harvey's turn to ask if she was sure.

'I'm positive. I recall it clearly now.'

Relief washed over Harvey like a tsunami. After two days of probing, he finally had something solid to work with, though he had no time to enjoy the moment. The X3 had been in the UK for more than four days, giving al-Hosni plenty of time to make his preparations.

Harvey picked up the folder and told Farsi to follow him. In the outer chamber, he asked Solomon to have Malika and Jalal returned to her cell.

'I need you and Gerald upstairs in five minutes. We won't be questioning her any further today.'

Harvey led Farsi up to the office and told him to assemble the team in the conference room, then knocked on Ellis's door and entered.

'It's definitely al-Hosni,' he told her. 'Malika confirmed it.'

'How did she know?'

'Hamad mentioned the name just now, and she said that was the one Karim had used when he was talking to one of his men.'

'Is it possible she's just saying that to keep you sweet?' Ellis asked.

'No way. Hamad only mentioned his surname, but Malika knew his first name.'

Ellis digested the information for a moment. 'Okay, how do you plan to proceed?'

'I'm assuming al-Hosni isn't stupid enough to have the X3 stashed under his bed, which means one of his acquaintances is in possession of it. We already have comprehensive logs of everyone he's met over the last few days, but we'll have to backtrack to follow the movements of each and every one of them. It's going to take thousands of man-hours to go through all the CCTV coverage, so we'll need everyone working double shifts.'

'Do it. In the meantime, I'll report in to Maynard. He's been bugging me every hour for updates, so this should keep him happy for a while.'

Harvey left her to make the call and returned to his own desk, where he looked up the surveillance logs on al-Hosni. One file contained a list of everyone he'd been in contact with since Friday: more than thirty confirmed names. Hundreds of others had attended the mosque at the same time as al-Hosni, but those names would have to wait until the prime suspects were eliminated.

He removed his laptop from the docking station and carried it through to the conference room, where he found the whole team waiting. After hooking his machine up to the wall-mounted screen, he brought up a picture of the main target.

'This is Imran al-Hosni,' he said, looking up at the image of a man in his late forties sporting a long, thin beard. 'He's the imam at Stockwell Green mosque. One of our female prisoners confirmed that he is part of the X3 plot. It's unlikely that he took delivery of the agent personally, but he's certainly pulling the strings. Our task is to uncover the movements of everyone in this file over the last four days.'

The image on the screen changed to the list of names. 'The surveillance logs show where and when al-Hosni met each of these people.

Use that date stamp as a starting point and use CCTV coverage to track their subsequent movements. If that leads nowhere, look backwards from their meeting to last Friday. In particular, we're looking for something changing hands. It could be as small as a paperback or larger than a briefcase, but chances are, one of these people has the X3, and it's our job to find it before they can use it.'

'Why don't we just bring al-Hosni in?' Gareth Bailey asked. 'It sounds like we've got enough evidence to arrest him.'

'We do, but we can't guarantee he'll talk. Our priority is finding the X3, and once we have it we can start pulling people in. Speaking of CCTV, Gareth, how did you get on with the A2 lorry search?'

'There's one vehicle outstanding. It failed to reach the second camera, so I checked the cameras on the off-ramps and there's no sign of it there, either.'

'When did you discover this?' Harvey asked.

Bailey looked down at his coffee. 'Yesterday evening.'

'And you didn't think to tell me?'

'I didn't want to come to you until I had something concrete to report.'

Harvey did his best to hide his frustration. 'Please tell me you at least ran the plates.'

'Of course! I'm not that stupid.'

Harvey bit his tongue. Chewing Bailey a new hole might make him feel better, but he needed everyone on board, not sitting in a corner nursing hurt feelings.

'Was the name Anjam Shah by any chance?'

Bailey didn't have to answer. The look on his face told Harvey all he needed to know.

'If you'd come to me with that information yesterday, we would be well on our way to finding the X3. Next time, I want to know every tiny detail, no matter how insignificant you think it is. That goes for everyone.'

Ellis entered the room and stood next to Harvey.

'I just got off the phone with the Home Secretary. He has authorised unlimited overtime and manpower, so we'll be absorbing a few people from Six until this is resolved. In the meantime, sleep is a luxury we can't afford. If you've got plans for the next few days, cancel them. There's a deadly agent out there, and we have no idea when they intend to use it. Let's just assume it's soon.'

Ellis handed the meeting back to Harvey, who began assigning the operatives with names from the list.

'Gerald, I want you in on this, too,' he said to Small. 'If you're working on anything, put it on hold. We need every able body tracking these people.'

Harvey dismissed the group and returned to his own desk, where he brought up the list of names. He'd opted to take the first five, and number one was Nasir Qureshi, the courier who had met al-Hosni days earlier. Because Qureshi had returned to Syria before the women had arrived in the UK, Harvey knew he couldn't possibly have the X3, so he scratched him and moved on to the next person of interest. He referenced the man's name in the surveillance log and, armed with the date and time of the meeting with al-Hosni, he looked up the nearest CCTV camera.

His stomach growled as he logged into the camera control room, and he fired off a quick message to Ellis, asking her to order sandwiches for the team. It promised to be a long night, and his next hot meal could be days away.

He stole a glance over to Sarah's desk, but she was deep in concentration. Whatever it was that she had to say to him, it would have to wait.

~

The imam sat in his office and looked at the clock on the wall as it ticked inexorably towards eight o'clock. His young charges would soon start to arrive, though there was only one he was interested in this evening. A young man who would carry out the act he had been working towards for the last few years.

The imam had arrived in Britain as a dependant of his late wife, a solicitor who had succumbed to cancer two years earlier. She had been the one to arrange his visa based on his documents, almost all of which were convincing forgeries. The university diploma was fake, as were his work history and references. They'd been created by his masters in order to facilitate his move to the heart of the enemy stronghold. Within hours of his arrival he'd sought out the local mosque and passed on the message he'd been told to convey.

The path to victory starts here.

The incumbent hierarchy had resisted the orders, and days later their leader had been found dead in an alleyway. The new imam had quickly been asked to step into his position, mostly by those who feared a similar fate. The old guard had soon been cleared out, and the new regime had set about the task of finding young blood willing to listen to the new teachings.

The kids he'd chosen had been those desperate for inclusion. They were the victims of bullying at school, or those whose fathers wielded a belt rather than offering a welcoming bosom. The imam had made them all feel wanted, needed, part of a new family.

Their daily lessons had consisted of his version of selected verses from the Quran:

And slay them wherever ye find them . . . Such is the reward of the disbelievers.

The actual text and preceding verses referred to the act of self-defence, but that didn't suit the imam's purpose. He used the following verses to show that jihad, far from being a 'spiritual struggle', was actually a call to arms:

Warfare is ordained for you, though it is hateful unto you; but it happen that ye hate a thing which is good for you, and it may happen that ye love a thing which is bad for you. Allah knoweth, ye know not.

There is no blame for the blind, nor is there blame for the lame, nor is there blame for the sick (that they go not forth to war). And whoso obeyeth Allah and His messenger, He will make him enter Gardens underneath which rivers flow; and whoso turneth back, him will He punish with a painful doom.

With the subtle omission of a few words and readings taken out of context, he had managed to convince his fledgling flock that Allah's only wish was for them to defeat the disbelievers.

These lessons were followed by first-hand accounts of the atrocities inflicted on their Muslim brethren over the last quarter of a century, from Iraq to Afghanistan, from Libya to Syria – tales backed up by graphic photos and the occasional video depicting crimes against Islam, each designed to instil further hatred of their oppressors.

Several of his protégés had gone to fight in the Middle East, while the more promising ones had been chosen to make England their battleground.

The imam watched as the first of the young men entered the mosque and took off their shoes. So far, three stood in front of him, all wearing hooded jumpers and carrying backpacks over their shoulders. He remained silent as he waited for the other five to turn up, and when the last one came through the door ten minutes late, he saw the nervous expression on the youth's face. He was clearly expecting a dressing-down, but the imam saved him the humiliation.

He'd sold the evening's exercise as a test of their counter-surveillance skills, and had set them a challenge: get from a set point to the mosque in three hours using the most circuitous route imaginable. Some had started in Holloway, others in Kensington and White City. All of them would be followed, he'd promised, and those who took the easy route would suffer his wrath.

In truth, he'd only had one boy tailed, a promising nineteen-year-old who had excelled at the training camp he'd attended in northern Pakistan. The trip was supposed to have been a pilgrimage to his parents' homeland during his gap year, but only the imam and a select few others knew the real reason for the six-month vacation.

Iqbal stood among the other boys, all looking at him expectantly, but he remained silent until Ghulam entered the building and offered the slightest of nods before disappearing into the imam's office.

'You have done well this evening. The reports I received have been very encouraging, and I am glad to see you have all been paying attention to the lessons you've been given. However, the test is not yet over.' He walked among them and handed each of them a twenty-pound note. 'As you make your way back home, I want you to take a different route. Again, your job will be to evade the man following you. At some point, I want you to change your clothes. Get rid of the top you are wearing now and change into the one you have in your backpack. Make sure you do this in an area with no CCTV coverage.'

He stood in front of Iqbal and looked him up and down. 'Go into my office. There is something about your performance this evening that needs to be addressed.'

Iqbal looked shaken but he did as instructed.

'Wait here,' the imam told the others, and followed Iqbal into the room, closing the door behind him. Ghulam was waiting, and had what looked like a silver fire extinguisher in his hand.

'Take a seat,' he said, and Iqbal sat in a chair opposite a large oak desk. He clasped his hands and held them between his knees, a nervous look on his face. The imam sat opposite him, resting his elbows on the desk and steepling his fingers.

'Relax,' he said. 'I asked you here because I have a special task for you. The one you've been training for.'

He paused to let the words sink in. He'd discussed this moment with Iqbal a few times, and now that the time had come, he wanted to make sure he could trust the boy to follow it through to its conclusion.

Iqbal looked up at him, determination etched on his face. 'What do you need me to do?'

It was just the reaction the imam was hoping for. He took the device from Ghulam. 'I want you to set this off on Friday.' He showed the boy how to arm the canister. 'Flick this guard up, move the switch to the "On" position and hold the button down for three seconds. Got it?'

Iqbal nodded. 'Will it hurt?'

'Only for a moment, but once it is activated, you can take another way out.'

Ghulam reached into his waistband and produced a small pistol. 'It is already loaded. Just remove the safety catch, like this, then point and fire.'

'I can do that.'

'Good. I won't see you again after tonight, but you will always be in my thoughts. When word spreads of your deed, none will be prouder than I. Your own reward awaits you in *Jannah*.'

He told Iqbal to place the device in his backpack, then gave strict instructions regarding the deployment site as well as the planned time.

'When you leave this room, you must look as if you have been admonished. Tell no-one about this conversation, not even your closest friend. As I told the others, I want you to take the long way home and change your clothes during the journey. Did you bring a spare hoodie?'

'I did,' Iqbal said, 'and I added these to my bag.'

He showed the imam the white designs that adorned his backpack. 'They are attached with Velcro, so when I change my top I can remove these, too. It will make it harder to spot me once I have changed.'

The imam beamed at the boy. 'You are more than ready. May Allah watch over your travels.'

He opened the door and let Iqbal walk through, then followed him out, a stern look on his face. The youths had been chatting among themselves, but stood to attention when they saw the imam.

'Go home, all of you. Ghulam will arrange the next test and will contact you at the weekend. Remember your instructions for tonight.'

The imam turned and walked back into the office, relieved that his part in Karim's plan was almost over.

CHAPTER 21

Wednesday, 16 August 2017

Harvey sipped at his second cup of coffee of the morning, hoping it would work faster at waking him up. It was barely seven and, despite going home dog-tired, he had managed little sleep.

He'd tried to get Sarah to open up to him, to reveal what it was that had caused their spat earlier in the day, but she'd insisted that it wasn't the time, and had quickly fallen asleep. Harvey hadn't been so lucky. He'd lain awake trying to figure out what he'd done wrong. He knew for a fact that he hadn't consciously been flirting with Malika, which is what seemed to have set her off, but could she have read something into it that he hadn't even noticed?

He'd finally drifted off after three, only to be shaken from his dream two hours later. After a quick shower, he'd tried once more to prise something out of Sarah, but she'd brushed him off again. At least she'd been her normal, bubbly self this morning, and while he was still puzzled as to what had brought on the sudden change in her, he was grateful for the return to the status quo.

His computer finished booting up, and he logged in and checked his messages. The Metropolitan Police had made no progress with the murder of the plastic surgeon. A van had been seen leaving the area, but the plates had turned out to be false. The rest of the team had sent in progress reports before clocking off for the night, and Harvey went through them one by one. Nine people had been eliminated from the suspect list, their actions nothing out of the ordinary. He finally came to Gerald Small's report. He'd given the technician an additional duty, and that had been to hack into the computers of the haulage company that employed Anjam Shah.

> *Shah had a delivery of motor parts to the south of France on Friday 11th August. No cargo on the return journey.*

It immediately struck Harvey as unusual. He had a friend who worked the roads and knew that on long trips, they only made their money if they took goods both ways. This was further proof that Shah was the one who had helped the women into Britain, and his ties to al-Hosni's mosque confirmed that they were on the right track.

It was the only positive, though. Everyone else on the team had struck dirt in their efforts to find anything on al-Hosni's associates. That was to be expected with such a laborious task, but going over old CCTV footage was their only way to discover who had the X3. Gareth Bailey had suggested pulling in one of the people al-Hosni had met with, just to see if they could get him to talk, but it was far too risky. For one, it would tip their hand. As soon as word got out that his friends were being arrested, al-Hosni would destroy any evidence connecting him to the nerve agent. The second stumbling block would be trying to get such a person to talk. The worst they could do was question the suspect; if he refused to answer, they could do nothing more.

With Shah's involvement confirmed, Harvey went over the surveillance reports from the previous day. Al-Hosni had left his house at the usual time and travelled to the mosque as normal, only this time he'd stayed inside after everyone else had left. When he'd emerged an hour later, it had been with four men. Harvey studied the pictures that had been taken with a telephoto lens, but didn't instantly recognise any of them, so he opened the facial recognition software and fed the images into the system. The search produced four confirmed matches, and he studied their files until he saw Ellis swipe her way onto the main floor.

'I think we may have something here,' he said, halting her progress. 'Al-Hosni was seen to meet four new people yesterday, and their profiles ring all sorts of alarm bells. This one in particular.'

Ellis bent to read the information on his screen. 'A chemical engineering student?'

'One who has just spent a year in Turkey, though I'll bet our friends in Ankara will have a hard time coming up with an address for him there. Most likely he used it as a gateway to Syria.'

'Check with them,' Ellis told him, 'and send details of all four to my screen.'

She continued on her way to her office, and Harvey composed and sent a quick message containing links to the relevant files. That done, he placed a call to the Turkish National Intelligence Organisation. Three minutes later, he had their promise to contact him with the man's details by lunchtime.

This latest suspect ticked all the right boxes, and Harvey decided to make him his priority. The previous night, he'd followed the first of his suspects around London, but at no point did he hand off anything that could possibly be the X3, nor did he receive anything. That scratched one off the list, but he faced another long day of it.

He was about to commence checking on the chemical engineer when a communication from GCHQ hit his inbox. He opened it and saw that a text message had been sent to al-Hosni's phone.

Two more days

The timestamp was thirteen minutes earlier, and Harvey knew he had just been privy to the start of the countdown. The sender was unidentified, but the location the text had been sent from was appended to the message.

Birmingham.

He would now have to move his meagre assets around, spreading them even more thinly. Maynard had promised unlimited resources, but that had been when they thought the threat was confined to the capital. There was no telling how he would react to a request to double their numbers.

Still, that would be for Ellis to deal with.

Harvey went over to Sarah's desk to pass on some instructions. While she got to work on it, he walked into the boss's office with a printout of the message and waited until Ellis had read it.

'We're going to need more people,' he said.

'Clearly. What connections does al-Hosni have up there?'

'Sarah is looking into that as we speak, but I'd like to get a small team assembled. They can head up there and we'll brief them once they arrive.'

'Take four men off their assignment down here and get them moving. I'll organise their replacements after speaking to Maynard.'

Harvey turned to leave, then stopped. 'I was thinking, maybe it would be a good idea to have a chat with al-Hosni and let him know that we're on to him.'

'You mean like Sarah did with Alexi Bessonov last year?'

Her reply was like a slap in the face. Sarah's decision to confront the Russian gangster had resulted in her torture, and if Ellis had taken a few more minutes to find Bessonov's hidden cellar, Harvey's girlfriend would most certainly have died.

'She did it alone, but I was thinking more of a cosy chat in the street, with plenty of backup. If we can make him nervous, he might make the mistake that leads us to the X3.'

'I'll consider it,' Ellis said, 'but only as a last resort.'

Harvey left her office and saw that more of the day shift had arrived, unsurprisingly none of them looking fresh or relaxed. He returned to his desk and greeted Hamad Farsi, who was too busy yawning to respond with anything but a grunt.

'Got a job for you,' Harvey said. 'This one's nice and easy.'

He gave Farsi the details of the phone that had been used to text al-Hosni and asked him to locate it on CCTV, specifically the place where the text message had originated. While his colleague got on with that task, he composed a message to the rest of the team, asking them to pay special attention to anyone on their list who made a journey north in the last few days. He sent it out, then looked through the duty roster to see who he could send to Birmingham. He cross-referenced them with the nine people who had been scrubbed from the list, then pulled them from their current assignments. Ten minutes later, he'd spoken to each one and given them their new instructions.

While he waited for them to battle the traffic on the M40 en route to their destination, Harvey checked the log to see when chemical engineer Malik Hansa had met with al-Hosni. From there, he backtracked through CCTV, another yawn escaping as he settled into what promised to be another marathon shift.

～

David Manners checked his tablet as his colleague pulled into the outside lane to overtake a slow-moving lorry. The motorway journey had taken an hour so far, and they still had another sixty miles to go. Commuter traffic and roadworks meant they wouldn't hit Birmingham until after ten, but he was at least grateful for the change of scenery. After days of watching people do nothing at all, moving felt good. The lead might turn out to be nothing, but it beat sitting in the back of a van for hours on end, waiting for a suspect to do something more sinister than put the bins out.

'It's stopped moving,' he said to Tom Gaines, who was sitting behind the wheel. They'd been tracking the suspect's phone reception since leaving London that morning, and it had been on the move up to this point.

'Where is it now?' Gaines asked.

Manners changed the view on the handset to show the satellite image rather than the computer-generated map, then selected 'Street View' and looked at the location from ground level.

'In a school.'

'I'll bet you twenty quid they dumped it and a kid picked it up. It's going to be a waste of time.'

'I agree, but we have to see it through. It could be a staff member.'

He entered the location of the school into the car's satnav. He hoped Gaines was wrong, but deep down he had a feeling this was going to be a fruitless journey. The people they were up against tended to know a thing or two about covering their tracks, as the information they'd received from Harvey confirmed. The text message had been sent from the middle of a park, hundreds of yards from any surveillance cameras, and it would be impossible to check everyone who left the area. If it had been dropped, the chances of finding the person who'd sent the text were slim to none.

He called Harvey to inform him of the situation; unsurprisingly, the section lead had the same misgivings.

'Park up outside the school and wait until the phone leaves the grounds. You'll probably have to wait until after three, but we might get lucky if they take a lunch break.'

With his orders confirmed, Manners settled in for the rest of the journey. He kept an eye on the device, but the signal never moved, and ninety minutes later they had parked fifty yards from the school entrance.

Manners told the driver to take the first watch while he went in search of food. Ten minutes later, he came back with coffee, sandwiches and an assortment of chocolate bars. They chatted about upcoming holidays and their impatient kids until the red dot on the screen caught Manners's attention.

'The phone is moving,' he said, noting the time for his report. It was 12:47, and they were fully alert. Kids began filing out of the building, heading in small groups towards the local shops, but the dot on the screen remained within the boundary of the main building. By the time one o'clock came round, it was clear that whoever had the phone wasn't going out to lunch.

They resigned themselves to another couple of hours in the car, and Manners took the opportunity to contact the other two members of the detail. The last time they'd checked in, Rob Best and Tony Booker had been stuck in a tailback on the M40.

'Where are you?'

'Still stuck in traffic,' Best replied. 'Apparently there was a pile-up about five miles up the road. We won't be going anywhere soon.'

'Okay, let me know when you're on your way.'

With half of the team out of action, Manners was going to have to deviate from normal procedure. Ideally, there would be two units, one trailing a suspect at a reasonable distance while the other hung further back. If the first unit got too close, they could peel off and hand the pursuit over to their partners. That was now out of the question. When the time came, they would have to take discreet to a whole new level.

Two hours later, Manners called Best again, but his colleague reported no change in their situation. 'It's just us,' he told Gaines as he waited for the signal on the screen to indicate movement. Children were beginning to make the journey home, but the red dot remained stationary, even as the steady flow of kids reduced to a trickle.

'Either the kid with the phone is in detention, or we've got a real player,' Manners said.

Forty minutes after the school day had ended, he finally saw the signal heading for the exit. He picked up his camera and opened the car door.

'I'm going to get some pictures. Wait for me here.'

Manners got out and jogged across the road to where bushes lined the inside of the perimeter fence. He found a spot that gave him a view of the school's double doors, then checked the handset. The suspect would be out in a few seconds, according to the display, and he raised the camera just as a man opened the door and walked out into the sunlight.

Manners got a dozen head-shots and a few of the leather briefcase the subject was carrying, then waited to see how the suspect planned to get home. He saw the man pull keys from his pocket. The hazard lights on a silver Honda flashed twice.

Manners had seen enough. He strolled calmly back to the Ford and got in.

'He's Asian, mid-thirties to early-forties, driving a silver Civic,' he said as he fastened his seat belt.

The car appeared at the gates, and Manners consulted the handset to confirm that they had the right man.

'That's him. Let him get round the corner before you set off. We can track him with this.'

Gaines waited until the Honda took a right at the end of the street, then started the engine and pulled away.

Manners connected the digital camera to his phone via Bluetooth and downloaded the pictures he'd taken, which he sent to Andrew Harvey with a request for ID.

'Take a left up ahead.'

Gaines followed his directions and pulled onto a dual carriageway. 'I see him, about twelve cars ahead of us.'

While traffic remained heavy there was every chance they would go undetected, but both were aware that things would get tougher once they reached residential streets and their cover thinned out.

They tracked the Honda for another mile before Manners saw it indicating to turn right. Gaines took the same route and stopped short when the suspect pulled up outside a police station.

'What's he up to?' Manners wondered aloud, and his phone beeped as a message from Harvey appeared on the screen. 'Pull in here.'

They watched the suspect enter the station, and while they waited for him to return to his car, Manners checked to see what Harvey had managed to uncover.

'His name's Syed Kahr,' he told Gaines. 'Been a teacher for twelve years, no known affiliation to any terror groups. Cleaner than clean, according to all records. He lives in Chapel Street, Aston, with a wife and eight-year-old daughter.'

Five minutes passed before Kahr emerged from the building. Gaines started the engine, but Manners told him to wait.

'The signal says the phone's still in the police station.'

Manners allowed the Honda to pull away, then got out and ran across the road to the station. Inside the reception, he saw two youths on a bench facing a young police officer sitting in a Perspex-fronted booth.

'The man who just left. What did he want?'

The officer behind the counter looked Manners up and down, then returned to the report he was writing. 'I'm afraid I can't tell you that, sir.'

Manners had expected as much. He would have shown the man his ID, but protocol dictated it wasn't to be carried in the field. Having tried the low-key approach, it was time to ratchet things up a little. He phoned Harvey to explain the situation, then hung up and waited.

Within two minutes, a senior officer burst through an internal door and walked over to Manners, his hand outstretched.

'Superintendent Edwards. How can I help you?'

Manners walked him over to the reception desk. 'A man came in a few minutes ago. I believe his name was Syed Kahr. I need to know what he was doing here.'

Edwards looked at the desk jockey expectantly.

'I was . . . er . . . just finishing up the report, sir. He just wanted to hand in a mobile phone.'

'Any particular reason?'

'He said one of his students found it on the way to school this morning. Mr Kahr is a teacher, sir.'

Manners felt deflated. After more than six hours of waiting, it seemed Gaines had been right. A kid had indeed picked it up, but at least this one had been honest enough to hand it in.

'What kind of forensic facilities do you have here?' he asked Edwards.

'Just the very basics.'

'Then I'll have to take it with me.'

Edwards instructed the officer to hand it over, and it turned out to be a cheap push-button model.

'I'll need a receipt,' the young policeman said.

'No problem. Fill one out and I'll sign it. I'll also need your fingerprints, as well as those of Kahr and the student so we can eliminate them from our enquiries.' He took out his phone and found Harvey's details in his contact list. 'Call this number when you have them, and preferably within the next two hours.'

Manners signed for the phone and had it placed in an evidence bag to preserve any prints, then called Thames House to tell Harvey about the find before returning to the car to update his colleague.

'What now?' Gaines asked.

'Back to London. Harvey wants this in the lab ASAP.'

CHAPTER 22

Wednesday, 16 August 2017

Veronica Ellis once again marvelled at how ugly the building that housed the Home Secretary's office looked. It had the same impression on her every time she had to visit John Maynard, and she wondered if it had been designed specifically to sap her morale before she set foot inside. The building was only eleven years old but looked like something out of the 1970s. In fact, she suspected the architect had originally proposed three designs, and then decided to incorporate all of them into one monstrosity.

She made her way to Maynard's office, and was surprised when his secretary ushered her straight in. The Home Secretary normally liked to keep her waiting for at least five minutes, so she was immediately on her guard.

She closed the door behind her and walked over to Maynard's desk, a regal-looking oak affair with polished brass trimmings. The man sitting behind it wasn't so fancily attired. Maynard wore a white shirt open at the collar, his tie hanging loosely around his neck, and had the appearance of a man much older than his fifty-five years. His usually immaculate haircut was disturbed, as if he'd been out in a high wind.

'I'm about to go and see the PM. He'll want to know why you haven't got your hands on the X3.'

And a good morning to you, too.

'We're following up every lead we have, but even with the extra resources, we're having a hard time pinning it down.'

'Then you're not trying hard enough! You yourself told me they plan to use it on Friday. That gives you a day and a half to find it.'

It was the first time she'd heard him raise his voice, and it didn't bode well. Maynard was unpredictable at the best of times, but in his current mood there was no telling what he might do. Removing her from her role as Director General of MI5 was his chief desire, as he had made clear on more than one occasion. For all his faults, though, he wasn't stupid enough to have her replaced in the middle of a major incident, but she knew that wasn't the only way he could make her miserable.

'We've done everything we can, and all by the book,' she countered. 'The results will come, I assure you.'

'By the book? By the *book*? I don't call mollycoddling prisoners and sending valuable staff around the country on wild goose chases by the *book*!'

Ellis thought he was going to explode. His face had taken on a crimson hue, and he appeared on the verge of apoplexy.

'Granted, Malika Ali was afforded certain concessions in return for her testimony, but it was because of this that we were able to focus our attention on Imran al-Hosni. As for the wasted journey, as you call it, we're still waiting for Forensics to see if they can extract anything from the phone. We should know within a couple of hours.'

'You haven't got a couple of hours. Your inept handling of this situation has forced my hand. When you get back to Thames House, I want you to pull your people off al-Hosni. He's my problem now.'

'He's our only lead to the X3. If we pull back now, we'll never find it.'

Maynard sat back in his chair, the hint of a smile suggesting nothing but malevolence. 'Your last report stated you had more suspects than you could cope with. Concentrate on those, but leave al-Hosni to the professionals.'

Ellis knew Maynard was trying to rile her, but she wasn't about to give him the satisfaction. 'You're talking about black ops,' she said calmly. 'I thought that was a thing of the past.'

'It's no longer your concern. I suggest you return to your office and get your house in order. I want everything you have on al-Hosni sent to me within the hour, and I mean *everything*. After that, you can prepare for the inquiry into your handling of this matter.'

'You're making a big mistake,' Ellis told him. 'We're so close, and whatever problems you have with me, you should let my people see this through.'

'You've had more than enough time to find the agent. Now go back and bring your team up to speed. While you're at it, it wouldn't hurt to update your CV.'

Ellis wanted to tear the man's throat out, but although it would make her feel much better, it wouldn't help the situation. She turned and left his office, taking the elevator down to the ground floor.

Her calm outer shell masked the thunder that brewed inside her. Maynard was right to be concerned about the looming deadline, but taking away access to their main suspect was a ludicrous decision. It didn't exactly paint a rosy picture for al-Hosni, either.

As far as she was aware, all black ops teams had been disbanded following the James Farrar saga, when a hit man had been sent to kill British citizens. That meant the only people Maynard could turn to would be E Squadron, a shadowy, hand-picked unit manned by experienced members of the SAS, Special Reconnaissance Regiment and Special Boat Service. The squadron primarily operated abroad on behalf of MI6, but Maynard clearly wasn't averse to having them ply their trade at home.

One thing was certain: once Imran al-Hosni was in their clutches, she'd lose any hope of finding the X3 and claiming the credit on behalf of her team. She knew Maynard wouldn't be satisfied merely with taking her scalp; he'd want a clean sweep to rid himself of anyone loyal to her.

Ellis half jogged the couple of blocks to Thames House, spurred on by the knowledge that the next couple of hours would be make-or-break.

～

Harvey was growing increasingly frustrated with the lack of progress. His team were working flat out, yet there was still no sign of the X3. To top it all, al-Hosni had cranked his social life into overdrive, visiting a dozen people in a single morning. Keeping tabs on all of them was proving harder each hour, and each person who met al-Hosni went on to meet a dozen others, the vast majority of whom remained unidentified. It was like a stone hitting a windscreen at speed. Al-Hosni was the epicentre, and one of the fractures led to the nerve agent. The trouble was, there were just too many cracks to follow, and the clock was ticking. Harvey had checked out the movements of the chemical engineer and come up empty, as had everyone else on the team. None of the people on their list had anything incriminating to say on the phone or over the internet, and apart from mingling in ever-larger circles, al-Hosni was keeping his nose clean.

He saw Ellis enter the office, shaking off her jacket as she headed to her glass palace, and decided it was time to revisit an earlier idea.

He followed his boss into her office and stood in front of her desk. 'We need to rattle al-Hosni's cage,' he said.

Ellis dumped her handbag on the floor and flopped into her chair. 'I just got back from Maynard's office, and he's told us to back off.'

'Are you serious?'

'I'm afraid so,' Ellis said. 'He's assigned someone else to deal with al-Hosni, and I suspect it's E Squadron. We're still on the case, but we're not allowed anywhere near him, effective immediately. We're to call our people off and concentrate on our other leads.'

Harvey studied her and saw a hint of rebellion in her eyes. 'I have a feeling that's one order you're in no rush to carry out.'

'Intuitive, as always. I'd like you to personally go and tell the surveillance teams to wrap things up. If you just happen to stumble across al-Hosni while you're there . . .'

Harvey was way ahead of her. 'How long do you think we have?'

'Hours, minutes . . . I have no idea.'

'I'm on it.'

Harvey turned to leave, but Ellis called him back.

'Be careful,' she said. 'We don't know for sure who Maynard is sending, or how al-Hosni's followers will react to your presence.'

'Understood.'

Harvey went to Farsi's desk to tell him he was leaving the office for a while.

'What are you working on?'

'Just getting a little background on one Muhammad Khan, imam at the Tower Hamlets mosque,' Farsi explained. 'I've got a meeting with one of my contacts in an hour. I told you about it yesterday.'

'Oh, right. Well, don't get too hooked up on what he tells you. We need to deal with al-Hosni first. Speaking of which, I'm about to go and meet him.'

Harvey called the unit tasked with keeping an eye on their prime suspect and asked where he could find them. They told him al-Hosni had just entered the mosque in Stockwell Green for prayers, and would be there for the next hour at least. Harvey was familiar with the building, and as it was a forty-minute drive, he had time to stop off at Sarah's desk to see how she was getting on.

As he approached, he saw that she too had abandoned her assigned duties.

'I thought you were comparing those entering that Birmingham park with facial recognition? Have you finished already?'

'No,' she said without looking up, 'I handed that off. I want to know more about Malika.'

Harvey's first thought was that it must have something to do with her outburst from the previous day. Had it been anyone else, he would have told her to drop it and return to her assigned duties, but once Sarah set her mind to something there was little he could do but let her run with it.

'Anything in particular?' he asked.

'I just don't trust her.'

'So nothing in particular.'

Sarah turned to face him. 'There's a lot about her answers that doesn't add up. For starters, I'm not buying the fact that she managed to convince Inas to stay and claim asylum when it would endanger her sisters back in Syria.'

'Okay, I admit that concerned me, too, but when I thought about it, Malika had days to talk to her.'

'That's not all. Malika refuses to talk, and then suddenly she can't wait to open up to you.'

'That's because we threatened to take her son away,' Harvey said.

Sarah snorted. 'So you think it's her maternal instinct that kicked in? Then why does she hold the baby as if it isn't hers?'

'What are you talking about? I've spent hours in there with her and the boy. She dotes on him.'

'Really? When was the last time you were around a mother and her baby? I've got sisters and friends who all have kids, and they don't hold them anything like she does.'

Harvey shrugged. 'It could be a cultural difference.'

'Nonsense. I'll bet any money that boy isn't hers. He doesn't even look like her.'

Harvey thought back to the many sessions he'd spent with Malika, but couldn't recall any behaviour that had seemed out of character. Then again, he hadn't spent much time around children, while Sarah was an aunt many times over.

Could there really have been some blatant clues that he'd missed? If there had been, there was only one way to get to the truth.

'If you're really that convinced, go downstairs and get DNA samples from both of them. If they don't match, you win. If they do, though, you drop it and concentrate on the man she fingered. Speaking of which, I'm going to meet al-Hosni now.'

'Wait! What? You're going to speak to him? Alone?'

'No, I'll have backup, and it'll be in public.' He told her about the conversation with Ellis. 'I have to try to convince him to come in. He's not likely to try anything.'

'You seem very sure,' Sarah said, and for the first time in days he could sense genuine concern in her voice.

'I am. There'll be four men watching over me, ready to pounce at a moment's notice.'

'I'd feel better if there were more. Can't you get SO15 involved?'

Harvey would indeed have felt better walking up to al-Hosni accompanied by several armed members of the Metropolitan Police's Counter Terrorism Command, but his plan was simply to let the suspect know he was being watched, not create panic on the streets.

'There's no need, I promise. I'll be back within a couple of hours.'

Sarah took his hand and squeezed tightly.

'You better, mister.'

CHAPTER 23

Wednesday, 16 August 2017

Harvey arrived at the mosque five minutes before prayers were due to end, and it didn't take long for him to find the first of the teams watching over their main suspect. He walked to their government-issue Ford and slipped into the back seat.

'What's he been up to?' he asked.

The front passenger consulted his notebook. 'He met two new faces outside the mosque. They chatted for a couple of minutes, then went in. We sent the photos to the office.'

Great, Harvey thought. *Another couple of names to add to the ever-growing list.*

'Did you manage to record the conversation?'

'Yeah, but they just chatted about the weather.'

Harvey checked his watch. 'Which is al-Hosni's car?'

'The blue Vauxhall.'

He asked to see the images the men had taken, all the while keeping an eye on the mosque's entrance. The faces were unfamiliar, but it helped to use up a couple of minutes.

When the first of the worshippers left the building, he handed the phone back to the front-seat passenger. 'We've got new instructions,' he said. 'We're to . . . Hang on, I know that guy. He used to be in my five-a-side football team. He still owes me fifty quid.'

Before the operatives could react, Harvey jumped out of the car and crossed the road, walking quickly towards the mosque. The less the operatives knew about his plan, the better. Any heat would come down on him, not the two men in the car.

'Hey! Gamal!' he shouted, more for the benefit of the directional microphone his people used. 'It's me, Andrew.'

The man turned and studied him. 'Do I know you?'

Harvey positioned himself so that he could see the door to the mosque. 'Sure you do. We used to play for the Hammersmith Harriers.'

'You must be mistaken.'

'Come on, man. You're just saying that because you owe me money.'

Harvey was fast running out of ways to keep the conversation going, but Imran al-Hosni came to his rescue. The man who held the key to finding the X3 was walking towards him accompanied by three others.

'My name is not Gamal,' said the stranger.

'Sorry,' said Harvey. 'My mistake.' He made for al-Hosni, and when he caught up with him, he gripped the man's arm.

'I'm with MI5, and we know all about the nerve agent,' he said quietly.

Al-Hosni stopped in his tracks and turned towards Harvey. At first he appeared confused, before a smirk appeared on his face. 'Do you have a name, Mister MI5 man?'

'Andrew. And I'm here to do you a huge favour.' He let go of al-Hosni, knowing he had his attention.

One of the imam's companions got between the two men and squared up to Harvey, but al-Hosni ushered him aside. 'Let him speak.'

Harvey kept his voice low. 'You can either voluntarily come to my office for a chat, or wait until the wet team pays you a visit. My way will avoid a lot of bloodshed. Yours, to be exact.'

The smirk became a full-blown smile, formed of nicotine-stained teeth. 'I am sorry to disappoint you, but I know nothing about any nerve agent. You must have the wrong man.'

'Last chance,' Harvey pressed. 'You can either come in and discuss it civilly over a cup of tea, or wait until your balls are in a nutcracker before you start talking.'

'If you had any reason to believe I had a biological weapon, we wouldn't be having this conversation on the street. I'm sure your colleagues in the black Mondeo can confirm that I've said or done nothing wrong, so I suggest you either arrest me now or let me go on my way.'

Harvey was about to respond when the roar of an engine announced the arrival of a black van. It screeched to a halt ten feet away from them and the side door slid open. Three men jumped out, and their military bearing confirmed Ellis's guess that Maynard had handed the matter over to E Squadron.

Two of the men pushed al-Hosni's companions aside as Harvey backed away, and the imam was dragged to the van. The third soldier stood with his hand on the butt of an automatic in a shoulder holster, the unspoken threat clear to all. Ten seconds after arriving, the vehicle pulled back into traffic, one passenger heavier.

Harvey turned in time to see the two men in the Ford set off in pursuit, and he ran in front of their car, relieved when it stopped a few inches from his knees.

'Forget it,' he said as he walked round to the driver's side window. 'We're officially off the case. Report back to Thames House right away.'

Harvey ignored their questions and returned to his own car, angry at Maynard for getting things moving so quickly. If he'd had another few minutes, he might have convinced al-Hosni to avoid any unpleasantness, but that was now out of his hands.

On the plus side, al-Hosni's new captors should have him talking within a few hours; he'd heard the stories about how they operated, their ruthless efficiency not always within the boundaries of the law. The downside was that his team's recent efforts would be overshadowed, and Maynard would seize the opportunity to unseat Ellis and replace her with some kiss-arse who would make their lives unbearable.

That was, if they managed to survive the cull.

Harvey started the car and drove back to the office, all the while trying to decide the best way to break the news to Ellis.

~

Aswan stood in the doorway of the estate agent's, his head down as he tapped at the keys on his mobile phone. To anyone passing by, he was just another slave to technology, banging out a text message, but he kept his eyes fixed firmly on the café across the road.

He'd followed Samir from the meeting at the mosque, and though he knew why Muhammad Khan had given him the task, it wasn't one he relished. Aswan had known Samir for several years, having lived close by when the boy had been at high school. The kid had a tendency to stray from the righteous path now and again, but Aswan had always found him trustworthy.

Clearly, Khan thought otherwise, which was why he'd told Aswan to tail Samir and report in. Aswan had sent a text minutes earlier with his location, and he'd been instructed to remain in place and wait to see if Samir met anyone.

Please be wrong, Aswan thought as he watched his friend sipping a hot beverage. The café was almost empty, and Samir was sitting at a table at the back, his eyes on the entrance. Every few seconds he would check his watch, and Aswan realised that Khan's suspicions were probably correct. It was a shame, because what lay in store for Samir was bound to be unpleasant.

Muhammad Khan was a feared man within the community, and he'd made it clear that the message he'd shared with his inner circle earlier that evening was to go no further. For obvious reasons. They finally had the means of launching an attack that would make 7/7 look like amateur hour, and with the schedule set for Friday, there was still plenty of time for things to go wrong.

Having someone talk about it, for one.

An elderly woman left the café, leaving only Samir and a couple of workmen enjoying a late fry-up. It remained that way for another few minutes, until a short, thickset man approached the door and checked the area before entering. When he sat opposite Samir, Aswan sighed. His friend's fate was all but sealed. He stopped the random key tapping and composed a fresh text message before firing it off to Khan's right-hand man.

~

Hamad Farsi scanned the area as he approached the rendezvous, but saw nothing out of the ordinary. There was one guy tucked into a shop doorway, but he was focused on his phone and didn't appear to have noticed his arrival. He entered the café and spotted Samir sitting at a table near the back of the room. He ordered a coffee from the counter before joining his informant.

'You're late,' Samir said quietly. One foot was tapping on the floor, a clear sign that he craved chemical stimulation.

'Yeah, traffic's a bitch. What have you got for me?'

Samir leaned in closer. 'There's going to be an attack on Friday.'

'I need names and a location.'

'Khan said the man behind it was Imran al-Hosni, but he didn't say what he was going to hit. All I know is that it's going to be big.'

'That's not good enough,' Farsi said. 'Did you manage to get a recording?'

'No, they made everyone hand in their phones before going into the meeting.'

'Then you'll have to tell me what he said, word for word.'

Farsi hoped to gain something new, but after five minutes it was clear Samir had nothing to add to what they already knew: al-Hosni had a nerve agent and planned to use it in less than two days' time. The only thing that seemed out of place was that Muhammad Khan had got wind of the plot. Farsi tried to remember seeing any mention of him in the al-Hosni files, but came up empty.

'So do I get paid?' Samir asked.

Farsi pulled a small bundle of notes from his pocket. 'There's two hundred. Get back to me with proof and I'll be back with a grand.'

Samir started to object but Farsi was already heading for the door, his mind set on finding the link between Khan and al-Hosni.

He left the café and walked around the corner to his car, all the while checking for signs that he was being watched, but the man in the doorway had gone and no-one else seemed interested in his presence.

When he reached his Ford, he called Harvey and gave him a concise summary of the meeting.

'I don't remember reading Khan's name in any of the reports,' Harvey said.

'That's what worried me, too. Al-Hosni hasn't contacted him by phone or email, and we've backtracked on everyone he's met. Is there a chance we missed someone?'

The line went quiet for a moment.

'You still there?'

'Yeah,' Harvey said. 'I might know who passed the info to Khan. Get back here as soon as you can. I've got plenty to update you on.'

~

Aswan watched as the two men chatted in the café. He'd already taken a photo on his phone and the picture was on its way to Khan's number two. All he could do now was await further instructions.

They came two minutes later in the form of a succinct text message:

```
Return to the mosque
```

Aswan put his phone away and took one last look at Samir – the stranger was handing him something. Aswan shook his head. This would probably be the last time he saw the young man. He spun and jogged to the end of the street, turned right, then joined the steady stream of people entering the Tube station. He rode the three stops to the mosque, then knocked on the imam's door.

When he was shown in, Aswan told Khan what he had witnessed, including the handing over of what could only have been money or drugs.

Khan remained impassive. 'I always had my doubts about that one,' he said.

'What will happen to him?' Aswan asked.

'Samir has decided to forsake us. He will witness Allah's wrath first-hand.' He handed Aswan a slip of paper with the address of a coffee shop written on it. 'Tomorrow, I want you to send him a text message and ask him to be there at midday on Friday. Tell him to take a seat outside. I will take care of matters once he arrives.'

With a wave of his hand, Khan signalled an end to the meeting. Aswan took his leave, weighed by the knowledge that he would be leading his friend to his death. He briefly considered warning him, but quickly realised that doing so would put his own life in jeopardy.

No, better to follow Khan's orders and pray that when the time came, Samir wouldn't suffer too long.

~

Harvey was going through CCTV footage when Farsi returned to the office. He'd managed to track his target from the moment he'd left al-Hosni's home to a nearby Tube station, but was having difficulty discovering which station he'd travelled to.

'Who did we miss?' Farsi asked as he stood at his side.

'The courier,' Harvey said. 'It was my fault. I was so hung up on who could have taken delivery of the X3 that I discounted him because he was back in Turkey by the time the women arrived here. I searched the database to find links between al-Hosni and Khan but there was nothing, so he must be the link between the two men. The trouble is, he didn't get off where I would have expected.'

'Maybe he got off a station early to check for a tail,' Farsi suggested. 'Send the details to my terminal and I'll check it out.'

Harvey fired off the information and resumed his facial-recognition search of the people leaving the Tube station nearest to the mosque where Khan led services. There were two exits, which would double the time it would take to locate Qureshi. He'd already covered the possibility that the courier had gone direct to Khan's home, but cameras covering the street had shown no sign of him that day.

He finished the first half of the task and he had switched to the camera covering the east exit when a message flashed on his screen. He opened it and saw that it was from the forensics team.

'They found no prints on the phone, other than the teacher and police in Birmingham who were known to have handled it,' he told Farsi.

'That's no surprise. With something this big, they're bound to be careful.'

Harvey was about to resume his search, but Farsi's words made him pause. 'Al-Hosni doesn't seem to be all that careful,' he said. 'He knows he's being watched. He told me when we met earlier, yet he's doing nothing to hide his activities.'

'Now that you mention it, it does seem strange. Unless he's confident that we don't know the whole picture. I've said from the moment we started tracking his associates that one of them might have just been a conduit, passing information to those who have the X3.'

It was something they'd discussed many times, but there was simply no way to watch everyone. With their limited resources, it would only need three or four people in the chain before the numbers became unmanageable. If al-Hosni met forty people, who each met forty people, who each met forty people, they would have to keep tabs on more than 60,000 suspects. Many could be ruled out quickly, but that would still leave tens of thousands who would need to be investigated. As it was, they barely had the manpower to cope with less than 1 per cent of that, even after drawing from the resource pool of MI6 and the Metropolitan Police.

'There's not a lot we can do about that now. Maynard has al-Hosni, but if we can fill in some of the blanks we might be able to save a few careers.'

'Maynard has him?' Farsi asked, a puzzled look on his face. 'Why?'

'I sent a memo round, but you were out at the time.' Harvey explained what had happened earlier that day, and how they'd been denied access to their top target.

Farsi went to his station, while Harvey set his new search running. He watched as the square flashed across the still image on the screen, looking for a face to match Qureshi's. Once the final face had been dismissed, Harvey fast-forwarded the footage a few seconds and tried again. He yawned and stretched as the computer worked its magic, trying to remember the last time he'd had a decent night's sleep.

He perked up when Sarah swiped her way into the office. The triumphant look on her face told him she'd found something.

'The DNA profiles,' she said, handing over a printout.

Harvey took it and skimmed the contents until he got to the section that compared mother with child.

'Looks like I owe you an apology,' he said. 'Is this a hundred per cent accurate?'

'Checked and double-checked,' she said with a smile. 'The kid isn't hers.'

Harvey rose. 'Let's go and have a word with her.'

'Wait.' Sarah pushed him back into his seat. 'It gets better. Remember Khadija Tawfeek, the woman who died in the back of the truck? The post-mortem showed a cerebral haemorrhage. The autopsy also revealed that Khadija was a haemophiliac, the reason for the bleed-out. As you know, standard toxicology tests are performed post-mortem, but they found nothing. I asked them to run the enhanced tests, and they got a hit.'

'What was it?'

'A combination of corticosteroid, amphetamine and warfarin. It was a big enough dose to induce acute hypertension and, coupled with her existing condition, was enough to cause the haemorrhage.'

'So she was killed?'

'That's the MD's opinion.'

'Which begs the question: why?'

Harvey logged into the police database and brought up Tawfeek's file. He clicked the tab to show the images, and found one of her final resting place. He'd seen it before, when the report had first come through, but he'd only glanced at it. Now he studied it more carefully, and immediately the scene looked all wrong.

'Look at this,' he said. 'There's a ditch three yards away from where she was dumped. It would have been a lot easier to throw her in there

Trojan

and cover the body than going to all the trouble of digging a shallow grave.'

'It's almost as if they wanted her to be found,' Sarah said.

'If that's the case, then why leave the X3 inside her? Surely they'd want to remove it first.'

'If they had, it would have been a simple homicide. It certainly wouldn't have reached our desks. Something tells me they wanted us to find her—'

'So that we could follow the trail to Malika and the others,' Harvey interrupted.

'Exactly.'

He sat back in his chair. 'But how could they be sure that we would even know about the X3 being stolen?'

'When Frank Dale briefed us about it, he said the source of the tip-off had been anonymous. What if it's been Nabil Karim all along? He could have been making sure we knew what we had and how important it was that we find the rest of it.'

'Let's backtrack,' Harvey said. 'We're saying Karim sends five women over here with the X3. He has one of them killed and left relatively out in the open so that she's easy to find, knowing we would be able to trace the others in the party. That sound right so far?'

'It does,' Sarah agreed. 'And having found the other four, one of them conveniently starts to spill the beans, and we swallow everything she says.'

Harvey looked up at her. 'Go ahead, you can say it.'

'I told you so.'

CHAPTER 24

Wednesday, 16 August 2017

Malika sat on the bed in her cell and looked over at the crib, where Jalal was sleeping off his most recent feed. He was a good boy, never any trouble, and that had made her task all that much easier. She was growing quite attached to him, but she knew it was too late for that.

She checked her watch. Less than thirty-six hours to hold out, and so far she had them eating out of her hand. They'd fallen for everything she'd told them, just as Nabil Karim had assured her they would. She just wished she could be a fly on the wall, watching them chase their tails as they focused their attention on Imran al-Hosni.

Karim's plan had been simple yet masterful. Give them all the clues they needed, but all pointing to the wrong man.

She'd been so grateful when the short MI5 agent had mentioned al-Hosni in the interrogation room. It not only showed that Karim's planning had been spot on, but it also provided her with the perfect opportunity to reinforce their suspicions. She'd mainly been left alone after that. No doubt the agents had their hands full keeping track of all their targets.

The only downside had been the death of Khadija. The other three women had been genuinely upset at the discovery of her body in the back of the truck, but Malika had known it was coming. Khadija's death had been manufactured to ensure the phial of X3 was discovered, leaving a trail back to her and the others – a trail the authorities would be sure to follow after Karim leaked news of the attack at the chemical-weapons storage facility. It had only been a matter of time before MI5 picked them up, and their asylum applications had helped the process along. All she'd had to do from that point on was convince them that the boy was the only thing she cared about. The other three women had done as they'd been instructed, and had said nothing beyond confirming their names.

Malika had often wondered what the target would be, but she would find out soon enough if the British agents' incompetence continued. The target was the one thing Karim hadn't told her, just in case they somehow managed to break her. The Friday deadline was fast approaching, and though she wouldn't be able to witness it herself, she hoped to live long enough to hear the glorious details.

The door to her cell opened and the blonde woman entered, an unfamiliar smile on her face. Up to this point, her manner had been cold, stand-offish. Malika was immediately on her guard.

'Time for another chat,' the woman said.

Malika went to pick up Jalal, but the blonde quickly got between her and the crib. 'Not this time.'

'I will only talk if my son is in there with me.'

The blonde seized her arm and twisted it, forcing Malika to double over in agony. 'That privilege has been revoked.'

The woman forced Malika out of the cell and along the corridor to the interrogation suite, where Agent Harvey waited.

The woman pushed Malika into the chair and stood behind her, out of sight but close enough that Malika could sense her presence.

'I want my son with me,' she told Harvey, rubbing her wrist.

'No problem. Tell us where he is.'

'He's in the cell.'

'Oh,' Harvey said. 'You mean Jalal. Well, I'm afraid I've got some bad news for you.'

So that's *what she was doing*, Malika thought. Someone in a nurse's uniform had come into her cell, supposedly to check that Jalal and she hadn't contracted a virus that had been prevalent in the building, but they clearly must have been conducting DNA checks.

There had always been the possibility that this moment would come, and Malika was prepared for it.

'So he isn't my son, what difference does it make?'

'Well, for starters, it means everything you've told us is lies,' Harvey said.

'I had to do it. My own son died two years ago, and Karim told me there would be no chance of getting into the country if I had been on my own. That's why he made me take Jalal.'

'So who does the boy really belong to?'

'He's an orphan. His parents were killed in a bombing months ago. I've been looking after him as if he were my own.'

She studied her adversary, but couldn't tell if her words had been believed. She soon got her answer, but from the blonde.

'Bullshit! You've been playing us from the start!'

'I swear, I'm telling you the truth.'

'If that's the case, tell me about when you were sealed into the heating units on the truck.'

'I already told you a hundred times.'

'Tell us again,' the blonde barked.

Malika had rehearsed the scene many times, and launched into her second rendition. It took her three minutes to tell them everything up to the point where Khadija's body had been discovered.

'Thanks,' Harvey said, and left the room, leaving Malika to ponder her next move.

~

Once the door was closed, Harvey asked Solomon to replay Malika's latest account of the truck stop. While listening, he read from the printed transcript. He made notes as he listened and, when the recording ended, he handed the sheet to Sarah.

'As I expected,' she said. 'Let's see what she has to say about it.'

They went back into the room and Harvey took his usual seat. Sarah stood behind him, arms crossed as she stared at Malika.

'I've just compared your last answer with the one you gave on Monday, and there are a few discrepancies,' Harvey said. 'How do you explain that?'

Malika shrugged. 'I can't be expected to remember every detail.'

'Well, that's the thing,' he said, passing her the transcript. 'The details were exactly the same. Your story only differed by a handful of words. I've never come across anything like that.'

'What he means,' Sarah added, 'is that it sounds like you're reciting something you've memorised. Like a song you sing to yourself over and over. I think you started rehearsing that speech before you even left Syria. We know Khadija was murdered by the truck driver and her body was left so that it would be easy to find, leading conveniently back to you.'

Malika swallowed nervously, a simple tell confirming that she'd been lying to them all along. A false trail for them to follow, which surely included the phone call from Birmingham: another way of misdirecting precious government resources to chase shadows.

'It's clear that Imran al-Hosni hasn't got the nerve agent,' he said. 'If you don't tell us who has it, you'll be charged with accessory to murder. You'll spend the rest of your days behind bars.'

Malika coughed and licked her lips. 'I'd like a Coca-Cola.'

'After you start talking,' Harvey said, but Malika coughed again and shook her head.

'I'll get one,' Sarah said, and swiped her card at the door, leaving the two of them alone.

'We know it's going to be used soon,' Harvey said. 'I need to know who has it and what the target is.'

Malika remained silent, and Harvey wondered what the next step would be. If she weren't forthcoming, there would be little he could threaten her with apart from harsh words. Not even the danger of losing her 'son' would get her talking. The only way to get her to open up would be to hand her over to E Squadron and let them work their magic, though doing so would mean admitting to the Home Secretary that they weren't capable of doing their job.

Harvey thought about Tom Gray, a good friend who believed in law and order but who wasn't afraid to overstep the mark in order to get results. He would be a great asset right about now, but he was somewhere in Italy and there simply wasn't time to track him down and get him on a plane.

No, if Malika were going to break, he would have to break her himself.

Sarah swiped her way back in and placed the unopened can of Coke on the table. 'Start talking. Who has the nerve agent?'

Malika opened the can and took a long sip, then held it in her hands as she stared at Harvey. 'I wasn't given that information. I admit I was told to give you al-Hosni, but that was all. Karim didn't tell me who actually had it. He said it would be safer for me if I didn't know.'

'So all the time you've been here, you've been pointing us towards the wrong man. Do you know what al-Hosni is going through at this very moment? I'd be surprised if he's still alive, to be honest. And if we feel at any moment that you're holding out on us, you'll be joining him.'

'You wouldn't do that,' Malika said, her demeanour suddenly stern. 'You British pride yourselves on operating within the law, and that will be part of your downfall. As for me, life in a cell will be no great hardship. I expected as much when I made my journey here.'

'Oh, trust me,' Sarah said. 'We might tell the world that we're the leaders in upholding human rights, but no-one's got a clue what goes on behind the scenes. Have you heard of waterboarding?'

'I have, but you don't have the stomach for it.'

'On the contrary,' Harvey said. 'We've been perfecting the art for years now. Al-Hosni was snatched off the street hours ago, and the news channels are blaming a fictitious anti-Muslim group we created. In a couple of days, his body will be found, but the police will have nothing to go on. In a couple of weeks, he'll be forgotten. You'll be next unless you give us what we need to stop the attack.'

Harvey let the words sink in, but Malika seemed unfazed. He was about to tighten the screw when Farsi appeared at the door and gestured for them to join him outside.

'I found the connection between Khan and al-Hosni,' he said when the door closed. 'The courier, Qureshi, met him three hours after leaving al-Hosni's place. He got off the Tube three stops late and took a taxi back to Khan's mosque. I've got people identifying Khan's main associates and we're tracking their movements over the last week.'

'Good work,' Harvey said, and was suggesting further measures when Solomon erupted.

'Andrew!'

Malika finished the Coke and held the empty can under the table, out of sight of those watching her through the one-way window. She squeezed the can in the middle, then gripped the ends and slowly worked them back and forth, the friction weakening the vessel at its most vulnerable point. After a few seconds, she was rewarded with a sharp *crack* as the can split in two, and she felt along the broken edges for the sharpest section.

Her time had come, as she knew it eventually would. All had seemed to be going so well, and though she hadn't been able to see it through to the end, she was proud to have led them a merry dance for so long. She wouldn't be around to learn of the destruction she had helped to cause, but it was enough to know that she had helped Karim in his fight. What little else she knew about the plot would follow her to the grave.

Malika discarded half of the can and rolled up her left sleeve. She knew this was going to hurt, but Nabil had assured her that the pain wouldn't last long. Once the adrenaline kicked in at the sight of the blood, her natural defences would block the pain. She placed the keen edge of the can against her radial artery, just as Nabil had shown her, and after taking a deep breath, she pressed down as hard as she could. She felt nothing more than a sharp prick as blood began to seep out of the wound, but the real pain came when she dragged the improvised blade up her arm. She managed to gouge a four-inch tear before the sensation became too much, and she switched her focus to her carotid artery. She placed the can against the side of her neck, two inches below her ear, and slashed sideways.

The sight of the blood spurting from her arm and neck made her feel faint, and she closed her eyes and thought of Nabil Karim. The image of her brother began to float in front of her, his face blurring and coming back into focus, and she believed she could hear him talking to her.

Malika! Malika!

'Malika!'

Harvey pulled a handkerchief from his pocket and stuffed it against the girl's neck, while Sarah and Farsi tried to stem the flow from Malika's arm. Solomon rushed into the room with a first-aid kit and told them that an ambulance was on its way.

'Malika!' Harvey repeated, slapping her face. Her eyes opened, and she smiled up at him. She spoke in Arabic, her voice low, but Harvey couldn't understand her.

'Hamad, what's she saying?'

Farsi put a hand up for him to be silent and listened to Malika.

'She thinks you're her brother,' he said. 'She hopes you're proud of her.'

Malika's breath became shallower as the blood seeped through the bandages. A tourniquet had been applied to her upper arm, but there was little they could do to stem the flow from her neck. Harvey kept the pressure on, but the puddle on the floor was growing bigger by the second.

Malika managed a few more words, and Farsi looked up at Harvey. 'She called you Nabil. She said your plan was almost perfect.'

'Nabil? You mean she's . . .'

'Karim's sister.'

The door buzzed open and two paramedics ran in. They took over and asked everyone to stand back, and Harvey watched as they put a cannula in her right hand and attached an IV line.

'There's nothing more we can do here,' Farsi said. 'I suggest we concentrate on Khan.'

Harvey agreed, but first he wanted to clean up. Malika's blood was all over his clothes, and his hands were dripping crimson.

The trio went to the washrooms while Solomon remained behind to collate the video for the inevitable inquiry.

Back in the office, Harvey, Sarah and Farsi went to the locker room to wash and change into spare clothes. They all had an overnight bag pre-packed in case they had to deploy at a moment's notice, and they were grateful that they wouldn't have to finish the shift in bloodstained apparel.

Once they were changed, Harvey told Sarah to call a meeting and have everyone gather in the conference room.

'I'm going to let Veronica know what's happened. I want all al-Hosni surveillance teams recalled and reassigned to Khan. Hamad, I need a list of his known associates. We'll do the same as we did with everyone al-Hosni met: trace their movements over the last six days.'

Harvey knocked on Ellis's door and walked in. 'There was an incident downstairs,' he said, standing in front of her desk. 'Malika tried to take her own life. The paramedics are with her now.'

'How the hell did that happen?' Ellis asked.

'She had a can of Coke, I left the room, it was over in seconds. She turned it into a blade and slashed herself pretty bad.'

'Damn it, Andrew, she's our best chance of finding the X3!'

'Thankfully, that isn't the case. It looks like she was a plant all along.'

Harvey explained how he and Sarah had come up with the theory, and Malika's answers had just about confirmed it. 'Everything now points to Muhammad Khan.'

Ellis sat back in her chair and crossed her legs. 'It's an interesting supposition, but why go to all the trouble of creating this false trail? Why not just sneak it into the country and use it? It seems they had everything in place, so why alert us that the X3 is on our soil?'

'I asked myself that, too,' Harvey admitted. 'Qureshi could have brought it with him and we'd have been none the wiser. Maybe they figured that with our people spread out all over the city, we might have got wind of it, but by concentrating all our efforts on al-Hosni, it gave them the freedom to weaponise the agent and set it off before we get a sniff of it. Or perhaps they don't know our capabilities and, rather than hope we wouldn't find out about it, they decided that the best option would be to swamp our resources.'

Ellis stared off to Harvey's right for a few moments, something she did when she was processing information.

'Let's say you're right,' she said at last. 'It's taken days to get everything we have on al-Hosni. How do you plan to prove Khan has the X3 in the limited time we have left?'

'We'll have to bring him in.'

CHAPTER 25

Wednesday, 16 August 2017

Muhammad Khan picked up his new passport and tucked it into the side pocket of his duffle bag, ensuring the zip was closed. He took one last look around the room and, confident that he hadn't forgotten anything, walked into the hallway, where a full-length mirror stood by the front door.

He checked his appearance. It was somewhat humiliating to see his reflection dressed in a black *burka* that covered him from head to toe, but recent events made the disguise necessary. News of Imran al-Hosni's abduction had reached him quickly, Nabil Karim's false trail working all too effectively. By now, al-Hosni would be at a secret location, being interrogated by the best Britain could muster. It would only be a matter of time before al-Hosni cracked and the truth came out, and when that happened, the police would be looking for the real name behind the upcoming attack.

The doorbell rang, startling him, but when he checked through the spyhole, he saw the two people he was expecting. He stood behind the door and opened it halfway to let them enter, careful not to expose himself to anyone who might be watching outside.

'Did you see anything suspicious?' Khan asked the tall, elderly male.

'No. We drove slowly and saw nothing.'

The woman who accompanied him was dressed exactly the same as Khan, and her height was a perfect match, too.

'Very well. Take my bag to the car.' He turned to the woman. 'Stay away from the windows and do not open the curtains.'

The old man struggled to lift the duffle bag, but the car was only a few yards away, and Khan was sure he could manage it. He followed the man's slow progress down the garden path and watched him bundle the bag into the back of an old Nissan. Khan climbed in behind the driver's seat and put his seat belt on.

'Is this the best you could manage?' Khan asked as he scanned the bleak interior.

'It is very reliable, and our journey is not that far,' the old man assured him.

It was too late to do anything about it, so Khan sat back and watched the suburbs flash past his window.

He wouldn't miss London. The free council accommodation had been adequate at best, and he had relied on government handouts for the last four years, but free money hadn't been enough to make up for the decadent society and anti-Muslim sentiment that flowed down every street and alleyway. There were those who preached inclusion and multiculturalism, but just because they used government buzzwords didn't mean that everyone had bought into them. He saw the cultural clashes day in, day out, and the slogans daubed on the walls near the mosque left no doubt as to the real feelings on the street. Despite its Muslim mayor, he had little hope for the city.

Muslims and infidels could not live happily side by side, that much was clear to him, and he was proud to have played his small part in widening the gulf between them. On Friday, his masters in Syria would claim a great victory, and anti-Muslim sentiment would ratchet up another notch. Young Islamic men would be persecuted for their beliefs, but there would always be someone willing to lend a sympathetic ear and steer them towards their true calling. The infidels would call them radical Islamists, but they were freedom fighters willing to lay down their lives so that Islam might rise in the West.

The car suddenly plunged into the darkness of an underground car park.

'There's no CCTV coverage in this area,' the driver said, handing over the keys to a BMW. 'It's the one to your right.'

Khan waited a couple of minutes to ensure they hadn't been followed into the car park. Once satisfied, he slipped out of his disguise and left it in the rear footwell.

'Is your accomplice ready?' he asked.

The plan called for the driver to walk around the shopping mall directly above them and a second woman, wearing the same clothes Khan had just discarded, to be waiting on the enclosed stairwell to take Khan's place and perpetuate the charade.

'I sent her a text message. She is in position.'

'Then enjoy your shopping,' Khan said with a smile. With one last check of the vicinity, he got out of the Nissan. He moved his bag to the boot of the BMW and climbed behind the wheel. The engine purred into life and the display told him he had a full tank.

Khan checked his reflection in the mirror. His long beard had been trimmed to a goatee, and the *kufi* he always wore on his head was gone, leaving him feeling slightly naked. It was all necessary, though. His appearance now matched the photo in his forged passport, one that would take him to Denmark initially, and eventually home to Syria.

He entered his destination into the satnav and turned on the police scanner he'd asked to have installed, then eased out of the parking space and headed for the exit.

~

While Sarah drove, Harvey called ahead to the team assigned the job of watching Khan's house.

'Are you in position yet?' he asked.

'We arrived about ten minutes ago, and there's already been some activity. An old man and a woman entered the house and stayed for about three minutes, then they left carrying a bag. It looked heavy. They got into a faded-green Nissan. I've sent you pictures and the plate number.'

'Okay, remain where you are, we'll be there in five minutes.'

Harvey checked his inbox and opened the message the team had sent. The old man wasn't anyone he recognised from Khan's list of known associates, and he had no existing relatives in the country. There wasn't a lot to be learned about the woman, dressed as she was. He decided the best thing to do was to forward the details to Farsi and have someone work them up.

'It's the next street on the left,' Sarah said, as she pulled up to the side of the road.

'Then we just wait for SO15,' Harvey replied. One of the downsides of the job was that he had no power to detain or arrest anyone. That task was left to the people of the Met's Counter Terrorism Command. While he waited, he took the automatic from his shoulder holster and checked that he had a round in the chamber before replacing it inside his jacket. It had been Ellis's idea to go armed and, given the stakes, he had been happy to sign the weapon out.

One thing that puzzled him, though, was Ellis's hesitance when he'd said he wanted Sarah along on the ride. They'd been out on assignment together scores of times; he wondered why his boss wasn't keen this time.

'Any idea why Veronica didn't want you to come along?' he asked.

Sarah shook her head. 'Just being overprotective, I expect.'

Both of them had read Khan's file, and the man had a reputation for violence. Still, that hadn't seemed enough to split up their pairing.

'But why all of a sudden? We've handled trickier cases than this.'

Sarah remained silent, staring out of the front window.

'Is it anything to do with what happened a few days ago?'

A tear formed in the corner of her left eye, and Harvey knew he'd hit the spot. He grabbed her hand and squeezed. 'Please, tell me what it is. You keep saying it's not the right time, but I have the feeling that day will never come. If I've done something to upset you, you have to tell me.'

Sarah turned to face him. 'Do you love me?'

'Of course I do. I wouldn't let anything come between us.'

'Not even a child?'

'No, of course n— Wait . . . Are you saying you're pregnant?'

Sarah managed the faintest of nods, and Harvey's jaw dropped. He was struggling for words when she snatched her hand away.

'I knew you'd react like that.'

'What? No, wait . . .'

Harvey searched for the right words but then realised he didn't know what he wanted to say. The revelation had been so far from what he'd expected, and he wasn't sure how he felt. Elation was the prevalent emotion, but confusion and fear were battling for dominion.

It wasn't as if they'd ever openly discussed having children, but it was far too late for that conversation. It was going to happen, and it was that certainty that gave him a burst of clarity.

'I'm so happy!' He threw his arms around her as best he could in the confined space and squeezed her close.

Sarah pulled back and looked him straight in the eye. 'Are you sure? You looked a bit gobsmacked for a minute.'

'I'm positive. If we were sitting here discussing the possibility, I might have had some doubts, but now that you have a little . . . Is it a boy or a girl?'

'I don't know yet. I'm only eight weeks. It'll be another three months or so before I find out.'

'Well, now that you have a little person growing inside you, I'm over the moon. We'll need—'

Harvey's phone buzzed, interrupting the moment, and he suddenly remembered the reason they were sitting in a car in East London.

'Harvey.'

'This is Sergeant Bury, SO15. We'll be at the location in fifteen seconds.'

'Roger that. We'll meet you at the door.'

Sarah pulled out and turned into Khan's street. She could see the two cars packed with armed officers stopping near the target house, and she screeched to a halt behind their vehicles.

'Wait here,' Harvey said, but Sarah ignored him and jumped out.

'Sarah, please.'

He got a glare in response, and knew further protestations would be useless.

Three men were sent to the rear of the building and Harvey waited impatiently for them to report in. When the call came, Bury, a tall, bluff veteran cop, marched up to the front door and rang the bell. He waited ten seconds, and when no-one answered he pressed it again and shouted through the letterbox.

'Khan, open the door!'

Bury gave the occupants a couple of seconds, then beckoned the officer carrying the enforcer, a red steel tube used to gain a quick – if undignified – entry.

'On my mark, go, go, go!'

The old wooden door caved on the first blow, and Bury was first inside, closely followed by several of his men. Harvey came next, and he could see the team entering the rear of the house, their weapons raised as they cleared the kitchen. A team went up the stairs, and when Harvey heard one of the officers shout something, he headed for the living room.

Four men were surrounding a woman, who was sitting on a couch. She was dressed completely in black and had her hands on her knees, as if she had been expecting them to call.

'Has she been searched?' Harvey asked.

'Not yet. We're waiting for a female officer to arrive.'

'I'll do it,' Sarah said, and gestured for the woman to get up. Her instructions ignored, Sarah grabbed the woman's arm and pulled her to her feet before patting her down.

'Where's Khan?' Harvey asked her, but the woman refused to speak.

A uniformed officer stuck his head through the door. 'The house is clear.'

'So is she,' Sarah added.

Harvey got on his phone and called the surveillance team, instructing them to join him in the already crowded house. They arrived within a minute.

'Is this the woman you saw entering the house?' he asked them.

'It's hard to tell, guv. She's certainly dressed the same way.'

Harvey turned to the occupant, who was still standing. She looked to be about five-nine, exactly the same height as Khan. It was clear that Khan had slipped away, and the manner in which he'd done so removed any doubt as to his guilt.

'Take her in,' Harvey told Bury. 'Khan's wife died a couple of years ago and he didn't remarry, so she'd better have a phenomenal reason for being here.'

Harvey got on the phone and called Farsi. 'I sent you details of a green Nissan a few minutes ago. I want you to check all CCTV cameras in this area and find out where it went. I think Khan switched places and is dressed as a woman. Also, enter his details into PAP.'

The Police, Airport and Port system had been introduced a year earlier. Prior to its inception, MI5 would have had to register a notice on the Police National Computer, which would have informed all forces. They would then have had to send out an All Ports Message, which covered the major air and maritime ports, and then contact each of the smaller airfields and marinas individually. PAP did away with all that, allowing them to flag suspects UK-wide within minutes.

Harvey added details about the clothes he suspected Khan to be wearing and asked to be updated as soon as they had anything.

'Let's get back to the office,' Harvey told Sarah. He led her out to the car and got into the passenger seat.

'What the hell was that all about?' Sarah asked as she slipped behind the wheel.

'What?' Harvey said, confused.

'Telling me to wait in the car, that's what.'

'You're about to have our baby,' Harvey said.

'In seven months' time! Do you plan to wrap me in cotton wool until then?'

'Of course not, but if I can keep you away from dangerous situations, I will.'

Sarah sighed as she started the car. 'If I'd known you were going to be like this, I wouldn't have told you until it became obvious. I hate the idea of spending the next six months tied to a desk.'

'I wasn't suggesting that. I just don't want anything happening to you.'

They drove the rest of the way back to Thames House in such silence that Harvey was glad to re-enter the chaos of the office.

$$\sim$$

Harvey swiped his way onto the office floor and walked over to Sarah's desk.

'As requested,' he said as he took a prawn sandwich and feta salad from the carrier bag he was holding.

Normally he would have let a subordinate do the food run, but after hours of sitting at a desk staring at his monitor, he was glad of the fresh air and exercise. It also gave him a chance to clear his head. Some people had an aptitude for sifting through CCTV footage, but after a couple of hours it turned Harvey's brain to mush.

'Maynard's here,' Sarah said.

As Harvey looked over towards Ellis's office, his boss opened the door and beckoned him over.

'Andrew, if you will . . .'

Harvey put the bag containing his own sandwich on Sarah's desk and walked over to the glass palace, where the Home Secretary stood next to Ellis's desk.

'Sit,' Maynard said.

Harvey would have preferred to remain standing, knowing Maynard wanted the psychological advantage of looking down at him, but one look from Ellis and he did as he was told.

'What the hell happened to my suspect?' Maynard barked.

'Al-Hosni? Your people grabbed him, from what I understand.'

'I'm talking about Malika Ali. I came here to instruct you to prepare a handover and I find out she's dead!'

News of Malika's demise had reached the office an hour earlier. No-one had shed a tear, but Harvey had seen it as the signal for the brown stuff to start flying, mostly in his direction.

'It wasn't something we could have predicted,' he said in his defence. 'She didn't come across as suicidal.'

'Well she clearly was!'

'Obviously,' Ellis said. 'But I've read the report and, while regrettable, there are lessons to be learned.'

'Lessons? You guys are supposed to know how to kill a man with a paper cup, and you didn't think there was anything wrong with leaving her alone in a room with a metal can?'

'That's not the business we're in,' Ellis shot back. 'And you know it. Malika's dead. It's time to move on.'

Maynard wasn't about to let them off the hook that easily. 'Someone is going to pay for their incompetence,' he said, directing the barb at Harvey. 'In the meantime, prepare the remaining three prisoners for departure. My men will be here in fifteen minutes. Do you think you can keep them alive that long?'

Ellis ignored the remark. 'You won't get much from them. You'd be better off concentrating your efforts on al-Hosni.'

'He's a dead end,' Maynard said, straightening his tie. 'Literally. I want transcripts of every interview you've conducted on the prisoners within the next half-hour, but before you start on that, I want to know what you're doing to dig yourself out of the shit pile you've created.'

'We've switched our efforts—'

'—to other members of the mosque al-Hosni attended.' Ellis cut Harvey off. 'Some have been on our radar for a while, and though we haven't actually seen them with al-Hosni, we haven't been able to ascertain who he's spoken to once inside the building. One of them holds the key, I'm sure of it. Everyone else he had contact with has been eliminated from our enquiries, which means one of these new names must have knowledge of the X3.'

'I hope you're right, for your sake. If the Friday deadline you told me about is accurate, that doesn't leave you long to save your career.'

Maynard stormed out, and Harvey waited until he'd been escorted off the main floor before turning to Ellis.

'You're not going to tell him about Khan?'

'Hell, no! The last thing we need is that egomaniac micromanaging our investigation. Let him chase ghosts all he wants, as long as it keeps him out of our hair.'

CHAPTER 26

Thursday, 17 August 2017

Harvey woke with a start and found Hamad standing over him.

'What is it?'

'I was following one of Khan's associates and found something interesting.'

Harvey looked at his watch. It was just before five in the morning – three hours of sleep would have to do.

'He took a cab,' Farsi continued, 'and stopped near a café. Someone else got in and they drove to a lock-up garage in the railway arches in Lambeth. Looks like they stayed for a few hours.'

Harvey eased himself off the travel cot, one of four that had been set up in the locker room to allow the staff to catch a few winks between sifting the huge pile of data. 'Do we know who these people are?'

'The guy I was tracking is Ghulam, one of Khan's right-hand men. He met someone called Badawi. I checked him out and he's a chemical engineer.'

'Where's Badawi now?' Harvey asked.

'Gone,' Farsi said. 'Flew to Turkey two days ago.'

'That's happening a lot recently. What do we know about him?'

'Lived in London for fifteen years and spent the last eight teaching chemistry at North Lodge College. He sold his house for cash last week and sent the proceeds to an account in Syria.'

'Sounds like he's not planning on coming back,' Harvey said. 'Tell me about the lock-up.'

'The registered owner is one Kasim Abdullah. I ran his name through the system and his cousin is in Khan's inner circle.'

'Get someone over there to check it out, and make sure they've got a Hazmat team with them.'

If a chemical engineer spent hours in a lock-up, it was unlikely he was playing video games. The last thing Harvey wanted was for London's finest to go snooping around inside without the hazardous material team giving it the all-clear first.

'Already organised,' Farsi told him. 'They should be there in a couple of hours.'

'Thanks. Keep tracking Ghulam and Badawi. I want to know where they went afterwards.'

Farsi disappeared, and Harvey went to the washroom. He splashed water on his face and a little on his hair to get rid of the just-woke look. Still feeling like crap, he made a couple of coffees and took them to Sarah's desk.

'What are you working on?' he asked, placing a cup next to her.

'Badawi. Hamad told me about the lock-up and I offered to split the workload. It looks like they stayed there for five hours, then got picked up by the same taxi just after midnight. I'm looking to see if he had anything with him when he was dropped off.'

Sarah took a sip of her coffee. 'Ew. What's this?'

'Decaf,' Harvey said, lowering his voice. 'Don't want the baby up all night.'

They hadn't told anyone about Sarah's condition, preferring to delay the announcement until things had returned to normal in the office.

Sarah placed the mug to one side. 'When this is all over, we really need to talk.'

'Agreed.' Harvey gave her a quick kiss, returned to his own station and entered his password on the PC. The screen presented him with the last thing he'd been working on: a list of vehicles that had left the shopping centre car park the previous day.

The team had tracked the green Nissan there and had seen the old man and a woman walking around the stores. They'd window-shopped for two hours, then driven back to a house in East London. Officers from SO15 had brought them in and the man had been briefly reunited with his wife, who had been picked up from Khan's house earlier.

At first, the man had denied any knowledge of Khan, but after being presented with photo evidence, his story changed. He'd conceded that, under duress, he'd driven Khan to the shopping centre, but insisted that after dropping him off, he had no idea where Khan had gone.

Harvey had read the full transcript of the interview, and didn't believe a word of it. He'd called the station and found that the suspect had been interviewed since, but wasn't changing his story.

Having tracked Khan to the shopping centre, Harvey had no option but to check the plates of every vehicle leaving the car park in the hope that one of them might have some connection to the imam. He'd counted more than ninety cars, vans and motorcycles leaving in the hour after the Nissan had arrived, but checks made against the DVLA database hadn't thrown up anyone even vaguely linked to Khan.

There was one hire car among them, but he wouldn't be able to find out who'd rented it until the firm's office opened later that morning. Just to be on the safe side, he entered a marker for it on ANPR. The automated number plate recognition system would alert him each time it passed one of the networked cameras, and he would at least be able to keep it in his sights until it could be eliminated as irrelevant.

Harvey had just finished entering the details when a yellow box flashed on the screen, showing the car's index along with the current time and location.

M90, junction 6.

Harvey brought up a map of the UK and searched for the location. 'What are you doing in Scotland?' he asked himself. It was hardly an offence to drive hundreds of miles in the middle of the night, but it certainly seemed suspicious.

He logged into the road-traffic-management system and located a camera a few miles further up the road. He was disappointed to see that it was static, so he moved on until he found one that could be controlled remotely.

The traffic was light, the cars nothing but dots on the screen. Thankfully, the sun had risen a quarter of an hour earlier, so he wasn't presented with oncoming headlights. Harvey zoomed in and concentrated on an approaching white van. The detail was so sharp that he could make out the logo on the disposable coffee cup sitting on the dashboard.

The van disappeared out of shot a second later, and Harvey repositioned the camera so that he had a good view of oncoming traffic. Several more vehicles passed the location, and he was beginning to think he'd missed the suspect when a black shape appeared at the top of the screen. As it grew larger he could make out the distinctive shape of the BMW and his pulse quickened as he zoomed in. There was only one person on board, and as it neared, he could see that the driver was Asian, but he looked nothing like Khan. No long beard, just a goatee, and this man wore glasses. Still, Harvey knew enough tradecraft to realise such subtle changes in appearance would be a decent disguise. The only way to be sure was to run the image through facial recognition.

Harvey took a dozen snaps before the car passed out of view, then looked for the clearest one and uploaded it. He set the match parameters to the most recent photo they had of Khan and hit the 'Enter' key. The result came back within three seconds:

98 per cent match.

'I've got Khan,' he said aloud, and his colleagues gathered round.

'Where?' Farsi asked.

'Scotland. I doubt he's got the X3, but he certainly knows who does. We need to alert every port north, east and west of him. Gareth, take over and keep an eye on him. Let me know if he turns off the motorway.'

He gave Bailey Khan's current location, then asked Sarah to contact Police Scotland and see if they could spare any armed units to help.

'From what I remember, they only have something like ten armed officers for every thousand on the beat,' Sarah told him.

'Try anyway.'

Harvey logged out of the RTMS and called up the PAP system. He checked the map overlay and saw that there were a dozen airstrips as well as a few marinas dotted along the coastline. If Khan were looking to skip the country, he was unlikely to be heading for a major port, but Harvey wanted to be thorough. The PAP alert he'd sent out had contained Khan's old photograph, and he needed to update it as soon as possible. That meant uploading the latest image he'd taken, but he also wanted to speak to someone at each of the locations to make sure they kept their eyes peeled. Some of these places had little more than a nightwatchman on duty at this hour, and he didn't want to have to rely on them being awake and alert enough to check the system for updates.

'Andrew, he just hit the A90, heading east towards Dundee. If he turns off before he gets there we could run out of coverage very soon.'

'Thanks, Gareth.'

Harvey was able to eliminate the sites to the west, which included most of the airports. That left just one strip and a handful of marinas, and Harvey started with the closest one.

'Hello?' a voice said after a few rings. It was the sound of a man who'd just woken up. Harvey introduced himself and asked who he was speaking to.

'Ross Matthews, air traffic control.'

'Do you usually sleep in the tower?' Harvey asked.

'Actually, the phone diverts to my home just outside the fence. We don't have any traffic before nine in the morning.'

'Well, I need you to go to work early today.' Harvey explained the reason for the call and gave Matthews his personal mobile number. 'When you get to the tower, call me with a list of flights scheduled to leave today, as well as any passenger details you may have.'

He hung up before Matthews could object, then started dialling the first of the marinas.

'There are no armed units in the area,' Sarah told him. 'The best they can offer is a couple of squad cars.'

It wasn't ideal, but sometimes you had to go with what you had. 'Okay, get Gareth to liaise with them. He can give them a running commentary and help set up a roadblock. I'll continue to notify the ports in case Khan manages to evade us.'

Ten minutes later, he'd just finished talking to the fourth marina on his list when Bailey came over to his desk.

'We lost him.'

Khan yawned as he passed a sign that indicated twelve miles to Dundee. His next turn-off was five minutes away, when he'd transition from the dual carriageway to the back roads. He was still fifty miles from his ultimate destination, but he still had time to make his rendezvous despite the setbacks he'd suffered on the journey.

The first had come just minutes after joining the M1. An accident involving a lorry and a coach had closed two lanes, causing miles of tailbacks. It had taken him over three hours to clear the traffic, but once back up to speed it was clear he'd driven over some of the debris from the crash. His rear right tyre had blown out, and it had taken another thirty minutes to replace it with the spare. The extra half-hour wasn't the problem; he'd been due to arrive seven hours early anyway. What concerned him the most was that the temporary spare tyre was supposedly only good for short distances at a maximum of 50 m.p.h.

A quick internet search on his new burner mobile had revealed a service station fifteen miles ahead, and he'd called a mobile tyre-replacement company and asked them to meet him there with a new wheel. That had used up another two hours, and four hundred pounds from the cash he was carrying.

Night had disappeared an hour earlier, and with light traffic, he'd been able to make up a lot of time, but the police scanner he'd been listening to revealed trouble ahead. Two patrol cars had been ordered to take up position at the junction with the A923 and intercept a black BMW. That was enough to make him nervous, but when they read out his licence plate he knew they were on to him. How, he had no idea. His first thought was that the old man who'd rented the car had rolled on him, but that was all they were likely to get out of him. Only one other person knew where he was heading, and that was the man he was supposed to meet in two hours' time.

Khan pulled into a lay-by to analyse the situation. If he was going to make the rendezvous, he would have to move quickly, but with the police waiting for him up ahead, his options were severely limited. He checked the online map and saw that the next main turn-off was the one the police were covering. There were many side roads, but these dead-ended at farms or small villages. A central barrier dividing the carriageways made turning round impossible, leaving him no choice but to continue down the road.

It didn't necessarily have to be in the same car, though.

Khan looked up the number for the largest roadside assistance company and placed a call. He gave them his location and said his car had suddenly died on him.

'No, there's plenty of petrol. I think it might be electrical,' he said.

The operator tapped at her keyboard and asked if he was a member. When Khan said he wasn't, the woman gave him a price for the callout. It seemed a little steep, but under the circumstances, Khan had no choice but to agree to it.

'I have a team member who can be with you in twenty minutes.'

'That's perfect,' Khan lied, and hung up. Twenty minutes was far from ideal. The police lying in wait were clearly expecting him, and if he didn't arrive at the junction soon they would no doubt come looking for him.

Seconds felt like minutes, minutes like hours, as he stood by the car, looking up and down the road. He was relieved that it was mild enough to require a jacket, because the long sleeves were perfect for hiding the tyre iron.

The recovery vehicle arrived two minutes early, and Khan positioned himself near the back of his car. Traffic was a little heavier now, and if he were going to make his move, he'd have to be careful not to do so in front of witnesses.

'Morning,' the van driver said as he walked to the front of the BMW. Khan was pleased to see that he was in his fifties and had a beer belly. A younger, fitter man might have been more difficult to deal with.

'What's the problem, then?'

'I was hoping you'd tell me,' Khan said. 'I was driving along and suddenly there was no power.'

The mechanic frowned. 'Can you get in and start it up?'

Khan got behind the wheel and turned the key in the ignition. He'd earlier popped open the fuse box and removed items until it rendered the car useless, so he wasn't surprised when his actions produced no result.

'Hmm, definitely electrical,' the mechanic said.

Khan got out, hoping to follow the man back to the van to collect some tools. It would be the ideal place to take the man down, out of sight of passing motorists. Unfortunately, the mechanic opened the front passenger door and knelt down to remove the fuse panel cover.

His handiwork was about to be discovered, leaving Khan no choice. He pulled the tyre iron from his sleeve and hit the man's skull as hard as he could. Bone crunched and the mechanic pitched forward, and Khan followed up with a few more blows for good measure.

His victim lay still, half inside the car. Khan quickly checked for a pulse but found none. He stripped off the man's high-visibility jacket and put it on, then searched him until he found his ID and the keys to the van. He started up the victim's vehicle and repositioned it so that he could dump the corpse in the BMW's boot without anyone witnessing the act.

Khan moved his bag from the boot of the car to the van, then pulled the corpse to the back of the saloon. The body was heavier than he'd expected, and Khan was sweating by the time he slammed the boot closed and locked it. It was worth the effort, as it would buy him some extra time. When the police found the car, it would take some time to discover the body in the boot, by which time he'd be miles away.

Khan started the van and pulled out into the road. He still had ninety minutes to reach his destination, and if the mechanic's body remained undiscovered for long enough, he might just make it.

'What do you mean you've lost him?'

'Vanished,' Bailey said. 'He passed one camera and didn't reach the next. There's a few turn-offs but they lead nowhere.'

'What about the local police?' Harvey asked.

'They were in position when Khan went past the last camera. He just didn't reach them.'

'How long should it have taken Khan to reach them?'

'About six minutes,' Bailey confirmed.

'And how long has it been?' Harvey asked, dreading the answer.

Bailey looked sheepish, confirming Harvey's fears. 'Twenty-three minutes.'

'Christ on a stick! What were you doing all that time?'

'I was looking to see if there was any way he could have turned off and joined up with a major road, but I came up empty.'

Harvey was almost purple by the time Bailey had finished his excuse, but chewing him out wasn't going to rectify the situation. He would deal with him later, once they'd reacquired Khan.

'Whoever you're liaising with, patch them through to my phone.'

Bailey scuttled off, and Harvey's phone rang a few moments later.

'Andrew Harvey.'

'This is PC Glen Cottrill of Police Scotland. I was just dealing with one of your colleagues.'

'Not anymore. What's your current location?'

'We're sitting at the junction of the A90 and A923 waiting for your man,' Cottrill said.

'I think it's pretty clear he's not coming. I suggest you go looking for him.'

'I'll have to wait for orders from control—'

Harvey slammed the phone down, vowing to check later to see if it really was National Idiot Day. In the meantime, he looked up the number for the chief constable of Police Scotland and dialled his mobile.

A two-minute conversation with the top man got the ball rolling, and Harvey was promised a dozen vehicles to help in the search for Khan. He'd requested helicopter support, too, but the chopper was temporarily out of action. The cop assured him that, given the small number of major roads in the area, finding the suspect shouldn't be that difficult.

Harvey didn't share his optimism, but thanked the brass for his help and hung up.

How Khan had managed to evade the roadblock he didn't know, but bringing him in wasn't going to be as easy as he'd expected. He would have preferred to be in Scotland overseeing the search, but time wasn't on his side and his presence was needed in the office. The local police would have to handle it, and hopefully his chat with the chief constable would result in a little more motivation on their part.

Harvey finished speaking to the marinas near Khan's last known location, then opened the list of Khan's associates. One of them had to either have the X3 or know where it was, and the time for sitting back and watching had come to an end. He dialled Ellis's mobile. She sounded wide awake, even at such an ungodly hour.

Harvey briefed her on Khan's movements and subsequent disappearance and Farsi's discovery at the lock-up garage, then explained the real reason for the call.

'I want to bring all of Khan's friends in,' he told her.

'Risky,' Ellis replied. 'If we cast the net that wide, there's a chance we'll miss the one we're really after, and that might force them to bring the deadline forward. Khan only has a few people in his inner circle, so spend the morning checking them out. The more we can eliminate, the better, but if you haven't got anything solid by lunchtime, get SO15 to round them all up. Ghulam looks the most likely, so concentrate your efforts on him. I'll be in the office by eight.'

Ellis ended the call, and Harvey's frustration was tempered by the fact that even if the suspects were brought in, it would be difficult to get them to talk. Handing them over to Maynard's goon squad would do his department no good either, as the Home Secretary would take all the credit.

Ellis was right, they had to narrow down the list of suspects, and Ghulam was the best lead they had so far.

'Andrew, check this out.'

Harvey walked around to Farsi's desk.

'What is it?'

'When Ghulam left the lock-up he took the taxi back to the mosque,' Farsi said. 'He was carrying a black briefcase when he went in, but not when he came out. I just checked with Sarah and she said Badawi wasn't carrying one when the same taxi dropped him near his home. I know he had one when he met Ghulam that afternoon. The X3 must be in that case.'

It was possibly the break Harvey had been looking for. He turned and addressed the room.

'Everyone, drop what you're doing and listen up. Hamad is going to send you details of the CCTV footage he's just been looking at. Adnan Ghulam entered his mosque at twelve-thirty on Wednesday morning and he was carrying a black briefcase, but it wasn't on him when he left . . .'

'. . . three minutes later,' Farsi confirmed.

'We think the X3 is in that case, and we need to know who picked it up. Hamad, you continue checking the coverage until midday. Sarah, you've got midday until midnight last night. Elaine, you've got everything from then until now.'

The team got to work, and Harvey placed another call to Ellis.

'We think Ghulam took the X3 to his mosque in Tower Hamlets,' he told her. 'I've got everyone looking to see if it was picked up by someone else, but chances are it's still there.'

'Run your checks first, but give SO15 a heads-up. If CCTV reveals nothing, we'll send them in.'

Harvey disconnected and called the counter-terrorism unit and put them on standby, then returned his attention to Khan. The chief constable of Police Scotland had given him the mobile number of the sergeant heading up the search.

Harvey called him for an update.

~

Sergeant Ben Davies pulled in behind the two patrol cars that were already on the scene and left his blues flashing as he got out of the car. The sun was beginning to make its presence felt, and he knew today was going to be a scorcher by local standards.

Two of his men were standing next to the black BMW while another pair marked the area off with crime-scene tape. One of the officers pointed out a faint trail of blood on the tarmac that led from the middle of the car to the rear.

'ETA on the SOCO?' Davies asked as he pulled on a pair of latex gloves.

'Twenty minutes.'

The scenes of crime officer would go ballistic if he interfered with the evidence, but his boss had made it clear that the suspect was to be apprehended as soon as possible, and Davies took that to mean corners were there to be cut.

He'd seen enough claret in his time to know what he was looking at. Drag marks.

He tried the boot lid using one finger but it was locked, and he didn't need to be a detective to figure out what had happened. The reports said there was only one person in the BMW, so either he was injured, dragged himself to the boot and locked himself in, or he'd done the deed to someone else.

'Get something to pry this open,' he said, and one of his men returned a minute later with a screwdriver.

'It's all we've got.'

Davies got to work, but the low-tech approach was a waste of time. After a few minutes, he gave up. He wanted to preserve as much evidence as he could, but was left with no alternative. He pulled out his baton, extended it and smashed the rear driver's-side window, then reached in and opened the door. That action popped all the locks, and he was able to lift the boot lid and see its grim contents.

While an officer called for an ambulance, Davies checked in vain for a pulse. He then went through the man's pockets, searching for identification, but came up empty.

'Fetch me the fingerprint kit,' Davies said.

An officer returned with a handheld device that was connected to the Police National Computer and Davies pressed the right index finger of the corpse onto the screen. A beep confirmed the capture, and he waited until it returned a match.

Nothing.

'Looks like he's never been arrested,' he said. He put his radio to his mouth but his mobile rang before he could call it in.

'Ben Davies,' he said.

'Sergeant, this is Andrew Harvey from MI5. Your chief constable gave me this number. I'm calling about the Khan case. Have you managed to locate him yet?'

'We've found the car but no sign of the suspect. He did leave a body behind, though.'

Davies explained the find, and asked if Harvey could help out.

'Send me a photo of the man's face and one of the fingerprint to this number. I'll run them through our systems.'

The line went dead, and Davies turned photographer. He sent the photos and waited for the response.

'That was quick,' he said when the phone rang two minutes later.

'His name is Albert Jennings and he works for the AA. Contact them and ask for the index of the van he signed out this morning.'

Davies thanked Harvey and looked up the AA on his phone, then called the contact centre and asked for the supervisor. Within minutes, he had the index and passed the details on to all units in the area. The discovery of the body added extra urgency to the investigation, and Khan had gone from possible terror suspect to murderer.

With all officers in the region looking for him, it was only a matter of time.

CHAPTER 27

Thursday, 17 August 2017

When Davies sent the van's plate number through, Harvey considered whom to assign the work to. Bailey was available, but his recent performance didn't instil a lot of confidence. He thought about passing the task to Sarah, but she was already working on a vital aspect of the investigation. Everyone else was otherwise engaged, too, leaving Bailey as the only one who could pick up the slack.

Resigned to his decision, he went over to Bailey's desk and gave him the van's licence plate and Davies's phone number. 'Input that into ANPR and let the sergeant know as soon as you get a hit.'

'Got it.'

'I hope so,' Harvey said. 'I want updates every ten minutes. Understood?'

Bailey nodded solemnly. Harvey hoped that his request for constant updates would keep the agent focused.

Harvey went to get a coffee, and by the time he got back to his desk, he found Bailey waiting for him.

'Got him.'

'Already? Excellent. Where is he?'

Bailey led Harvey over to his desk and pointed to a dot on the screen. 'Heading north-west on the B954.'

Harvey frowned. 'We've got ANPR cameras on a remote Scottish B-road?'

'Nope.' Bailey smiled smugly. 'I called the AA and asked them for the van's transponder number. They all have tracking devices fitted so that the control centre know how far they are from a call-out.'

It was so obvious that Harvey kicked himself for not thinking of it first. The long shifts and lack of sleep were no doubt affecting his judgement.

'Nice work,' he told Bailey. 'Let Davies know right away.'

Harvey went to his own PC and looked up the location, then zoomed out and scanned the surrounding area. The road would take Khan away from the east coast, leaving only one possible destination.

He jogged over to Bailey and interrupted his phone call. 'Tell Davies to send some of his men to Nimping Airfield.'

Harvey checked the time. Having spoken to Ross Matthews, the air traffic controller at Nimping, he knew that no flights were due in until after nine, which gave Davies ninety minutes to secure Khan. Matthews had provided a schedule for the day: all bar one were domestic flights. The exception was a hop across the North Sea to Denmark, but that wasn't due to arrive until early in the afternoon. If that was the one Khan planned to catch, it made time even less of an issue.

'Done,' Bailey announced. 'He's sending an armed unit now, along with two other cars.'

'Good work. If Khan deviates, let me know immediately.'

Khan peered up at the sky, but apart from a few wisps of white cloud, it was empty. His watch said he was a few minutes early, and the GPS showed the airstrip a mile ahead.

It had been a tense half-hour, and he was convinced the danger wasn't over. The radio in the van had constantly requested confirmation that the driver had completed his latest assignment, but after twenty minutes that had stopped. There had been silence ever since, an ominous sign that could only point to one thing: they had found the car and Jennings's body. Every cop in the area would be looking for him, but if he could evade them for another few minutes, he'd be on his way to Denmark, the first leg of his journey home.

When he was half a mile from the airstrip Khan pulled over onto the grass verge and wound his window down. He didn't want to arrive too early and have to answer any awkward questions. He'd been assured that the place was unmanned before nine, but wasn't going to take any chances. Sometimes eager employees arrived at work early, and he wanted to avoid any further confrontations.

The drone of a light aircraft's engine caught his attention. Khan looked to the east and saw a Cessna in the distance. He started his engine and drove towards the strip, but as he turned a corner he found himself facing more than a worker with time on his hands.

Khan slammed on the brakes. A hundred yards ahead, two police cars were parked across the road, and half of the officers in front of them were carrying automatic weapons. He saw the Cessna grow bigger as it neared the runway, then returned his attention to the roadblock. His ride to freedom was tantalisingly close, and he'd been warned that if he wasn't ready to board as soon as the plane touched down, he could kiss his ride goodbye. It was an unscheduled flight, and therefore imperative that they get off the ground as soon as they could.

There was no point turning around now; the police cars would easily catch the lumbering van. Surrender wasn't an option, either.

Even with the best legal defence, he was facing the rest of his life behind bars.

If he even made it that far.

The police could only be after him for one reason, and that was the X3. Imran al-Hosni had been snatched off the street because they thought he had it. By now, al-Hosni would have been broken, leaving the authorities determined to secure the nerve agent at any cost.

The plane was down to two hundred feet, leaving Khan just seconds to make his move. He put the van in first gear and hit the accelerator, aiming for the small gap between the police cars. The unarmed officers ran for cover while the others raised their rifles and aimed at his vehicle, but Khan had no intention of stopping. After all the years of preaching about sacrifice to his young audience, it was his turn to fight. He'd either make it to the plane, or die trying.

He was thirty yards from the roadblock when the first bullet hit his windscreen. The glass spider-webbed, and Khan ducked as more rounds slammed into the vehicle. The van tilted as a tyre blew out, but he kept his foot down.

When the van hit the stationary car, Khan flew across the cab like a pinball. His head struck the dashboard, but the adrenaline coursing through him blocked the pain. He regained his seat as blood trickled from a gash in his forehead. In the side mirror, he could see the police chasing him on foot, and he gunned the engine once more. He managed to reach 40 m.p.h. by the time he crashed through the wire gate, and he could see the runway ahead.

The Cessna's wheels touched down as Khan drove alongside it, frantically waving for the pilot to stop. He matched the plane's speed until both came to a halt, then jumped out with his bag over his shoulder. He struggled to the plane under the heavy weight, and when the pilot opened the passenger door from the inside, he heaved his luggage into the aircraft. If it hadn't been for his passport, tucked into the bag's side pocket, he would have left the bag in the van.

That decision cost him dearly.

He'd taken one police car out of the equation, but the other had quickly taken up the chase. Two officers had jumped out as the police Volvo screeched to a halt behind the Cessna, and their shouts for him to desist were lost in the whine of the propeller.

Khan had one leg inside the cockpit when the other exploded in agony. A bullet had ripped through his thigh and shattered the femur with such force that even the surging adrenaline could not numb the pain.

'Go!' he urged the pilot through clenched teeth as he dragged himself into his seat.

The pilot gunned the engine as more rounds peppered the fuselage, then slowed as they reached the end of the runway.

'What are you doing?!' Khan yelled.

'I've got to turn around. There isn't enough runway.'

The plane's nose spun to the right and Khan could see the police standing a few hundred yards in front of them.

'Run them down!' he ordered, his mangled leg forgotten for the moment.

The engine roared as the power kicked in, and Khan watched the figures in the distance grow bigger by the second. More bullets flew from their weapons as the Cessna hurtled towards them, but apart from a hit in the top corner of the windscreen, their aim was defective.

The police scattered as the plane reached take-off speed. Khan felt immense relief as the nose came up and the ride smoothed out.

The moment was short-lived.

More rounds hammered against the side of the plane, and the pilot's scream told Khan that one of them had found its mark.

'Where are you hit?' Khan cried. He had no idea how to control an aircraft; without the pilot, this was going to be the shortest flight of his life.

'My ribs,' the other man managed. 'I'm hurt bad.'

Khan had only one thing on his mind. 'Can you make it to Denmark?'

The response was a wince, then the pilot coughed and blood splattered the windscreen and control panel. He tried to suck air into his blood-filled lungs but only succeeded in ejecting more frothing crimson before falling forward on the control column.

The nose of the aircraft pointed towards the ground. Khan seized the yoke and pulled back with all his strength, but the gurgling pilot's weight made it impossible to move it.

All he could do was curse until the propeller bit into the ground and the ensuing fireball silenced him forever.

Harvey put the phone down, ran his hands through his hair and stared up at the ceiling. He did his best to control his emotions, but the words refused to be held back.

'For fuck's sake!' he yelled.

The room went silent until Farsi recovered from the shock of the outburst to ask what had happened.

'Khan's dead.'

The one man who knew where the X3 could be found was now a charred lump in a remote Scottish field. All they had left were numerous possibilities and a looming deadline.

'What have we got, people?' he asked while he had their attention. 'Have you seen anyone leaving the mosque with a bag?'

The silence told him all he needed to know.

Harvey got up and walked into Ellis's office. The case for bringing in the remainder of Khan's network had just strengthened immeasurably, and the sooner he got the ball rolling, the better. He told her what had happened, and her reaction was much the same as his had been.

'I want to bring Ghulam in now,' he said. 'We're making no progress with the people who attended the mosque, and time is running out.'

'Do it.'

Harvey hesitated by the door. 'I also want to send SO15 to the mosque.'

Ellis started to speak, but Harvey stopped her. 'I know you're going to say it's a sensitive issue liable to raise tensions in the community, but everything points to the X3 still being there.'

'I was going to mention that,' Ellis said, 'but I agree that it has to be done. My only concern is that once news hits the media, Maynard will come asking questions. He's going to want to know why we haven't told him about Khan.'

'An anonymous last-minute tip-off?' Harvey suggested.

Ellis looked unenthusiastic but agreed that it was the best they had.

Harvey hurried back to his desk and passed the instructions on to Sergeant Bury at SO15. He thought about stressing the need to take Ghulam alive, given the fiasco in Scotland, but the only way to ensure that happened would be to take charge at the scene.

'Have your men standing by in Leopold Road,' he told Bury. 'You're not to make a move until I get there.'

The location was two streets away from Khan's semi-detached home. It was as good a place as any to meet without tipping their hand.

Harvey retrieved his jacket from the coat stand, but found his path to the exit blocked.

'And just where do you think you're going?' Sarah asked, her arms crossed tightly against her chest.

'I need to make sure they don't get trigger-happy.'

'I'm coming with you.'

Harvey took Sarah by the elbow and led her to a quiet corner. 'We've been over this. I don't want you in harm's way.'

'In case I lose the baby?'

'Exactly.'

'And what if I don't want *you* in harm's way in case the baby loses its father? Did you ever consider that?'

Harvey had to admit that the thought hadn't crossed his mind. 'I'll be staying in the background,' he promised. 'There'll be no danger.'

'Great,' she said triumphantly. 'So there's no reason not to take me along.'

Sarah got her coat and was waiting at the door by the time Harvey reached it.

CHAPTER 28

Adnan Ghulam ignored the chimes of his mobile phone as he sat glued to the television. The picture on the news channel was of the burnt wreckage of a light aircraft, and the news ticker said that two passengers had died in the crash. It hadn't been a particularly interesting item until a photo of Khan had appeared in the top corner and an air traffic controller had eagerly explained what had happened to the on-site reporter.

'*The police were waiting for this guy but he rammed their cars and then crashed through the gate. I was in the tower trying to communicate with the pilot when it happened, and I saw this van driving up to the Cessna, and a guy got out and tried to get in the plane. I think the police shot and wounded him, but he got in and the plane took off. They shot at it as it went by, then about thirty seconds later it nosedived into the ground.*'

So Khan hadn't made it home after all. Ghulam felt even better about his decision to remain behind. He'd been offered a seat on the flight but had graciously declined. His health problems precluded him from going back to Syria, where specialist care was non-existent. Even staying in London would not do him much good in the long run, but he'd decided to make one last stand before his body succumbed to the ulcerative colitis that was plaguing him. The next step in his treatment was an ileostomy, and Ghulam had long ago decided that when the time came to carry his crap around in a plastic bag, he'd say goodbye to this world in fitting style.

He turned the television off and walked over to the window. Inching the lace curtains aside, Ghulam looked out into the street, which was typically deserted.

The police had somehow managed to see past the ruse fingering al-Hosni as the man in possession of the X3, but there had always been a slight chance that would happen. That they had fooled them for this long was a blessing, and the precautions they had taken would mean the attack would still go ahead before the authorities had a chance to stop it.

It also meant the police would be looking for Ghulam next. As Khan's right-hand man, he was the logical choice, but their efforts would be in vain. He had no intention of being taken in, never mind talking.

The phone rang again.

'Adnan, did you hear the news about Muhammad?'

Ghulam recognised the voice, and could barely contain his fury. Iqbal, the boy tasked with delivering the nerve agent, had been forbidden from contacting anyone until his mission had been completed.

'Is this your own phone?' he growled.

'No, I bought a burner, just as I was taught.'

The fact that the phone would be hard to trace back to the boy was one thing in Iqbal's favour, but there was no excuse for breaking protocol.

'Khan is dead,' Iqbal continued. 'Does that affect tomorrow's plan?'

'No!' Ghulam shouted. 'Proceed as directed. Now destroy that phone and speak to no-one!'

Ghulam ended the call and threw the handset across the room. It struck a wall with such force that the plastic casing shattered, but he had already resumed his watch on the street by the time the pieces hit the floor.

The entire operation was now in jeopardy because of one foolish child. Burner or not, the conversation had no doubt been captured by the government snoopers, and they would be concentrating all of their efforts on finding the person who had made the call. If Iqbal did as instructed and destroyed the handset, they wouldn't be able to track his current location. All they would have was the tower the call was routed through, and that would be too large an area to search in the time that remained. However, as a person of interest, everyone Ghulam had been in communication with over the last few months would be in MI5's database, and that would help to narrow the search considerably.

Movement in the street caught his eye, and all thoughts of Iqbal were immediately cast aside. A line of black-clad figures was inching towards his house, and the assault weapons they were carrying told him all he needed to know about their intentions.

Ghulam moved to the side wall of the living room and pulled back a rug to reveal a trapdoor. He swung it open and looked at the contraption he'd created a week earlier.

Three butane gas canisters lay next to a small black box, which had a blinking red LED light on the top. Wires ran from the detonator to an ice-cream container that held a few pounds of homemade explosives; not enough to destroy the house on its own, but combined with the butane it would create a blast large enough to kill anyone within a hundred feet.

Ghulam flipped a switch on the box, then opened the quick-release valves on the gas bottles. He put the trapdoor back in place and smoothed out the carpet, then sat on the sofa, awaiting the inevitable. He tried to listen for the escaping gas, but as had been the case with his trial run, the leaks were silent, the small shag pile and the overhead fan masking the sound. With butane being heavier than air, it wouldn't rise through the floor and give away his little secret. The timer was set for eight minutes, which would be more than enough time for the police to search the house and declare it clear of any threats before bringing in a team to look for the X3.

He looked up at the clock and calculated the time for detonation just as the front door caved in and a sea of black flooded into the room.

~

Harvey pulled up behind the two police vans in Leopold Road and didn't bother asking Sarah to remain in the car. They were far enough away from any danger at this point, and he decided to save his efforts for when they were really needed.

He got out of the car as Sergeant Bury walked over to him and explained what his unit planned to do.

'I'll send four men in first. Their job is to secure the premises. Once we have the all-clear, we'll send the rest of the team in to help with the search.'

'I'll leave the operational side to you, but I just want to stress how important it is that we take Ghulam alive.'

'I'll pass that on,' Bury said. 'But my men have families waiting for them. They'll do what's necessary to get home tonight.'

It was the best Harvey could hope for, short of sending unarmed men in to pick up Ghulam, but there was no telling what a man capable of releasing such a deadly nerve agent would do when confronted by the police. Better the officers protected themselves than be exposed to unnecessary danger.

Harvey followed Bury over to the quartet of armed officers and listened while he briefed them. A couple of them shot looks at Harvey, but none questioned the orders.

Bury had the men board the vans. 'We'll drive to the end of Ghulam's street and wait up there. Once the house is secure, we'll call you in,' he told Harvey, who walked back to his own car.

He started the engine and tucked in behind the police vehicles. One of them peeled off to block off the other end of the road and, when they reached their destination, Harvey eased the Ford onto the pavement and switched the engine off. The strike team could be seen jogging to within twenty yards of Ghulam's house, then stopping to radio in their status.

'Here we go,' Harvey said as the men formed a line and made their way to the suspect's house, the man in front carrying a bright red battering ram. Harvey watched him reach the door and take one swing before the frame gave way and the team were inside.

Harvey cranked his window down to listen for gunshots, but the street remained silent except for the sound of the occasional passing car. He began to worry that Ghulam wasn't home, that he'd followed Khan's example and made a run for it.

Seconds ticked agonisingly by, until Bury left the van and came over to the car.

'What's happening?' Harvey asked.

'They've got Ghulam,' Bury told him. 'He offered no resistance, and the rest of the house is clear. I'm about to send up the search team.'

Harvey slapped the steering wheel. 'Yes!'

'Don't get too carried away,' Sarah warned him. 'We've still got to get him to talk.'

Bury returned to the van and ordered the rest of his men up to the house, while Harvey considered Sarah's words. She was right; he was getting a little ahead of himself. Having Ghulam in custody was one thing, but there were limits to what they could do to get information out of him.

'Give me fifteen minutes with him,' Harvey said. 'If I can't get him to talk, we'll have to let Maynard's goons have a crack.'

'If we hand him over to Maynard, he'll take all the credit. He'll get rid of Veronica in a heartbeat.'

'Not necessarily. If we're the ones that deliver Ghulam, that must go some way towards redeeming ourselves.'

He could see that Sarah wasn't convinced, but as far as he was concerned it was the only remaining option.

'Let's go and help out,' Sarah said. 'There's a chance the X3 is in his house.'

She put her hand on the door release, but Harvey grabbed her elbow. 'Not this time. I want you to stay in the car.'

'Your concern is noted, but it's not going to happen. He's in cuffs, for God's sake. What's he going to do? Look at me strangely?'

Harvey's phone rang, and he gestured for her to stay put while he answered it.

'Harvey.'

'We intercepted a call to Ghulam's phone,' Farsi said.

Harvey listened as his colleague read from the transcript. 'It sounds like the caller is the one who's going to release the X3. Have you got a location?'

'We can only narrow it down to an area three miles wide,' Farsi said. 'We tried tracking it further but the signal's dead. He must have obeyed the instructions from Ghulam and destroyed the phone.'

'Then check all of Khan's associates and see if any of them live within that area. Get your snitch on it, too.'

Harvey hung up the phone and told Sarah what he'd learned.

'I still think we should check out Ghulam's house. There might be something there that could indicate who the caller is.'

Harvey had to agree, but despite her earlier speech, he remained reluctant to take her along. There wasn't much Ghulam could do to her, but Harvey still felt an overwhelming need to protect her.

It was as if Sarah could sense his inner turmoil.

'If you don't let me go in, where does this stop?' she asked. 'Will you refuse to let me do the grocery shopping, or will you force me to quit my yoga classes in case I get hit by an expanding consciousness? I'm telling you, this is going to get tiresome very quickly.'

Harvey looked at her for a moment, then sighed. 'You're right,' he apologised. 'I guess I'm still getting used to the idea of being a daddy.'

'Who says you're the father?' Sarah winked, and reached for the door handle.

The explosion lifted the car a foot off the ground and sent it tumbling across the road. Neither of them were wearing their seat belts, and they bounced around the interior like teddy bears in a tumble dryer.

When the car finally settled on its roof, Harvey found himself on his back, and the right-hand side of his face felt numb. He put a hand up to his cheek and found debris that had embedded itself in his cheek. His limbs all seemed to work, but things got worse as he looked over to Sarah. She was crumpled in a heap on the car ceiling, rivulets of blood seeping through her blonde hair.

'Sarah!'

Harvey righted himself, ignoring the jolt of pain from his right hip. He moved Sarah's hair aside and felt for a pulse. It was there, but weak.

Through the shattered window, he saw that little remained of Ghulam's house. Half of the adjoining building had disappeared, leaving just a couple of devastated rooms overlooking a smouldering crater.

'Are you two okay?'

An upside-down Bury knelt next to Harvey's window.

'I'm . . . I think so. Sarah needs an ambulance.'

'There's one on its way.'

Thoughts of Bury's men leapt into Harvey's head, but the time to mourn them would have to wait. The only thing that mattered was making sure Sarah lived. She lay face down with her backside in the air, and his first thought was to get her into the recovery position, but that meant moving her, and there was no telling what damage had been done to her spine. Even shifting her a couple of inches could be enough to paralyse her permanently, so he made do with smoothing her hair out of the way and checking to make sure she was breathing. He found a piece of shattered mirror and held it to her nose and saw it cloud slightly, confirming that she was alive.

'Sarah? Can you hear me?'

Sarah remained unresponsive, and all Harvey could do was hold her hand gently until the sirens heralded the arrival of the ambulances. Three arrived within a minute, and the first of the paramedics helped Harvey from the car while the others determined how best to remove Sarah. One of them wanted to take a look at his facial wounds, but Harvey waved him off, pointing at Sarah.

'Be careful, she's pregnant.'

One medic crawled into the car and checked her over while Harvey stood back watching the men and women do their work. After a few minutes, a collar was placed around Sarah's neck before she was rolled gently onto a spine board and carried to a waiting ambulance. Harvey climbed inside with her and sat in a corner so that the staff could continue working on her.

'How is she?' he asked as the siren wailed and the vehicle pulled away.

'Responses are good, but we'll know more once she's had a proper examination. We've radioed ahead so they'll be expecting us.'

The medic asked Harvey what had happened, and he gave a full account of the explosion and the brief aftermath.

'You were lucky to get away with just a few cuts and bruises,' he said, but Harvey wasn't listening. He was staring at Sarah, who looked so vulnerable lying unconscious on the gurney.

The ambulance made short work of the traffic and stopped outside the A & E department six minutes later. Harvey followed the trolley through the maze of hallways as the ambulance staff passed on details of Sarah's condition. When they reached the trauma unit, he tried to enter but a nurse blocked his way.

'She'll be looked after. Come with me and we'll sort you out.'

Harvey watched the double doors close and reluctantly accepted the fact that Sarah's fate was out of his hands. He let the nurse lead him to a cubicle where she offered him a seat and asked what had happened. As Harvey recounted the incident, he suddenly realised that he owed an update to someone else. He took out his phone, but the screen was cracked and it refused to turn on.

'I need to make a call,' he said. 'It's urgent.'

'Let me take a look at that face of yours first.'

'It can't wait that long.' He explained who he worked for and was rewarded with a look of sardonic disbelief. Harvey guessed she'd heard a few tall tales in her time, and claiming to be working for MI5 on a matter of national security clearly hadn't convinced her.

'Just sit still while I remove these,' she said, picking a piece of glass from his cheek with a pair of tweezers. She placed it in a kidney dish and told him to close his eyes while she worked on a fragment near the top of his cheek.

After ten minutes, Harvey had received a tetanus shot and half a dozen butterfly stitches for his troubles. He thanked the nurse and went to the reception area to find a phone.

'What the hell happened?' Ellis asked when the call connected. 'It's all over the news.'

'I don't know. We were sitting fifty yards away when the house went up. There were about eight officers in there at the time. There's no way they could have survived that blast.'

'Are you both okay?'

'I'm fine,' Harvey said, 'but Sarah was knocked out. They're assessing her now.'

The line went quiet for a moment. 'Andrew, did Sarah confide in you in the last few days?'

Harvey immediately sensed that Ellis was talking about the baby, and felt a little hurt that he hadn't been the first to know. 'Yes, she told me that she's pregnant,' he said a little more abruptly than intended.

'She's a strong girl,' Ellis replied, unperturbed. 'Did anyone manage to speak to Ghulam before the explosion?'

'Whatever he said to the arresting officers died with them. They're gone, all eight of them. The place must have been rigged to blow.'

Another silence followed, and Harvey once again thought of the families who would be waiting for their fathers and husbands to come home, only to receive a visit from a ranking officer instead. The children waiting for Daddy to tuck them into bed and read them a story, and the wives awaiting their life partners, so they could share a meal and snuggle in front of the television.

'I want you back here as soon as Sarah's stable,' Ellis said, interrupting his thoughts. 'Godspeed, Andrew.'

The phone went dead, and Harvey went back to the trauma unit. He stood outside the room for a few minutes, until eventually a doctor appeared through the doors.

Harvey stepped in front of him. 'How's Sarah?'

'She's fine,' the doctor told him. 'She has a concussion and dislocated two fingers, but there's no internal bleeding. I understand you were sitting closest to the blast?'

'I was.'

'That was fortunate. For her, I mean. No offence.'

'None taken. Is the baby okay?'

'Absolutely fine. We did a scan and found a healthy heartbeat. There was no damage to her abdomen, but she has a nasty cut to the head that I want to keep an eye on, so we'll be keeping her in overnight.'

'Can I see her?' Harvey asked.

'In about half an hour. I've arranged for her to be taken up to the AMU. You can wait for her there.'

The doctor gave him directions to the acute medical unit, and Harvey stopped off for a coffee on the way.

Ellis's request for him to return to the office would have to wait.

CHAPTER 29

Thursday, 17 August 2017

As Harvey entered the office floor, several people left their desks to walk over and ask about Sarah.

'She's fine,' he assured them. 'She'll be out tomorrow, maybe the day after. In the meantime, we've got work to do. Hamad, did they find anything at the mosque?'

'No word yet.'

'Okay, in five minutes I want you to update me on everyone's progress with the mosque CCTV.'

Harvey walked over to the glass palace and Ellis waved him in.

'She's fine,' he pre-empted her. 'Home in a couple of days, back to work in a week or so.'

'Good to hear. I spoke with Bury over at SO15. Such a terrible loss. He confirmed that none of his men reported anything of use before the explosion.'

'That doesn't leave us much to work with, unless the CCTV we've been looking at throws up any clues. All I can suggest is that we bring in everyone else who was known to Khan, but this time take proper precautions. No more home visits, for a start.'

'What do you have in mind?'

'We're tracking their phones, which tells us where they are. Anyone out in the open can be picked up, but if they're at home we risk another explosion. I suggest we use Hamad's snitch, Samir, to lure anyone holed up out in the open. Make up some excuse for why he has to meet them. That way we can take them down before they cause any damage.'

'Sounds good to me,' Ellis agreed. 'While you do that, I have to go and see Maynard. It's time we briefed him on Khan's role in this.'

'Are you sure that's wise at this point?' Harvey asked. 'Granted, his men would be more likely to extract the information we need – *if* we manage to bring anyone in alive – but it would be an admission that we aren't up to the task.'

'I know, but what with the plane crash and now this bombing, he's demanding to know what's going on. Besides which, my priority is making sure we get the X3 before they get a chance to use it. I'll deal with the fallout afterwards. Now get Hamad to contact his informant and get things in motion.'

Ellis put on her coat and led Harvey out of her office, locking it behind them. While she headed for the exit, Harvey made his way to Farsi's desk.

'Have we identified anyone who could have taken the X3 from the mosque?'

'We may have. I gave Gareth Sarah's workload and it looks like he might have found something.'

Harvey walked over to Bailey's desk and stood behind him. On the screen, he saw images showing the platform of an Underground station.

'I thought Hamad asked you to cover Sarah's load.'

'He did,' Bailey confirmed. 'And I am. I sent you an email ten minutes ago.'

Harvey patted his pockets for his missing phone before remembering that it had been destroyed. 'I haven't had time to log in yet. What did it say?'

'At about ten to eight last night, people started arriving at the mosque. There were eight of them all together, all carrying backpacks. We weren't able to identify any of them as they were all wearing hoodies, as if to deliberately hide their faces. They stayed inside for about fifteen minutes, then they all left together and headed in different directions.'

'Sounds suspicious,' Harvey noted. Unfortunately, his people had been focusing on al-Hosni at the time, otherwise he would have had people on the ground who could have called it in.

'It gets better. I tracked the first one to a Tube station and watched him get on a train. Thing is, he never got off again. I checked every station on the line, and there's no sign of him.'

Harvey turned to Farsi. 'I'll get everyone working on these eight suspects. While we're doing that, get a real-time feed from GCHQ and track all known phones. If you spot anyone out and about, liaise with SO15 and pull them. I also need you to meet with Samir. We have to get him to lure the others in Khan's clique out into the open, otherwise there may be a repeat of what happened at Ghulam's place.'

'Samir's not that good an actor,' Farsi objected. 'And he'd need a damn convincing reason before anyone would drop what they're doing to meet up with him.'

'His addiction makes him sound permanently nervous anyway, so he doesn't need to be Laurence Olivier, but I want at least one person in the cells in the next hour. If SO15 can't provide any, it's up to Samir. Come up with something.'

Farsi went to make his calls while Harvey asked Bailey to show him the people leaving the mosque. After viewing the footage, he gathered everyone round and designated each suspect before assigning them to team members.

'According to Gareth, the one he followed didn't appear to get off the Tube, so we can assume he changed his appearance at some point. If you come up blank, go back and look for matching bags, build, height, whatever you can. We need to find these people.'

~

Aswan chewed ruefully on his chicken sandwich, barely tasting the mass-produced filling. His mind wouldn't let go of what lay in store for Samir, and he couldn't help but wonder how Khan planned to deal with his friend.

He'd thought long and hard about sending the text as instructed, but his fear of the imam had been the deciding factor. The message had been sent, and Samir had even replied to say he'd be at the coffee shop the following day.

Why did you have to do it, Samir?

He knew the answer even as the question formed in his mind. The heroin. He couldn't be sure when Samir had first fallen under its spell, but it had been at least a year. The transformation had been subtle, starting with the weight loss and followed by the sallow look and skin infection that affected his arms and face. During that time Samir had had a couple of menial labour jobs and was now being supported by government handouts, though it wasn't nearly enough to feed his habit. That explained the secret meeting he'd witnessed; the bundle Samir had accepted had to be payment in exchange for information about Khan.

Aswan had tried to get his friend off the stuff, offering to go with him to a support group, but Samir had attended the first session and skipped the rest, always finding an excuse not to show. In the end, he'd given up trying, but still kept an eye out for Samir.

Until now.

He thought about going round to see Samir and giving him enough money for one last hit, but he knew he wouldn't be able to hide his concern if Samir started asking questions about the upcoming meeting. It would also put himself in jeopardy if Khan had someone else watching Samir and, given the imam's cautious nature, that was a real possibility.

Aswan swallowed the last mouthful and drained his drink, then walked out of the fast-food restaurant and towards the music shop.

'Get down on the ground!'

The armed police officers had appeared from nowhere, weapons pointing at his head.

Aswan briefly considered running, but the chances of him getting more than a few feet were slim to none. Four officers were now screaming at him to drop, and he slowly raised his hands and fell to his knees before lying face down on the pavement. Two of the cops held their weapons on him while the other pair performed a perfunctory search and applied the handcuffs.

'What is this?' Aswan asked as he was hauled to his feet. 'What's going on?'

The police ignored his questions and bundled him into the back of a car, then hit the sirens as it weaved its way through afternoon traffic.

After a ten-minute dash, the driver pulled into an underground car park and stopped near an open metal door. Aswan was pulled out of the car and marched to the entrance to the building, which looked newly painted in sterile white emulsion. He was led to a cell and forced inside, his escorts remaining silent throughout.

As the door clanged shut, Aswan sat on the bunk that was built into the wall. It didn't seem like any police station he'd ever been in, and the fact that he hadn't been booked in was strange, too. He'd had a couple of run-ins with the law, once for refusing to move on when a demonstration had turned ugly and the other time for being driven in a stolen car, so he was familiar with normal police procedures.

This was not normal.

The cell door opened and two armed guards ushered him to his feet. They led Aswan along a corridor and pushed him into a room where a metal table took centre stage. Two chairs faced each other, and Aswan's cuffs were removed before he was forced into the one with the leads dangling from it. He started bucking as he imagined being strapped into an electric chair, but two more guards appeared and held him down while his wrists and ankles were secured.

'Is someone going to tell me what the fuck is going on?' Aswan shouted, but the guards ignored him and attached electrodes to his temple and arms. That done, they left the room and Aswan alone with his fear.

He was now certain that he wasn't in the hands of the police. If he had been, he would have expected them to read him his rights and offer access to a lawyer, but so far no-one had said a word to him. He didn't think a phone call would be on the cards any time soon, either.

Could these be the same people who had abducted Imran al-Hosni? Whoever they were, it smelled a lot like the security services.

Aswan tried to think what they could possibly have on him, but nothing leapt to mind. He certainly wasn't stupid enough to have incriminating evidence on his phone or computer, and a search of his house wouldn't reveal anything to link him to terrorism. All they really had was the fact that he attended the same place of worship as Muhammad Khan, who was well known to the police. It certainly wasn't enough to arrest him. Aswan felt more confident as he processed the thought.

Then he remembered Samir. The man his friend had met at the café must have been from the police or MI5, which meant they knew about the plan to use the nerve agent. Aswan had been there the night Khan had told the small congregation about al-Hosni's plot, which put him in a tough position. He'd known a woman who had been jailed for not alerting the authorities to her husband's activities – some law about not informing the police about a possible terror attack. If they were going to level the same charge at him, it would be his word against Samir's.

Could he convince them that Samir was lying simply to feed his addiction? It was worth a try, but it would almost certainly go to trial, and convincing twelve jurors that Samir was unreliable would be difficult. In fact, if the agent were released as planned, it would prove that Samir had been telling the truth, leaving him with no defence whatsoever.

Aswan desperately sought a way out of the mess. He could try to bluff his way through it, or come clean and help in any way he could. The former option, if it failed, would see him spend the vast majority of his life behind bars, and for what? It wasn't as if he truly believed Khan's rhetoric. The reason he remained loyal was down to fear of the man, not any deep belief in his teachings. He'd read enough of the Quran as a boy to know the true meaning of the scriptures, but once he'd heard Khan's sermons, he'd soon realised that the new imam was manipulating the verses to his own ends. By the time he saw the true intent of the man, it was too late to do anything but go with the flow for fear of retribution.

An idea formed in his head, relaxing him slightly by the time the door opened and a tall, fit-looking man entered. The newcomer took the seat opposite him.

'My name's Andrew,' he said. 'I want to ask you some questions about Muhammad Khan.'

'Only if you tell me what organisation you're from,' Aswan said. 'You're not the police, I know that much.'

'I'm with MI5.'

Aswan sat back in his chair and exhaled loudly, hoping to give the impression that he was relieved. 'You're just the people I was coming to speak to.'

The man opposite looked at him questioningly. 'Really?'

'Yeah. I've got news about an attack. It's gonna take place tomorrow.'

'And when did you discover this?'

'Yesterday. Khan held a meeting and told us that Imran al-Hosni has something in place. I was coming to tell you when I got arrested.'

'If you heard yesterday, why didn't you come to us sooner?'

'I was scared,' Aswan said. 'If Khan finds out I've spoken to you, he'll kill me. I need protection.'

Andrew stared at him, and Aswan was beginning to feel like his bluff was about to be called.

'Why would a man in your position suddenly decide to tell us about the attack?'

'It's the right thing to do. Khan is using Islam as an excuse to promote his own dangerous ideology. If you can protect me from him, I'll tell you everything I know.'

The man opposite him mulled it over for a while. 'Okay,' he eventually said, 'I promise Khan will never hear about your co-operation.'

'I want a guarantee, in writing.'

'I can do better than that. Khan's dead.'

The news stunned Aswan. He wondered how it would affect his story. Would it be a benefit, or conspire against him? With Khan dead, there was no-one to contradict him, so that was a bonus.

If his interrogator were telling the truth.

'How do I know you're not lying?'

Andrew turned towards the large mirror on the wall. 'Bring his phone in here.'

The door buzzed open and a guard entered carrying Aswan's mobile.

'Free one of his arms so that he can use it,' Andrew said, 'but keep your gun on him.'

Once Aswan's right arm was unrestrained, Andrew handed him his phone. 'Do a search for Muhammad Khan and see what comes up.'

Aswan held the phone in his left hand while he searched online for the imam. One of the first hits was the BBC news website, and he clicked on the link to see an image of a burnt-out light aircraft. He quickly read the story, then looked up at Andrew.

'How do I know you didn't plant this so that I would believe you?'

'Search again,' Andrew told him. 'Putting a fake story on the BBC news website would be one thing, but to get every news outlet to pick it up would be impossible.'

That made sense. To be sure, Aswan went back to his search results and saw hundreds of listings from news organisations around the world. He went to the third page and clicked on a link. Sure enough, Khan was dead.

'Tell me how it happened,' Aswan said.

'He was trying to leave the country,' Andrew said, indicating to the guard to take the phone and restrain Aswan once more. 'That plane was supposed to pick him up and take him to Denmark but it was shot down by the local police.'

Aswan frowned; something didn't add up. He recalled his last conversation with Khan, when he'd been ordered to send the text message to Samir.

Tell him to take a seat outside. I will take care of matters once he arrives.

If Khan intended to kill Samir, why had he tried to leave the country? It could only mean that the imam planned to have someone else deal with him. Which meant Aswan had the chance to save his friend's life without repercussions. That was, if he could convince Andrew to take down Khan's right-hand man.

'I don't know anything else about the attack, only that al-Hosni was going to carry it out tomorrow. But Khan had me set someone up. He's going to be killed tomorrow, too. At lunchtime.'

'Are you talking about Samir?'

Aswan was initially taken aback, but then he remembered Samir's meeting with the mystery man who paid him. Also MI5, as he'd suspected. Of course MI5 would know about his text message to Samir.

They probably had a record of every text he'd ever sent, as well as recordings of all his conversations.

'Yes, Samir. I thought Khan was going to do it personally, but clearly not. The only other person I can think of is Adnan Ghulam. He does enforcement work for Khan.'

'Then I think Samir's quite safe. Ghulam killed himself today.'

Aswan looked at his phone for a moment, then decided to believe Agent Harvey. He'd never liked Ghulam; it was a blessing that both he and Khan were dead.

'I'm glad to hear it.'

'He took eight officers with him,' Andrew added, and Aswan's head dropped.

'I'm sorry. You might still want to warn Samir, though. I could've been wrong about Ghulam.'

'I will, but first tell me about the rest of Khan's friends. We know Ghulam brought a nerve agent to the mosque, but the police have turned the place upside down and there's no sign of it. Do you know who he might have given it to?'

'Wait. *Khan* had a nerve agent?'

'That's right,' Andrew said. 'Al-Hosni was a decoy, designed to make us concentrate on the wrong man while Khan made his preparations, but he gave it to someone. I need to know who.'

Aswan racked his brains. There were quite a few who associated with Khan – at least, they had before his death – but none of them seemed the kind to take part in an attack. Still, he reeled their names off, aware that someone behind the fake mirror was probably taking notes.

'We're already in the process of rounding them up, but none of them fit the profile. The youngest is in his mid-forties, whereas you're barely into your twenties.'

Aswan frowned. 'You think I've got this nerve agent?'

'You're in the right age bracket, you've been one of Khan's followers for quite a while, and after the run-around we've been given, it wouldn't surprise me if this "confession" of yours is just another attempt to steer us in the wrong direction.'

'So keep me here until someone else uses the stuff,' Aswan said confidently, 'and then you'll see I'm innocent.'

'Unless it's set to go off remotely,' Andrew said, his eyes fixed on Aswan's. 'Then you'll be back in the frame.'

Aswan hadn't considered that possibility, and for a brief moment he felt panic begin to claw at his chest. But something told him it wasn't the imam's style.

'I've listened to enough of Khan's sermons,' he said. 'He pushes the idea of martyrdom too hard to rely on a timer or anything like that. Having someone sacrifice their life makes more of a statement about commitment to Islam than planting a bomb and detonating it remotely.'

'Then tell me who has it so that we can stop them. In particular, I want to know about eight people who showed up at the mosque yesterday at eight in the evening.'

That was news to Aswan. The building was normally closed at that time on a Wednesday night, which made these visitors highly suspicious. The trouble was, he had no idea who they could be.

'If you show me their pictures, I might recognise some of them.'

'If we had pictures, I wouldn't be asking you,' Andrew said, clearly annoyed with his answer. 'All we have is CCTV of them entering and then leaving again a few minutes later. They were deliberately covering their faces.' The agent shrugged and gave Aswan a hard stare.

Damn. Aswan felt as frustrated as Harvey looked. If MI5 couldn't identify the men from the footage, though, it was unlikely that he'd recognise any of them.

Still, he had to try. If he could be seen to be helping, they might start believing the truth: that he had nothing to do with any attack.

'Can I see the footage? There might be something about them that rings a bell.'

Andrew thought about it for some time, and just as Aswan was expecting to have his request denied, he looked over to the mirror.

'Bring me a laptop.'

A couple of minutes later the door buzzed open and a woman placed a notebook in front of Andrew. He tapped at the keys, then turned it to face Aswan.

Aswan saw the familiar entrance to the building, and almost immediately the first figure entered the shot. It was soon apparent that Andrew had been right: the person on the screen was dressed for anonymity. More people appeared on the screen, but as with the first, there was nothing distinguishable about them.

It wasn't until the sixth person arrived that Aswan had anything to go on. The man only entered the shot for a couple of seconds, but there was something about the hoodie he was wearing that struck a chord.

'Can you rewind that bit?'

Andrew, who had been staring at him again – probably looking for tell-tale facial indicators – came around the table and moved the recording back a few seconds.

'There!' Aswan said. 'Pause it.'

The screen froze, and Aswan leaned in for a closer look. 'Can you zoom in?'

Andrew used the touch pad to enlarge the image, and Aswan was convinced that he knew the boy on the screen.

'That's Faysal Nejem. He never goes anywhere without that hoodie.'

Andrew panned out and restarted the footage. 'Let me know if you spot anyone else.'

Aswan watched the feed to the end. He shook his head; nothing else stood out.

'Tell me about Faysal,' Andrew said.

'He's one of the kids that hangs around the mosque. There's a few from troubled backgrounds, and Khan held private sessions with them most days. I don't know what went on, but Khan said they were lost souls, and he was leading them back to the righteous path.'

Even as he spoke the words, the true meaning became apparent. He'd met some of the kids, and they weren't the sharpest tools in the box. A couple came from broken homes, while Faysal himself had run away from an abusive father when he was fifteen. After being introduced to Khan and explaining his plight, Faysal had been given accommodation in return for attending regular religious counselling.

'I want the names of all of them,' Andrew said, moving the laptop over to his own side of the table.

Aswan listed as many as he could remember. 'I didn't meet all of them. They'd turn up for prayers, then go straight into their sessions with Khan. We weren't exactly encouraged to talk to them.'

Andrew closed down the laptop, then carried it to the door, where he paused.

'If I bring these kids in, what are the chances they'll be as co-operative as you?'

Aswan shrugged. 'Hard to say. A couple were happy to talk about their problems at home, but when I asked them about the private sessions, they clammed up. One said it was extra prayers, that's it.'

Aswan heard the door buzz and then lock again a few seconds later, and he wondered if he'd done enough to end this nightmare.

~

Harvey took the lift back up to the office and swiped his way in.

'I've got some names,' he said, getting everyone's attention. 'First step, match them to addresses and use CCTV to see if they arrived home late yesterday evening. If they did, track their movements. I want to see if we can place any of them at the mosque at eight o'clock. Let me know the second you get a hit.'

He read off the names Aswan had provided, then went to fill Ellis in.

'We're making progress,' he told her as he closed the glass door behind him. After a rundown on developments, he voiced his only concern.

'We're fast running out of time, and even if we bring them in, I'm not sure we'll be able to get them talking before it's too late.'

'Something tells me you have an idea.' Ellis frowned. 'One I'm not going to like.'

'The Home Secretary is happy to use E Squadron to interrogate prisoners. I suggest we do the same.'

'Hand everything over to Maynard?'

'God, no! I might as well resign now. No, I was thinking of using our own specialists.'

Ellis looked uneasy. 'If you're talking about Tom Gray, forget it. For one, we'd never get him here in time, and two, trouble follows him around. Nothing is ever black and white with Gray, if you'll pardon the pun.'

Harvey knew Ellis wasn't keen in involving Gray in any official work, despite the debt they both owed him. Gray and a handful of friends had risked their lives to free Harvey from Russian separatists, and although the man had a chequered history, he was as loyal as they came.

'Not Tom, but a couple of his friends.'

'Smart and Baines?'

'The very same. You told me yourself that they had no hesitation in volunteering their services when I was stuck in Tagrilistan. I'm sure they wouldn't mind taking part in a less dangerous mission a little closer to home.'

'Oh, I'm sure they'd jump at the chance, but if we ask SO15 to pick up the suspects and drop them off at the offices of two men who were once the subject of a nationwide manhunt, someone's going to start asking questions.'

'What if I told you I had a way around that?'

Ellis sighed. 'I was afraid you were going to say that.'

Harvey smiled, then let her know what he had in mind. Ellis picked a few holes in his idea, but after a few minutes, they had something both agreed was workable.

'When you call them, use a clean phone. I don't want this coming back to bite us.'

'I'll have to. Mine was destroyed in the blast. Still, I'd prefer to meet them in person. I'll sound them out, and once we get a hit on a suspect we'll get moving.'

When Harvey returned to the main floor, he learned that they had matched addresses to four of the six names, and the team had identified two of the hooded subjects entering their homes at just after ten at night. They were currently backtracking to see where they'd been that evening.

'How did we get on with the earlier tracking?' Harvey asked Farsi.

'We lost all eight when they got on public transport. I've requested on-board CCTV coverage, but they want a court order before they release anything.'

'You explained how serious it was?'

'I did,' Farsi said, 'but the jobsworths have forms to complete and boxes to tick. We won't be able to speak to a judge until tomorrow morning, then another couple of hours to study the footage. It'll be too late by then.'

'Then forget it. If we lost them on public transport, it's because they changed their appearance. You say we tracked two of them to their homes?'

Farsi nodded.

'Then backtrack their journeys that night. Once you lose them, make a note of the train or bus they used and cross-reference it with the eight youths from the mosque. If one of those used the same transport, we have our match.'

'You hope.'

'It's all we've got,' Harvey said. 'If that doesn't work, we have to pull them all in and make them feel chatty.'

'Even if we do get a hit, there's no guarantee they'll co-operate.'

Harvey smiled. 'Let's get a coffee and meet some old friends.'

~

Len Smart looked up from his Kindle as the door to his office opened and a short, blond man walked in and dumped himself in the chair opposite his desk.

'Don't you ever knock?' Smart asked.

'If I did, would you let me in?'

Smart briefly considered the question. 'No, I wouldn't.'

He returned to his e-reader, but Simon 'Sonny' Baines wasn't about to give him the peace he desired.

'Whatcha reading, boss?'

Smart still hadn't got used to the title, and when it came from Sonny it somehow sounded like an insult. Even though Smart looked the part, with his balding head and bushy moustache – and, he had to admit, he felt comfortable in the suit and tie – he sometimes yearned for the days when he'd been up to his neck in mud or sand rather than negotiating international contracts.

Up until a couple of years ago, he'd been just another name on a long list of ex-soldiers doing security work for Tom Gray's company Minotaur Logistics. After his name hit the headlines for all the wrong reasons, Gray had been forced to restructure his entire business in a bid to obfuscate his identity as owner. It had worked for a while, until a tenacious tabloid reporter dug deep enough to reveal Gray's involvement. In the days following publication of the article, clients had jumped ship rather than be seen associating with a man who had

240

once held five criminals to ransom. Gray had seen no alternative but to resign his position and dub his most trusted friend Len Smart the new managing director. Gray still had shares in the business, but these were managed anonymously by an overseas holding company, with Gray drawing a monthly salary that was paid via his solicitor.

Now and again, Gray would call to catch up and see how the business was doing, but for the most part, he left Smart to manage things. From what Tom said, the country life in rural Italy seemed to be fitting him and his young daughter well.

'It's called *Wicked Game* by Matt Johnson. It's about an ex-22 who had a part to play in Operation Nimrod, and his past comes back to haunt him.'

Sonny snorted. 'Those books are never realistic.'

'It's a lot more gripping and believable than the bullshit you use to pull women.'

'Hey, those are all true stories.'

Smart cocked an eye. 'Like the time you single-handedly wiped out an entire company of Revolutionary Guard during Desert Storm?'

'I did so!' Sonny objected. 'Well, granted, the company had been reduced to just a couple of blokes by the time the American A-10s were done with them, but they put up a hell of a fight.'

'I was there, remember? It was two guys standing in the open and firing in your general direction. Gray's three-year-old daughter could have taken them down.'

It hadn't really been that simple, and Sonny's shooting had been exemplary, but Smart had learned long ago not to feed his friend's ego.

Sonny, so named because he'd looked like a fresh-faced fifteen-year-old when he'd tackled the SAS selection process, despite being in his late twenties at the time, still retained his boyish countenance today. Smart marvelled at how kind time had been to him. While his own waist seemed to grow with each passing day, Sonny still looked like a fitness coach in his early thirties, though in reality they were both creeping up on their fiftieth birthdays.

Despite all the banter, Smart could not have wished for a better friend.

'So what brings you here?' he asked.

'I'm a little short.'

'You're telling me,' Smart said. 'You're the only man I know who had to use a step ladder to reach puberty!'

'Ah, the old ones are the best. But seriously, my salary didn't go in this month.'

'Yeah, there was an issue at the bank, but I sorted it. The money should be in your account by the end of the day.'

The phone on Smart's desk buzzed and Gill, the receptionist, announced the arrival of two visitors.

'We've got company,' Smart told Sonny, and his face lit up when he walked out of the room. 'Andrew! Hamad! Good to see you!'

He gave them each a bear hug, then asked Gill to provide some coffee as he showed them into his office. Sonny likewise greeted them with a hug, then ushered them into chairs before sitting on Smart's desk.

'What can we do for you guys?' Smart asked. 'Is this a social visit, or have you finally come to arrest Sonny for crimes against my sanity?'

'It's business,' Harvey said, as Gill arrived with a pot of Smart's favourite roast and four cups. He waited until she'd left the room before continuing. 'We have a delicate matter that needs to be kept off the books, if you know what I mean.'

Sonny smacked Smart's desktop. 'Count us in!'

'Hold on,' Smart said, raising a hand. 'We haven't heard the proposal yet.'

'Whatever it is, it has to be more exhilarating than screwing up the payroll. We're in.'

'Len's right,' Harvey said. 'You should hear us out first.'

'If you insist, but you're just prolonging the inevitable.'

Harvey spent the next five minutes briefing them on the current operation, then explained the role he wanted them to undertake.

'Like I said, we'll do it,' Sonny said.

This time, Smart agreed.

They spent another ten minutes tweaking the plan, which entailed bringing in a third person, then Harvey stood and drained his cup. 'Gentlemen, a pleasure, as always. I'll be in touch when we're ready to go.'

Smart walked them to the front door. When he returned, he found Sonny grinning like a Cheshire cat.

'I don't know what you're smiling at. I'm not paying you overtime for this.'

~

They were ten minutes from Thames House when Harvey's phone rang.

'It's Elaine,' he told Farsi, who was driving.

He answered the call and listened while Solomon brought him up to speed.

'Okay, put SO15 on standby. I'll call you back.'

He told Farsi that they'd traced one of the mystery eight, Faysal Nejem, to his home. He looked up the address on a replacement phone he'd got from Gerald Small.

'It's near Armistone Park. Call Samir and tell him to text this guy for a meet there in one hour. That'll give us time to get into position.'

Farsi used his hands-free kit to make the call while Harvey phoned Solomon back with detailed instructions. Once he'd done that, he checked the map again and used a burner phone he'd picked up to call Len Smart. The conversation was short, and ten minutes later Farsi pulled over near the entrance to the park. His phone beeped twice, and he checked the incoming text message.

'Samir says Nejem will be here at seven. That gives us forty-five minutes to get everyone in place.'

With a quarter of an hour to go, there was a knock on Harvey's window and he recognised Sergeant Bury from SO15. He was glad to see the man had followed his suggestion and changed into plain clothes.

'I've got three men with me,' Bury said when Harvey wound his window down. 'Two are dressed as joggers and the other one is walking his German shepherd. We borrowed him from the Met's dog squad.'

'Good. Have them standing by. Once the suspects arrive we'll make ourselves scarce, then I'll call you and you take them down when you're ready.'

He'd already informed Bury that Samir was working on their behalf, but in order to protect the snitch, he would be arrested as well. It would mean, at most, a couple of hours spent in a cell before being released without charge. Samir also knew the score; for an extra couple of hundred pounds, he'd readily agreed.

Bury returned to his unmarked car, and the waiting began.

CHAPTER 30

Thursday, 17 August 2017

Faysal Nejem wore his hoodie up, despite the warm evening. It was something Khan had drilled into him, especially when he was due to meet anyone away from the mosque.

He took a bus to within two hundred yards of Armistone Park, then walked with his head down to defeat the gaze of the street cameras. Now and again he would stop to peer into a shop window, looking for any sign that he was being followed. He repeated the manoeuvre half a dozen times before he was happy that he hadn't picked up a tail.

As he reached the entrance to the park, a Ford containing two men pulled away without giving him a second glance. Still, he scanned the area for anyone taking an interest in him.

All clear.

Faysal checked his watch. He was five minutes early, and he began to wonder what last-minute instructions Khan had passed to Samir. Of all people, he couldn't understand why the imam would entrust a drug addict like Samir with anything more important than a shopping list, never mind instructions to be carried out in the event of his death.

He'd seen the announcement on the news, and while it had saddened him, Samir's text message had been a timely reminder that he still had work to do.

Faysal entered the park and saw Samir sitting on a bench a hundred yards away to his right. As he strolled towards him, he kept checking the trees and bushes but saw no hidden cameramen or snipers waiting to take him down.

When he reached the bench, he sat and took in the people making the most of the glorious evening. A couple with a young child were enjoying a late picnic on the grass, while a dog walker struggled with half a dozen hounds of varying breeds and sizes. Nobody looked out of place. Faysal began to relax a little.

'What did you need to tell me?' he asked Samir, who looked desperately in need of another fix. He was sweating, not just because of the heat, and his hands wouldn't stop moving.

'Khan left you a message, but he told me not to bring it with me or tell you about it over the phone. You're to go to . . .'

Faysal stopped listening as someone walking an Alsatian approached from his left. The man couldn't seem to take his eyes off the pair, and Faysal immediately sensed danger.

The message from Khan forgotten, he got up and started walking away. When the dog began barking, he broke into a sprint. Two joggers were heading towards him, and he ran onto the grass to avoid them, but they mirrored his move and produced handguns.

'Stop! Police!'

Faysal had no intention of obeying them, despite the weapons pointing at him. He dashed to their left and awaited the sound of their firearms, but all he heard was his own rapid breathing as he ran for his life.

He was twenty yards from the exit when his escape came to an abrupt halt. One minute his arms were pumping freely, and the next he was anchored by a hundred pounds of snarling German shepherd.

The animal clamped its jaws around his lower arm and dragged him to the ground, where it continued to growl as it shook its head violently. Faysal tried digging his thumb into the beast's eye, but it easily shook off his clumsy attempts.

The two panting joggers arrived and stood over him, their pistols trained on his head despite his predicament. The dog handler finally turned up and persuaded the hound to release him, and Faysal clutched his mangled arm. Blood was already seeping through the sleeve of his hoodie, but before he could examine the damage, one of the cops slapped cuffs on his good hand and flipped him over onto his stomach. His other arm was cuffed, and then the policeman patted him down before slipping a hand under his armpit and hoisting him to his feet.

Faysal looked around and saw that Samir had also been cuffed and was being led away to the park's entrance.

Don't tell them anything.

Khan's warning came back in a rush. So far, it had been unnecessary. Even now, as the cops forced him out of the park, his escorts remained silent. That suited him fine. Once they reached the police station, he would demand treatment for his injuries, and after that, he would exercise his right to silence.

When they exited the park, Faysal saw the same Ford that had pulled away when he'd arrived, two men standing next to it. More plain-clothed officers, he assumed.

One of them opened the rear door and forced Faysal inside. The taller of the two joined him on the back seat while the other took the wheel. Neither spoke as the car pulled away.

What could they possibly want with me?

He hadn't accessed any prohibited material on the internet, nor had he ever used his phone for anything even remotely incriminating. Perhaps they wanted to know what had gone on in his private sessions with Khan, but if that was the case, they were going to be sorely disappointed.

'We've got a tail,' the driver said. 'White Transit van.'

'You sure?' the other asked.

'He's been behind us for the last three turns, but I'll try the back streets, just to be sure.'

The driver turned off the main road and drove down residential streets, all the while checking his mirrors.

'He's still with us. Should we call it in?'

'I think we should. It might be DTI, in which case Faysal here could be in real trouble. Remember what they did to al-Hosni.'

'Yeah, poor bastard. No-one deserves to go like that.'

'Who are DTI?' Faysal asked before he could stop himself.

'Death to Islam,' the rear passenger said. 'They're a splinter neo-Nazi group, most of 'em ex-military, and they hate everything about your people. They have quite a network, and we believe they have contacts within the police, because they tend to target people who are under investigation. DTI think we spend too much time and money building cases against terror suspects who either won't talk or are released due to lack of evidence. Their preferred method is to snatch 'em, torture 'em to death and move on to the next person in the chain.'

'I've never heard of them,' Faysal said.

'That's because we make a huge effort to keep them out of the news. Giving them airtime is what they crave, so we monitor the net for signs of their activity and close them down. Unfortunately, that's only made 'em bolder. They've kidnapped four terror suspects in the last six months and all of them turned up dead.'

'I called it in,' the driver said. 'They're sending a weapons team to the industrial estate near here. They don't want to take them down where there's lots of witnesses, otherwise the press might get wind of it.'

'Okay, let's lead them there, but make sure . . .'

A Transit van pulled out of a side street, blocking the road, and the driver slammed on the brakes to avoid a collision. Faysal was restrained by his seat belt, but his face still struck the back of the seat in front of him, breaking his nose. By the time his vision had cleared, the door was open and he was being pulled out of the car, blood pouring down his face and neck. He heard a pop as a silenced pistol blew a hole in the tyre, then the warm barrel of the gun was shoved into the side of his neck.

'Move!'

The balaclava-clad gunman didn't wait for him to respond. He marched Faysal towards the van that had been following them, pushed him into the back and slammed the door closed.

'Go!'

Tyres screeched as the vehicle reversed at speed, then spun around and took off. Every time it went round a corner, Faysal was thrown up against the side walls, and with his hands secured behind his back, he was powerless to prevent his head pounding against metal. The punishment continued for another five minutes, when the van came to a halt and the rear doors opened.

Faysal was dragged out by his feet, and his head inevitably hit the concrete floor, sending a bolt of pain through his body. His captors pulled him to his feet and led him into a dark hallway, then down a set of wooden stairs to a dank basement. The smaller one turned on a light and Faysal could see a metal chair in the centre of the room, and next to it was a table adorned with an array of tools.

The fear that had been growing inside him turned to full-blown panic. He tried to twist out of the big man's grip, but his strength was no match for the hooded figure, who spun him around and forced him into the seat. Just as quickly, a rope looped around his chest, pinning him to the backrest. He made one last attempt at freedom as they tried to secure his ankles, but a punch to the head knocked the last of the fight out of him.

The two men stood before him, unreadable eyes staring at him from beneath the balaclavas, the silence almost unbearable. To Faysal, the glare felt as excruciating as the pain he knew was coming. He glanced over at the table, and immediately regretted it. Just thinking about the agony they could inflict with the hammer, knives and pliers was enough to loosen his sphincter.

'You're scared,' the smaller one said. 'That's a good thing. Give in to the fear, answer our questions and we'll let you go. You're not the one we want, but you have the information we need.'

Something in Faysal wanted to nod his agreement, but Khan's words once again played in his head.

Pain is temporary, fleeting, a reminder that while you walk among the living you will never be truly at peace. Only through self-sacrifice will you receive Allah's blessings and eternal bliss.

'We'll give you a couple of minutes to think about it,' the larger one told him, 'then we'll start asking questions. If you tell us what we want to know, we'll set you free. If you don't, we'll remove these.' He pointed to his headgear. 'Once you've seen our faces, your fate's sealed. Then it's just a matter of how much pain you can endure before you die.'

Silence descended once more, and conflicting thoughts battled for control of Faysal's mind.

Pain is temporary, fleeting . . .

The words suddenly sounded hollow, spoken by a man who wasn't facing an agonising death . . . but to give in now meant relinquishing his place in the afterlife for eternity.

'You visited the mosque at eight o'clock last night. Who else was there?'

Faysal looked up at his captors, and a single tear ran down his bloodstained cheek.

'I have nothing to say.'

The taller one removed his balaclava, revealing a balding head and moustache. It wasn't what Faysal had been expecting. He'd envisioned a tattooed Neanderthal, not someone who looked like they'd come from a boardroom meeting.

'Pity,' the man said, tossing his mask aside. 'Sonny, gag him. I think we'll start with the pliers . . .'

~

Harvey finished typing up his report into Faysal's abduction and printed out a hard copy for Ellis to check and sign. He'd omitted his conversation with Farsi regarding DTI, nor had he mentioned the van that had been following them. He'd simply stated that Hamad had taken to the side roads to avoid traffic and the van had pulled out in front of them. Before they knew it, an armed man with dark forearms had snatched Nejem, blown out their tyre and driven off. Unfortunately, the dashboard camera had been knocked out of position at some point during the day, and all it managed to capture was black plastic and a tiny sliver of the bottom of the windscreen. Harvey had made the description of the attacker as vague as possible, underestimating the height by six inches and taking fifty pounds off Smart's actual weight.

It was the same story he'd told Bury when he'd turned up, though Harvey had given Smart a few minutes to clear the area before calling it in.

Harvey took the printout to Ellis's office and stood silently while she read through it.

'Sounds plausible to me. Nice touch on the description, too. That'll make them think one of Faysal's friends came to his rescue.' Ellis put down the paper and looked up at Harvey. 'How did it actually go?'

'Like clockwork. We planted the seed of fear in the kid's mind. Hopefully he'll talk before Len and Sonny have to get physical.'

'And you're okay with it if they do?'

'We need to find the nerve agent,' Harvey shrugged. 'If Faysal isn't helping us, he's against us. I'm not sorry, if that's what you're asking.'

'Good. I don't want you getting squeamish on me. Did the police find anything at Nejem's house?'

'Nothing. Looks like one of the other seven has the X3. We've identified one of them and SO15 will take him down tonight. We're just waiting on Len to get the names of the other six.'

Ellis looked at her watch. 'They've had him for a few hours. We'd have heard by now if he was being helpful.'

'Then it's just a matter of time,' Harvey said, as the clock on the wall ticked past midnight and into Friday morning.

CHAPTER 31

Friday, 18 August 2017

Harvey awakened to the sound of an unfamiliar buzzing, and it took him a moment to realise that it was coming from his untraceable mobile phone.

'Did you get it?' he asked, careful not to mention Smart's name.

'All seven.'

'Thanks,' Harvey said, very much relieved. 'I'll meet you in twenty minutes.'

He went to the bathroom and threw cold water on his face, then checked his watch. It was far too early to call for an update on Sarah, but he couldn't stop thinking about her, despite the fact that she was in safe hands. He'd managed a few minutes on the phone with her the previous evening and that had only made him miss her more. Thankfully, she would be released from hospital later in the morning, and he'd be able to fuss over her himself.

Once he'd eliminated the threat of the X3.

Harvey made his way down to the underground car park. It was a short drive to the rendezvous point, and traffic was almost non-existent at four in the morning. Smart was already waiting by the time he arrived.

'Judging by the time, I'm guessing you had to be persuasive.'

'He was a brave kid,' Smart said, as he handed over a sheet of paper, and Harvey thought he detected a note of respect in the ex-soldier's voice.

'Is everything clean?'

'We used false plates for the vans and took the route you gave us, so we avoided CCTV cameras. Sonny's dealing with the last loose end as we speak.'

'As long as it won't be discovered for a few years, I don't need to know the details.'

'No chance of that happening,' Smart said. 'Unless someone decides to dredge five miles off the Kent coast.'

Harvey was sure that Sonny would be more thorough than to just dump the body overboard, so the chances of anyone coming across the corpse would indeed be remote.

Harvey shook Smart's hand. 'Thanks. We'll be in touch in a couple of months to offer you some legitimate work. Say, forty hours of security consultation at two hundred an hour? That should more than cover your expenses for today.'

'Much appreciated,' Smart said. 'I just hope it was worth it.'

Me, too, Harvey thought as he walked back towards his car, mindful that on top of a kidnapping charge, he was now an accessory to murder.

It wasn't something he would have ever foreseen when he'd joined the service nearly two decades earlier, but the threats they now faced were quite different. Peace had broken out in Northern Ireland back in the late nineties, and the PIRA ceasefire meant a switch of focus to the Middle East, though that had generally been seen as an issue affecting the US rather than Western Europe.

That had all changed following 9/11, which led to the US/UK invasion of Iraq. That in turn made Britain a legitimate target in Al-Qaeda's eyes, and the Islamic terror organisation was a completely different proposition to the Provisional IRA. For one, the Irish would telephone warnings before detonating a bomb, whereas Al-Qaeda would strike without notice.

The geographical difference was immense, too. The PIRA had been concentrated in a relatively small area, while Bin Laden's people were a global phenomenon.

Perhaps the biggest contrast, though, was loyalty to the cause. From the early eighties, dozens of arrested paramilitaries had turned on their own and divulged the identities of compatriots in exchange for immunity from prosecution. In the realm of Islamic extremists, the supergrass was unheard of. Now and then, MI5 would get access to someone low in the food chain, unfortunate souls like Samir, but it was rare for them to come up with anything of major value. Experience had taught him that those more closely involved in operations would rather die than give up information, and Faysal Nejem had been a prime example.

It hadn't given him any pleasure arranging the boy's death, but unless they adapted to the enemy's strengths, the battles – and perhaps the war itself – would be lost.

He thought of Sarah once more, and wondered what she would have had to say about Nejem's fate. Would she have gone along with it, agreeing that the end justified the means? Harvey wasn't so sure. Sarah had a social conscience, and while his opinion sometimes differed from hers, he respected her stance. In this case, he felt sure that she'd have stood in the opposite corner and argued against torturing the boy . . . which begged the question: should he tell her about it?

The easy answer was no, but could he trust Farsi and Ellis to keep it between them? He felt he could, for now at least. That would give him time to revisit the issue, once the current crisis was over.

Harvey got into his car and drove back to the office. Ellis would be back in at six, preferring to sleep in her own bed rather than the makeshift sleeping quarters at Thames House.

He had a feeling she wouldn't be distraught at Nejem's death, either.

~

It was eight in the morning by the time SO15 were ready to execute warrants at the homes of the remaining six subjects. The locations were spread out over London, and Harvey had decided to remain in the office to oversee matters rather than try to guess which one might have the X3.

His cell phone rang, and the commander of SO15, Elias Burke, informed him that the teams had been given the go-ahead, which meant half a dozen people were about to choke on their cornflakes as their front doors smashed in. Harvey kept the line open so that the commander could feed him real-time updates, and within a couple of minutes, four teams had reported arrests. Another one came in shortly afterwards, but the news from the last address was less than stellar.

'The flat's empty,' Burke reported.

'Which one was it?'

'Iqbal al-Mubari.'

Harvey jotted down the name. 'Let's hope one of the other five have what we're looking for.'

Even as he said it, Harvey had a strong feeling that it wasn't to be. He handed Farsi the name and asked him to track the boy's movements.

It was another twenty-five minutes before his worst fears were confirmed. Searches of all six addresses had failed to turn up anything remotely like a nerve agent, which meant Iqbal must have it on him.

'Any sign of him?' Harvey asked.

'Nothing,' Farsi replied. 'There are no cameras on his street, and I haven't been able to locate him in the immediate area.'

'Shit!'

Harvey returned to the open line with SO15 and was asking if Iqbal's bed looked slept in when Gareth Bailey jumped up from his chair and started waving his arms frantically.

Probably just found the truck he was looking for last week, Harvey thought. 'Hamad, go and see what he wants, will you?'

Harvey turned his back on Bailey as he waited for a response from Commander Burke.

'Doesn't look like anyone's been there for a few days,' he finally heard. 'Apparently the milk bottle on the kitchen table looks more like yoghurt.'

Harvey turned to ask Farsi to check if there was an alternative address for Iqbal al-Mubari, and saw that Farsi too was now beckoning him over to Bailey's workstation.

His curiosity piqued, Harvey walked over. 'What is it?'

'Remember the eight people from the mosque?' Bailey asked. 'We were only able to track two of them home. Well, I was curious about one because he had a distinctive backpack. It's easy to change your top, but not your accessories—'

'The point being?' Harvey interrupted. They already had identities for the eight suspects, and he didn't have time to listen to Bailey wittering on about inconsequential matters.

'Sorry. I managed to pick him up again – by his backpack, see?' Bailey pointed to a still image on his monitor. 'I tracked him to an address we didn't have: a flat on the Crockford Estate.'

The address wasn't one they'd been working on that morning. 'How can you be sure it's one of our suspects?'

'I went to the coverage forty minutes before he boarded the Tube and noted everyone with a backpack. For everyone getting off the train, I had the same person getting on, except for this one. Someone got on with a white-trimmed backpack but wasn't seen getting off. This guy has a plain backpack, but wasn't seen getting on.'

Harvey slapped him on the back. 'Great work!'

He made a mental note to remember this moment when the annual appraisals came around, and he could almost forgive Bailey's earlier mistakes if this panned out and he managed to keep his nose clean from now on.

'Does CCTV cover the entrance to his flat?' Harvey asked.

'It does.'

'Perfect. I'll send SO15 round. In the meantime, keep an eye on the place in case he leaves.'

'That's what I called you over for. I already checked the feed, and he left the flat just after seven this morning.'

Ninety minutes – he could be anywhere!

'Hamad, share that feed with everyone. He could be just going out for breakfast, but we have to assume he's got the X3 on him.'

Harvey asked Commander Burke to send a team round to search al-Mubari's place, then ended the call and returned to his own desk, where he found details of the feed in a pop-up on his screen. He clicked the link and logged into the CCTV database, then set the time for 7:02 a.m. as indicated in Bailey's message. Seconds later, he saw movement on the screen as a hooded figure wearing a white-trimmed backpack emerged from a flat and pulled the door closed behind him.

'Okay, guys, listen up. If you see him get on a bus or enter a Tube station, shout it out. Chances are he's going to try to alter his appearance again, so I want all eyes on him. Gareth, share all the images with everyone and send copies to the police.'

Three minutes later, the first update came from Bailey.

'I've got him entering East Ham Tube station at 7:14.'

Harvey closed down his current feed and opened the one for the ticket area of the station, then rewound to 7:13 a.m. A minute later, he saw the distinct backpack appear on the screen, and he watched Iqbal al-Mubari swipe his way through the turnstile.

'He used an Oyster card! Elaine, log into the TfL database and see if he registered one under his own name.'

It was a long shot, but cases had been solved due to people making rudimentary mistakes. If al-Mubari had provided his own details, they'd be able to see which station he travelled to, eliminating a lot of time-intensive work on their part.

While he waited for Solomon to come back to him, Harvey followed al-Mubari to the platform and watched him board a train.

'He's on the 7:18 District line train, heading westbound,' he told his colleagues. 'Gareth, check everyone getting off at Upton Park. Hamad, you take Plaistow and I've got West Ham.'

Harvey switched his feed once more. 'Elaine, anything on the Oyster card?'

'Yes, I just got in. It's registered in his name and was last used at 7:14 this morning.'

'That means he's still on the Underground!'

But where? And was the Tube his ultimate target? It wouldn't be the first time the London Underground had been attacked. Even in the current state of high alert, no-one was searching bags before letting people into the stations.

Harvey rose from his desk and jogged over to Ellis's office, opening the door without knocking.

'Al-Mubari's still on the Tube. I want to evacuate it.'

'That's a big ask,' his boss said. 'Which station?'

'All of them.'

'You can't be serious.'

'I'm afraid it's the only option.' He explained how the suspect had swiped his pre-paid Oyster travel card at the start of his journey, and that it hadn't been used since. 'If we close down every station, he'll have to get off and swipe his way out. That'll give us a real-time fix on him. Once he's out in the open, we can guide SO15 in to pick him up. I don't need to close it for long. As soon as each station is completely evacuated, they can call it in. Once each line is ready, we can re-open them. We should only need fifteen minutes, twenty at the most.'

He told Ellis what else he would need, and then waited while she juggled the pros and cons. As always, she was quick to come to a sensible solution. She picked up the phone and scrolled through the contact list until she found the mobile number for the Mayor of London.

'I just hope we're doing the right thing,' she said as she waited for the call to connect. 'If his target really is the Underground, we might just end up forcing his hand at the height of rush hour.'

'Then let's pray he has other plans.'

CHAPTER 32

Friday, 18 August 2017

Iqbal al-Mubari waited for the doors to close and the train to move once more before looking up from his book and scanning the other passengers in the carriage. He'd made a note of everyone present when he'd boarded nine stops earlier and taken off his hooded top, placing it in his backpack. Finally, the last of those people had disembarked and he felt comfortable enough to reach into the bag and pull out a different top. Changing in front of people might have looked suspicious, and the last thing he wanted to do was draw attention to himself.

This was his fourth train of the morning, and while he hadn't seen anything to indicate that he was being followed, he wasn't prepared to take any chances. After taking the District line to Victoria, he'd switched to the Victoria line to King's Cross St Pancras, where he'd ridden the Hammersmith & City line before reversing direction and heading east on the Circle line.

The carriage was packed tight with people heading to work. Those standing in the aisle served to hide his actions from everyone apart from the passengers seated either side of him, both of them too engrossed in their phones to pay him any attention.

Iqbal slowly toyed with the Velcro fastener that held the white stripe on to the side of his backpack. It took a minute to silently ease it off, and he slipped the thin strip of material into the top of his bag as he turned it to repeat the action on the other side.

Cannon Street station came and went, and Iqbal finally got to work on the ship's wheel design on the front of the backpack, all the while checking to see if anyone was interested in what he was doing.

No-one cared.

It seemed he wasn't as interesting as the latest Facebook status update or incoming text messages, and he had the wheel design off and stowed by the time the train reached Blackfriars.

Just two more stops and he would be at Embankment, where he would change to the Bakerloo line for his last ever Tube journey.

The man standing in front of him broke wind, and if it hadn't smelled so bad, Iqbal might have laughed at the irony. Here he was, about to deliver a deadly nerve agent, and he was being subjected to a biological attack!

As the doors closed at Temple station, Iqbal rose and nudged his way through the throng to stand by the exit. He caught a woman looking at him in disgust, as if he'd been responsible for the foul odour, and he felt tempted to set off the gas now, just to watch the look of revulsion transform into abject horror as she choked on her last breath . . .

Iqbal ignored the temptation. In truth, he had no idea what effect the agent would have, just that he would feel little pain when he unleashed it. For Iqbal, who'd been raised by a father who had favoured a leather belt over encouragement and forgiveness, a little pain for a short period felt almost a blessing.

The train pulled in at Embankment and Iqbal followed the crowd towards the exit, peeling off when he saw the signs for the Bakerloo line.

He made his way to the northbound platform, and within two minutes, the train arrived. His destination was only two stops away, so he ignored the empty seats and stood by the doors.

They didn't close.

For the first time that day, Iqbal felt uneasy. Two full minutes passed and the doors remained open, and he tried not to let panic grip him.

'Ladies and gentlemen, this is your driver speaking. Due to an incident at the next station we will not be able to continue. This train will terminate here. Please make your way to the exits where bus services . . .'

The rest of the announcement was drowned out by groans from his fellow passengers, but Iqbal was just glad that there had been a valid explanation for the delay. He let the tide of disgruntled commuters drag him towards the exit, where he produced a second Oyster card and held it against the turnstile.

It's all part of the subterfuge, Khan had explained. *There's more than one way to track a person; don't assume it will be a man or woman following you down the street. Electronic surveillance is their greatest weapon, be it cameras or tracking your credit cards and phones. They rely on it heavily, but that can be used against them. With a little foresight, it is easy to create a false or confusing trail.*

Iqbal had spent many days thinking about how to implement this advice, and had come up with the perfect answer. As well as the Oyster card he'd registered online, he'd purchased another one in a shop using fake details. If anyone were tracking his journey, the trail would leave them scratching their heads.

He walked out of the station into bright sunshine. Frustrated travellers were demanding to know when the station would be open again, but Iqbal didn't hang around to hear the answer. He still had three hours to go before his task would be completed, and it wouldn't hurt to walk the short distance to Piccadilly Circus to complete his transformation.

Then again, walking around with his hood up was going to get him noticed, especially as everyone else was dressed for the glorious weather.

He found a sports shop nearby and purchased a black baseball cap and plain white T-shirt, then strolled into a coffee shop and ordered a cappuccino. Once served, he put the drink down on a table and went into the toilet, where he found an empty stall. He changed into the new T-shirt and put his hoodie into the backpack, then returned to his coffee.

The shop began to fill up as more commuters sought sustenance while they waited for the Tube to re-open. Two men in suits sat down at his table and immediately glued their eyes to their phones, and Iqbal took the book from his bag and pretended to read. It was either that or stare into space, and he didn't want to stand out. If he'd brought his phone along he could have blended in better, but he knew it was one of the easiest ways to be tracked. He'd taken the battery out the previous day, and the burner he'd used to call Ghulam had also been disassembled, with the pieces discarded in separate waste bins.

'Looks like it's not just Embankment,' one of the suits said. 'According to Facebook, the whole Tube's closed.'

Iqbal couldn't help but look up at the pair seated across from him.

'Of course the whole Bakerloo line will be closed if there was an accident,' the other said.

'It's not just the Bakerloo line. My mate Tony said he got the same message on the Circle line, and others heard it on the District and Victoria lines, too. "Accident at the next station, can't go any further".'

Iqbal's stomach almost performed a somersault. There could only be one reason for closing down the entire Underground system, and that was fear of an imminent terror attack.

Somehow, they were on to him.

Had they evacuated the Tube because they thought it was his target? It would be the obvious move.

'Grab your coffee,' the first suit said. 'They're opening the stations again.'

Both men got up and left, and Iqbal wondered what to make of it all. Why close the stations for just fifteen minutes? And, if they'd been searching for him, wouldn't they have had police at the exit, scanning the crowd? Fifteen minutes was barely enough time to empty the station, never mind search for . . .

There's more than one way to track a person.

They must have known he'd got on the Tube, either through CCTV or his Oyster card, and the more he thought about it, the more convinced he was that it was the card. His entry at East Ham would have been recorded on a database, but when he hadn't swiped it again, they'd decided to flush him out.

A smile played across his face as he imagined the bewildered security services trying to figure out how they'd lost him, and all because of the second Oyster card.

Khan would have been proud of him, he could feel it, and it made him more determined than ever to complete his mission.

Iqbal finished his coffee and left the shop. With over two and a half hours to go, he had plenty of time to reach his destination on foot.

~

'How the hell did he get off without using his card?'

Harvey paced next to Solomon's desk as she double-checked the Transport for London database.

'He could have hid in the station,' Farsi offered, but Harvey dismissed the idea.

'I instructed them to send staff down to every platform to check for stragglers. No, he got out somehow.'

'In cases of evacuation, wouldn't they open the turnstiles so that people can keep their ticket to use on the buses?' Bailey offered.

'Normally, but they also have an override that spits tickets back out instead of keeping them. That should have been in place, so he would have had to use his Oyster card.'

Harvey stood behind Solomon and asked her to refresh the data, but the resulting display still showed no new entry on al-Mubari's account.

'He got off, I know it,' Harvey murmured to himself.

'He looks to be following the same protocol as Wednesday night,' Bailey said. 'He's aware of CCTV, so he probably knows that we can track his phone, bank cards, Oyster card, everything.'

'What are you suggesting?'

'I'm just wondering why he would go to all the trouble of changing his appearance if he's going to leave an electronic trail for us to follow.'

'We already checked for his phone, and there's no signal. He hasn't got any credit or debit cards, either, just his Oyster.'

'Yeah, but if you're looking to avoid detection, wouldn't you buy a ticket instead of flagging yourself up on the system? It's as if he wanted us to know he got on the Tube—'

'—because he has another way of getting off! Gareth, that's twice in one day. You'll be turning into James Bond next!'

Harvey rushed over to Bailey's desk. 'Bring up the log of his movements on Wednesday night.'

Bailey opened the file on his screen, and Harvey told him to scroll down to the point where al-Mubari had exited the Tube. Next to the entry was a note describing the CCTV footage.

'Open that. I want to see him leaving the station.'

Bailey played the recording, which showed a hooded man tapping a card against the sensor on the turnstile.

'Elaine, do we have a record of al-Mubari clocking out of East Ham station at 22:23 on Wednesday?'

Solomon checked the database. 'No. He got on at 20:19, but there are no other entries that day. The next one we have is a penalty fare, then he used it again this morning.'

'Penalty fare?'

'Yeah. If you don't tap in and out, it's classed as an incomplete journey and they charge you the maximum fare.'

'But I just saw him tap to get out,' Harvey said.

'Then he must have used another card, because there's no record of it here.'

A second card? Could it be that simple? 'Start another search. I want all penalty fares incurred at 22.23 at East Ham on Wednesday.'

Solomon's fingers danced on the keyboard. 'Got it! One entry at 22:23.'

'Check to see if that card was used again this morning.'

Seconds later, he had the answer. '08:54, a penalty fare at Embankment.'

Nice try, he thought. But they hadn't caught him yet.

'We're getting close. I want all eyes on footage of the turnstiles at Embankment. You know the drill; if you see something, shout it out!'

∼

By the time Iqbal arrived at Piccadilly Circus, a large crowd had already congregated. At least two hundred people were standing around chatting or making last-minute adjustments to banners and placards. Some of them proclaimed 'ISIS is NOT Islam' and 'Proud British Muslim', and Iqbal could see why Khan had chosen it as his target.

And slay them where ye find them . . . such is the reward of the disbelievers.

The people gathered around him had abandoned Islam and embraced the materialist worship of the West. In doing so, they had brought Allah's wrath down upon themselves.

Iqbal found a fast-food restaurant and went straight into the toilet. Inside a stall, he removed all of his clothes and replaced them with the *salwar kameez* he'd brought along in his backpack. He emerged a few minutes later wearing olive-green baggy trousers and a loose-fitting top. The baseball cap had been replaced with a *kufi*, and he now wore sandals instead of training shoes. Most importantly, the nerve agent was now in a cloth bag with a drawstring neck, and he wore it over his shoulder and across his chest.

After leaving the toilet, he hung around inside until an opportunity presented itself. A group of five men stood and headed towards the exit, and Iqbal followed them closely, keeping the backpack low so that it wouldn't be easily seen.

Back out in the sunlight, he followed the men to the memorial fountain, then peeled off and found a space up against the side of a building, where he put the backpack down. It had served its purpose, and he intended to start chatting with someone close by and gradually distance himself from it. Hopefully some thief would come along and do him a favour once the march began.

According to Khan, the route would take them down Haymarket and along Pall Mall to Trafalgar Square, where the rest of the protesters would be waiting. After joining up, they would march down Whitehall before turning left and crossing Westminster Bridge. It was there, near the junction, that he should release the gas.

Why that spot in particular, Iqbal neither knew nor cared. He was familiar with the area, and apart from a couple of shops and Westminster Tube station, there was nothing of any significance, but the imam had been specific.

Stay near the front of the march, and once it nears the bridge make your way to your left, activate the device and walk back in the opposite direction. Don't run, or you'll draw attention to yourself, but do not dawdle, either. The aim is to expose as many people as possible, and it will take about two minutes to empty the canister.

If he followed the instructions, not only would he punish the apostates, he would also demonstrate to the West how vengeful Allah could be. They would pay for their devotion to the corporate coffee chains and fast-food empires whose taxes helped fund the war on Islam.

The crowd in Piccadilly Circus had swollen to more than a thousand while he'd been going over the plan in his head, and he walked among them, striking up conversations and listening attentively as they insulted Allah's very being with talk of compassion for the infidels. Words like 'integration' and 'multiculturalism' were tossed around as if they had any real meaning, but Iqbal knew they were just terms coined by the government to appease the ignorant. To be fully integrated meant allowing marriages between Muslims and Christians, and Iqbal couldn't imagine even the tiniest percentage of truly religious parents permitting their children to do such a heinous thing.

No, these people had shunned Allah, and they would pay the price.

∿

It hadn't taken long for the team to spot al-Mubari at the exit of Embankment station, and they'd seen him spend a few minutes in the sports shop before entering the coffee house. Once more, it had been Bailey who'd spotted him emerging in yet another disguise, and they'd tracked him to a burger joint in Piccadilly Circus before losing him again.

'It looks busier than normal,' Harvey noted. 'Is something planned for today?'

It took Solomon just a couple of minutes to confirm that a march had been organised to condemn the recent attacks that had killed more than a hundred Shia Muslims in Nigeria.

'It's the same people who co-ordinate the Arbaeen Procession every December.'

Harvey wondered if it were a coincidence that al-Mubari had chosen this location in which to go into hiding again.

'What's the route?' Ellis asked. With the net closing, she'd come out onto the floor to ensure their quarry didn't slip free, though Harvey knew she wouldn't interfere with his running of the show.

'Trafalgar Square, down Whitehall, across the bridge and ending at Jubilee Gardens.'

That would take them past Downing Street. Could Number 10 be the target? Was al-Mubari planning to use the march to get close enough for that? Unlikely, Harvey thought. He might get as far as the gates, but would need some impressive firepower to get past the armed-protection detail. The march would also skirt the Houses of Parliament, but the Commons was in summer recess, and a building devoid of MPs wouldn't be a worthwhile proposition.

'The Met are on the line,' Farsi said. 'They've got a dozen plain-clothed officers en route to Piccadilly Circus.'

'Get them to check out that restaurant and find out if there's a back exit. He's got to be around there somewhere.'

Twelve sets of eyes was a start, but they were still talking haystacks and needles. They were also running facial recognition against the growing assembly, but so far it had only thrown up three false alarms. The sole picture they had of al-Mubari was three years old, taken during a high school trip, lifted from the council's website.

'We need more people on the ground,' Harvey said.

'I'll head down there,' Farsi offered. 'I've got my bike downstairs. I could be there in ten minutes.'

'With your bad leg?'

'The exercise does it good.'

'Okay,' Harvey conceded. 'But no heroics. If you spot him, call it in and let the police handle it.'

'No problem. I'll call Samir, too. He could do with the money, and he might recognise al-Mubari.'

'Yes, call – wait, did you tell him about his meeting today?'

'What meeting?'

Harvey could have kicked himself. With all that was going on, he'd forgotten to share the information he'd got from the prisoner, Aswan.

'Samir has been set up. Khan must have found out he was working for us. Someone's going to take him out at lunchtime. He'll be on his way there now.'

'Where's the meet?'

Harvey looked up the log containing a list of Aswan's text messages. 'The coffee shop opposite . . . Westminster station. That's part of the route!'

Farsi frowned. 'Then he plans to release the X3 there,' he said. 'Khan wouldn't have someone else take Samir out so close to the march. The place would be crawling with police, and it would jeopardise his main objective.'

Harvey knew his friend was right. Khan must have planned to kill Samir with the nerve agent, and the meeting had been set up for ninety minutes from now.

'We've got about an hour and a half to find al-Mubari. Hamad, call Samir and tell him to meet you opposite the Cenotaph. When the march reaches you, get in among them and see if you can spot him. Again, no heroics.'

271

Farsi flipped him a mock salute and left the office.

'Elaine, you're now the police liaison. Let me know what they find at the restaurant.'

~

Iqbal had searched out the tallest members of the congregation and was now marching close behind them. He was about fifteen yards from the front of the procession, further back than he would have liked, but shielded from street cameras.

Progress seemed painfully slow, and the chants he was forced to echo felt like bile in his throat, but he had to keep up the pretence.

He glanced at his watch and saw that the march was on schedule. He'd feared it would run late when they'd reached Trafalgar Square and everyone seemed to stop and mingle with the crowd that had congregated there, but within ten minutes they moved off again, their numbers swelling.

They were now in Whitehall, and coming up on his right he could see the prime minister's official residence, protected by impenetrable gates and armed police. He wondered if, one day, someone might manage to breach the security cordon and get inside Number 10. It would be a fantastic achievement if they did, but he wouldn't be around to witness it. He even briefly considered running to the gates and activating the device he was carrying, but by the time it carried to the front door of the famous building, the PM would have been whisked away to safety in some secret bunker.

Iqbal snapped out of the daydream as something caught his eye. Away to his right, a few yards past the entrance to Downing Street, a man was paying more than a passing interest in the march. What made him stand out was the leather jacket, which must have been extremely uncomfortable with the temperature nudging thirty degrees centigrade.

Iqbal averted his eyes, turning his head to the left. The man had been scanning the crowd, there was no doubt about it, but was it just a standard security measure, or was he looking for someone in particular?

Someone like him.

Don't get paranoid.

In such a high-profile area there was bound to be a covert police presence. The only two other people who knew about his mission, Khan and Ghulam, were dead, so there was no way anyone could have any reason to be looking for him. Even if someone had discovered the plot, he'd taken more than enough precautions over the last few days to ensure that no-one could track his movements.

The logic made him relax a little, until he spotted Samir. Khan had spoken of him many times, and had used the drug addict as a prime example of all that was wrong with Britain. And here he was, scouring the procession as if his next fix depended on it.

Iqbal instinctively knew he was the one they were looking for, especially now that Samir had joined the search. How they had found out was beyond him, and at this point it no longer mattered.

But I'm so close . . .

They would turn left at the end of the street, only about two hundred yards away, and fifty yards after that he would release the gas. At the rate they were going, it would take five minutes at the most, but he would need to remain undetected until then.

Iqbal skipped forward a few steps until he was marching arm to arm with the taller men, and he prayed their bodies would shield him the view of those at street level. It made him vulnerable to the CCTV cameras, but the trade-off was worth it. The immediate danger came from those nearby, and he stole a glance behind him as he passed the point where Samir stood. The junkie's focus had shifted to those further back in the parade, and once he disappeared from sight, Iqbal slowed his pace and walked behind the tall figures once more.

Although that threat had passed, Iqbal didn't intend to let himself relax again. His eyes flitted from side to side, and he saw another face, this time on his right, peering into the marchers. Iqbal turned his face away and glanced up ahead. Only fifty yards until they turned towards the bridge.

A couple of minutes . . .

~

'Got him!'

Bailey's announcement grabbed everyone's attention, and Harvey hurried over to the junior operative's desk. On the screen was the facial recognition software showing a 96 per cent match.

'Where is he?' Harvey asked.

'About ten rows from the front. He's wearing a white skullcap, grey top and green trousers.'

'I can't see him,' Harvey said, looking at the live feed.

'He's walking behind this guy,' Bailey told him, pointing to a man on the screen. 'Wait, I'll show you the recording.'

Bailey double-clicked an icon and dragged the resulting window to his second monitor, then rewound the recording to two minutes earlier. When he pressed 'Play', Harvey watched the man Bailey had described step between two men.

'That's him.'

Harvey leaned over and hit the 'Pause' button. 'Let me in for a second.'

Bailey gave up his seat and Harvey sat, zooming in and restarting the footage. Al-Mubari seemed agitated, continually glancing to his left; then, as suddenly as he'd appeared, he vanished behind the taller figure.

'Why did you show your face?' Harvey asked himself.

Harvey played it back again and concentrated on the people lining the route. He easily recognised Farsi, and the person standing next to him looked like Samir. Just before al-Mubari drew level with the pair, he appeared on the screen.

'Damn! He knows we're looking for him!'

The element of surprise was lost. Harvey activated the comms unit he was wearing in his left ear. 'Hamad, we've spotted him, but he knows you're there. I want you and Samir to hang back while I guide SO15 in.'

'Understood.'

Harvey switched channels. 'Sergeant Bury, we have the suspect, but he's aware of your presence. You'll have to sneak up on him. He's carrying a cloth bag over his shoulder, and I think the nerve agent is inside. He can't be given the chance to activate it.'

Harvey rattled off a description of al-Mubari and described his position in the procession.

'Roger that. We're moving in now.'

'Just make sure you take him out before he reaches the end of the street.'

~

A shout from behind made him turn, and Iqbal saw three men forcing their way through the crowd, their eyes drilling into him.

Iqbal froze, but only for an instant. There had always been the possibility that the police might try to stop him before he saw the task through. Whether it turned out to be a random search at a Tube station or an instance like this, he had created a simple backup plan.

Release the gas.

The only problem was, they were closing too fast. He wouldn't have time to get the device out of the bag, never mind go through the arming sequence.

There was still a way.

Iqbal turned and pushed people aside as he fought his way to the side of the road, and once in the clear he burst into a sprint. If he could put some distance between himself and his pursuers, he would have enough time to trigger the mechanism, but a uniformed policeman stepped out into the road ahead. Knowing he had to get past him or admit defeat, Iqbal dug into the waistband of his trousers and pulled out the pistol. He aimed it at the cop, who raised his hands and stepped aside, leaving Iqbal with a clear run. He opened the bag and took out the metal canister as he turned the corner, but his final hope of setting it off vanished at the sight of four armed officers in a line across the road. They were less than ten yards away, kneeling with their Heckler & Koch MP5s aimed directly at him.

Iqbal pulled up, the canister in one hand and the gun in the other. His heart still wanted to find a way to set off the gas, but his mind told him he had no chance. He would have to drop the gun, in which case they would swarm him before he completed the task. The alternative would be to try to shoot all four of them, but he suspected that as soon as he raised the pistol he'd be cut down before he got a shot away.

Iqbal's eyes welled at the thought of failure. To die here, in the middle of the road, mere yards from his ultimate target.

If only he'd been able to release the gas. Perhaps when they shot him they would puncture . . .

A third option popped into his head, and it was so deliciously simple: shoot the canister himself!

The police were shouting at him, but Iqbal blanked them out, the gnawing sensation of disappointment replaced by an inner calm, as if his soul had already commenced the journey to *Jannah*. He so wanted to sing Allah's praises at that moment, but knew that doing so might signal his intentions.

Instead, he simply smiled as he brought the pistol up to meet the bottom of the device.

~

Farsi was fifty yards behind al-Mubari when the suspect broke away from the march and sprinted down the empty street. Farsi took off in pursuit, but his hip couldn't handle the burning pace. His quarry eased ahead, taking something from his bag as he ran.

It had to be the X3, and he was seconds away from using it.

'All units, take him down, now!'

Farsi screamed the command into his throat mic, but got no response. Confused, he checked the pack on his belt and saw that it was set to Harvey's frequency. He was switching it to the one for SO15 when a single shot rang out.

Farsi forgot about the radio and ran as fast as his dodgy hip would allow. When he reached the corner, he saw Iqbal lying on his back, a pool of blood forming around his head. On closer inspection, he could see the entry wound just above the boy's right eye, but the thing that would stay with him longest was the angelic smile on al-Mubari's face.

'He refused to put them down, and when his gun hand came up, one of my men opened up.'

Farsi turned to see Sergeant Bury standing next to him.

'Where's the canister?'

'Over there.' Bury pointed to his left. 'Exactly where he dropped it.'

'I'm going to need gloves, an evidence bag and a lift to Thames House.'

'Sorry, but we need to preserve the scene. Besides, I've got Hazmat en route.'

'How soon will they be here?'

'Fifteen minutes,' Bury told him.

'You know what's in that thing, don't you? Because if there's the tiniest puncture in that thing, you're exposing all these people to the worst death you could possibly imagine, not to mention leaving it exposed to any of al-Mubari's friends who might be backing him up.'

Bury blinked a couple of times, then ordered one of his men to fetch the items Farsi had requested. He used his phone to take pictures of the scene while it remained intact, and then called the Hazmat team and told them to head to Thames House instead.

Two minutes later, Farsi sat in the back of a squad car as it made the short trip back to the office, aided by lights and siren. He called ahead and suggested they contact Frank Dale at Porton Down to come and collect the X3, which he would hand over to the hazardous material guys once they reached the underground car park.

His heart skipped a couple of beats when the bag containing the lethal chemical almost bounced off his lap as the car hit a pothole.

'Do me a favour,' he said to the driver. 'Keep it under twenty till I get out.'

CHAPTER 33

Monday, 21 August 2017

For the first time in weeks, dark clouds filled the sky over Thames House. The forecast was for thunderstorms after the recent mini-heatwave, but Ellis felt a more portentous reason for their sudden appearance.

The message she'd received from the Home Secretary that morning gave no indication as to his mood, but despite the excellent work her team had done in foiling Nabil Karim's plot, she wasn't expecting a pat on the back.

Ellis used her pass to gain access to the main floor, which seemed almost deserted after the hubbub of the previous week. A few people had arrived early. They were a mixture of the usual early crowd and a couple who had got behind before the weekend, but most of the desks were deserted.

'Morning, Sarah,' she said, stopping at Thompson's station. 'How are you feeling?'

The only outward sign that Thompson had been caught in the bomb blast was the butterfly stitch above her right eye, but Ellis knew the real damage was often more psychological than physical. It had taken her a while to recover from the torture inflicted by Alexi Bessonov's thugs six months earlier, but this was different, and Ellis saw none of the post-traumatic anxiety in her this time around.

'I'm good.' Thompson smiled.

'And your little bundle of joy?'

'Andrew's fine, too.'

Ellis managed a smile of her own. 'But really, how's the little one?'

'No damage, according to the doctor. I'll be having regular scans over the coming weeks, but they told me it's just for reassurance.'

'That's good to hear. I imagine Andrew has been trying to molly-coddle you all weekend. He's only thinking of your well-being.'

'He has, and he's right. At first I didn't think so, but after what happened, I'm happy to let him pamper me for the next year or so.'

Harvey emerged from the break room with two mugs. 'Morning.'

'Speak of the Devil, and he shall bring you a lemon green tea.' Thompson beamed.

'Stewed for exactly two minutes,' Harvey said, 'just as you ordered.'

'I'll leave you lovebirds to it. Maynard will be here in ten minutes, probably to discuss our actions over the last couple of weeks.'

'We got a result,' Thompson said. 'What's to discuss?'

'With Maynard, there's always something.'

Ellis entered her office, and had barely had time to boot up her computer when she saw the Home Secretary being escorted onto the main floor. She went to the door and held it open, hoping that one day the show of courtesy might rub off on him. The rotund Yorkshireman took a seat opposite her desk and placed his briefcase on the floor beside his chair, and she once again marvelled at how he could make a Savile Row suit look like a cloth sack. The only thing about him that looked vaguely stately was his £100 haircut.

'To what do I owe the pleasure?' Ellis asked amicably, knowing her civility would grate on Maynard. 'I thought perhaps you might be here to commend my team on the tremendous job they did securing the X3.'

'Cut the crap, Ellis. You may have prevented an attack, but you also blatantly disregarded orders given to you by one of Her Majesty's cabinet ministers, namely me.'

'Oh? And just how did I do that?'

'I gave you clear instructions to keep me up to date with every aspect of the investigation, yet I didn't hear about Iqbal al-Mubari until after his arrest. Are you going to tell me it was another spur-of-the-moment thing?'

'On the contrary,' Ellis said. 'We knew about him eight hours before we managed to take him down.'

'During which time you made no effort to contact me.'

'And say what, exactly?' Ellis sat back in her chair, enjoying the battle. 'You would have had a name, nothing more. Unless you're saying you would have been able to track him down quicker than my team did, because you'd need a lot of infrastructure and resources to do that, and I haven't heard anything at the ISC meetings to suggest a rival agency is operating on British soil.'

'Of course there isn't,' Maynard blustered. 'But that's no excuse for not passing on the information.'

Ellis adopted a puzzled look. 'So you admit you wouldn't have been able to do anything with the name, but you wanted my team to spend hours creating detailed reports for you rather than stopping him? What would that have achieved, I wonder? Oh, I know: the attack would have gone ahead, I would have failed, and you would have a legitimate excuse to get rid of me. Well, I'm sorry, John, but it'll take more than that to prise me out of this chair.'

Maynard adjusted his tie. 'It was never about that.'

'Of course it was!' Ellis said, going on the offensive. 'You're the fourth Home Secretary I've served under, and none of your predecessors ever tried to hamstring my department the way you have. They knew our capabilities and limitations but trusted us to do our job without it ever becoming personal. Sure, we had our differences, but we saw past them to get things done. With you, though, everything is geared towards hampering our efforts.'

'If you're so disgruntled, why don't you just resign?'

Ellis looked him in the eye. 'Because you'd enjoy it too much, and you're the last man I'd give any pleasure to.' She couldn't resist the personal dig.

'Well, regardless of how you feel, I'll be submitting a report prior to the next Intelligence and Security Committee meeting, and it'll be particularly scathing.'

'Submit away,' Ellis said, waving a dismissive hand. 'Once they read it, they can ask you about E Squadron's recent activities.'

'They are mandated to aid and assist the security—'

'Ya-da, ya-da, ya-da,' Ellis interrupted. 'I know the script, John, and it doesn't mention actions against British passport holders on British soil. You overstepped the mark.'

'I don't believe I ever discussed them with you,' Maynard said smugly. 'You must be mistaken.'

'Perhaps. Just to be sure, though, I'm going to request the personnel files of all active members on the date Imran al-Hosni was abducted. My team was there and got some very clear footage. It is currently sitting in a database with a false entry date and innocuous file name, so there's no point doing a search for it. Needless to say, I have the usual backups as well. So, really, it's up to you. Either tell the ISC why you had al-Hosni snatched – and subsequently killed, I might add – or claim the unit went rogue and hang *them* out to dry.'

Maynard looked concerned at having had the tables turned on him, and Ellis drove home her advantage. 'A word of warning. If you make E Squadron take the fall, it'll be on your own head. You'll be deliberately ending their careers to protect your own, and some of them might take that personally.'

It wasn't an idle threat. Ellis knew that to make E Squadron, you had to attain the rank of sergeant as well as be in the top 2 per cent in the regiment. Anyone who had spent many years to achieve such a distinguished role only to have it snatched from them to save a politician's malodorous hide would naturally feel aggrieved. Whether or not they would seek retribution was another thing, but they would certainly have the motive and capability.

Maynard appeared to be coming to the same conclusion.

'It seems we have a stalemate,' he finally said.

Ellis considered it more of a win. She'd staved off another attempt to deprive her of her position, and with a cabinet reshuffle planned for early next year, there was a good chance he'd be shifted sideways and out of her hair.

'It appears so,' Ellis agreed. Still, no matter how neatly they'd sewn up the case, one loose thread dangled tantalisingly out of reach. 'What about Nabil Karim? Did al-Hosni give you anything useful on him?'

'We're working on that. He gave up one of their communication methods, an encrypted phone app, and I've asked Six to look into it. Hopefully it'll lead to the man behind all this.'

Ellis hoped so, too. Karim's plan had been well thought out and, if it hadn't been for Thompson's intuition, might well have succeeded. As long as Karim lived, he would remain a danger, and they might not be so lucky next time.

'I'll liaise with Martin over at Six,' she said. 'We'll help in any way we can.'

Another attempt to show that co-operation, not contention, was the best way to defeat the enemy, but it seemed lost on Maynard. He simply told her to have a detailed report ready by the end of the day, then picked up his briefcase and left without so much as a goodbye.

Ellis was grateful to see the back of him, and the moment he was gone, she called Harvey into her office to give him his assignment for the day.

EPILOGUE

Friday, 15 September 2017

Sergeant Dan Mitchell saw the plume of dust on the horizon and asked the sniper on the ridge above to confirm the numbers.

'Two cars, both four up.'

Eight men in total, against the four men in his patrol. It was hardly a fair fight, but Mitchell didn't mind having the advantage.

Especially today.

In his five years as an SAS sergeant, Mitchell had never been given such precise orders. Normally he'd be given an objective and the type of mission – reconnaissance, destroy, capture, et cetera – with the method of execution left to him. Not this time. The orders had arrived with the latest resupply, a typed message hidden among their rations and ammunition. He'd thought it a joke at first, but after reading what the target had done to Mohammad Abdulrashid, he could understand why they wanted him to get up close and personal.

Still, Mitchell had wondered why he hadn't been ordered to capture Karim for transport and interrogation. The terror leader sounded like the ideal candidate for rendition, but his superiors apparently thought otherwise.

'Which one is Karim in?' Mitchell asked.

'Second vehicle, rear seat, right-hand side.'

'Roger that.'

The small convoy drew nearer, now barely a kilometre away, and Mitchell scanned the area in front of him once more. Two of his men had spent the best part of the morning on their disguises, and for the last hour they'd been lying under the baking Syrian sun, waiting for the target to arrive.

'Thirty seconds . . .'

Mitchell received bursts of static in reply, which told him his men were ready to go. Seconds ticked by, and Mitchell waited until the first vehicle reached its marker, then pressed down on the handheld detonator.

The 4×4 was thrown into the air and flipped nose over tail before crashing back down to earth on its roof. Fire already engulfed the interior, and the second SUV skidded to a halt behind it.

One of two things would now happen, and Mitchell had prepared for both eventualities. Either the passengers would get out to check on the people in the mangled wreck, or they'd run.

As he expected, it was the latter.

The driver had barely started backing up before a .50-calibre round from the sniper's rifle hit him above the ear and removed most of his head. The remaining passengers piled out and took cover behind the vehicle, firing wildly into the hills.

With their attention focused on the threat from on high, none noticed the two men emerging from the ground behind them.

When Nabil Karim stopped to change magazines, four more shots rang out. The men either side of him collapsed, and Karim turned to see two heavily armed foreign soldiers standing feet away.

'Drop it!'

Although shocked by the swift and brutal attack, Karim seemed to regain his composure and slammed a new magazine into his AK-47, but before he could chamber a round, two bullets thumped into him. His right shoulder exploded, quickly followed by his left shin, and the weapon slipped from his grasp as he fell to the sand. He scrambled towards the rifle, but a dusty boot kicked it out of range. Rough hands flipped him onto his back and searched him thoroughly. Finding nothing, the soldier turned him once more and secured his hands behind his back with FlexiCuffs, then pulled him to his knees.

Mitchell called the sniper down from the hill and jogged over to the other troopers, a collapsible camera tripod in his hand.

'Get the battery,' he ordered one of the men as he set up a small camcorder. A minute later, the man returned from working under the SUV's hood. He unscrewed the plastic stoppers and carefully poured the contents of the battery into a wide-necked bottle. The other produced a plastic funnel, and Mitchell zoomed in so that Karim's face filled the shot, then hit the 'Record' button.

'Nabil Karim,' he said, 'this is for Mohammad Abdulrashid, who you knew as Abdul al-Aziz.'

He nodded to the soldiers, and one of them forced the funnel into Karim's mouth while the other slowly emptied the bottle into it.

Karim bucked and choked, but was unable to prevent the sulphuric-acid-and-water solution from entering his body. Mitchell could only imagine the damage it was doing to the man's throat and stomach, never mind his lungs, but it still wasn't enough to make up for what Karim had done to Abdulrashid. People died in wars – a soldier accepted that – but there were certain boundaries that shouldn't be crossed, and Karim had overstepped the mark.

He ordered the two men to stand aside, then panned out to show Karim convulsing on the ground. The acid might kill him, or it might not, but if he got to meet Allah, his final few minutes on the planet would be a real conversation piece.

Mitchell let the camera roll for another minute, then turned it off and dismantled the equipment. The recording would be sent by flash-burst message to the UK, where he had been assured it would be forwarded to MI6. It wouldn't bring Abdulrashid back, but it just might give his handlers some needed closure.

Mitchell's last act was to make a note of the location on his GPS before calling in the air strike.

If you enjoyed this novel and would like to know about Alan's future releases, just send an email to alanmac@ntlworld.com with Next Book in the subject line to be added to his mailing list. Alan picks five people on the list to receive a signed paperback a month before the official release date, and he only sends out a couple of emails a year, so you won't be bombarded with spam. Alan replies to all emails, so check your spam folder if you don't hear from him within twenty-four hours.

ABOUT THE AUTHOR

Alan McDermott is a husband and a father to beautiful twin girls, and currently lives in the south of England. Born in West Germany to Scottish parents, Alan spent his early years moving from town to town as his father was posted to different army units around the United Kingdom. Alan has had a number of jobs since leaving school, including working on a cruise ship in Hong Kong and Singapore, where he met his wife, and as a software developer creating clinical applications for the National Health Service. Alan gave up his day job in December 2014 to become a full-time author. Alan's writing career began in 2011 with the action thriller *Gray Justice*, his first full-length novel.

21505713R00176

Printed in Great Britain
by Amazon